W9-BJU-436

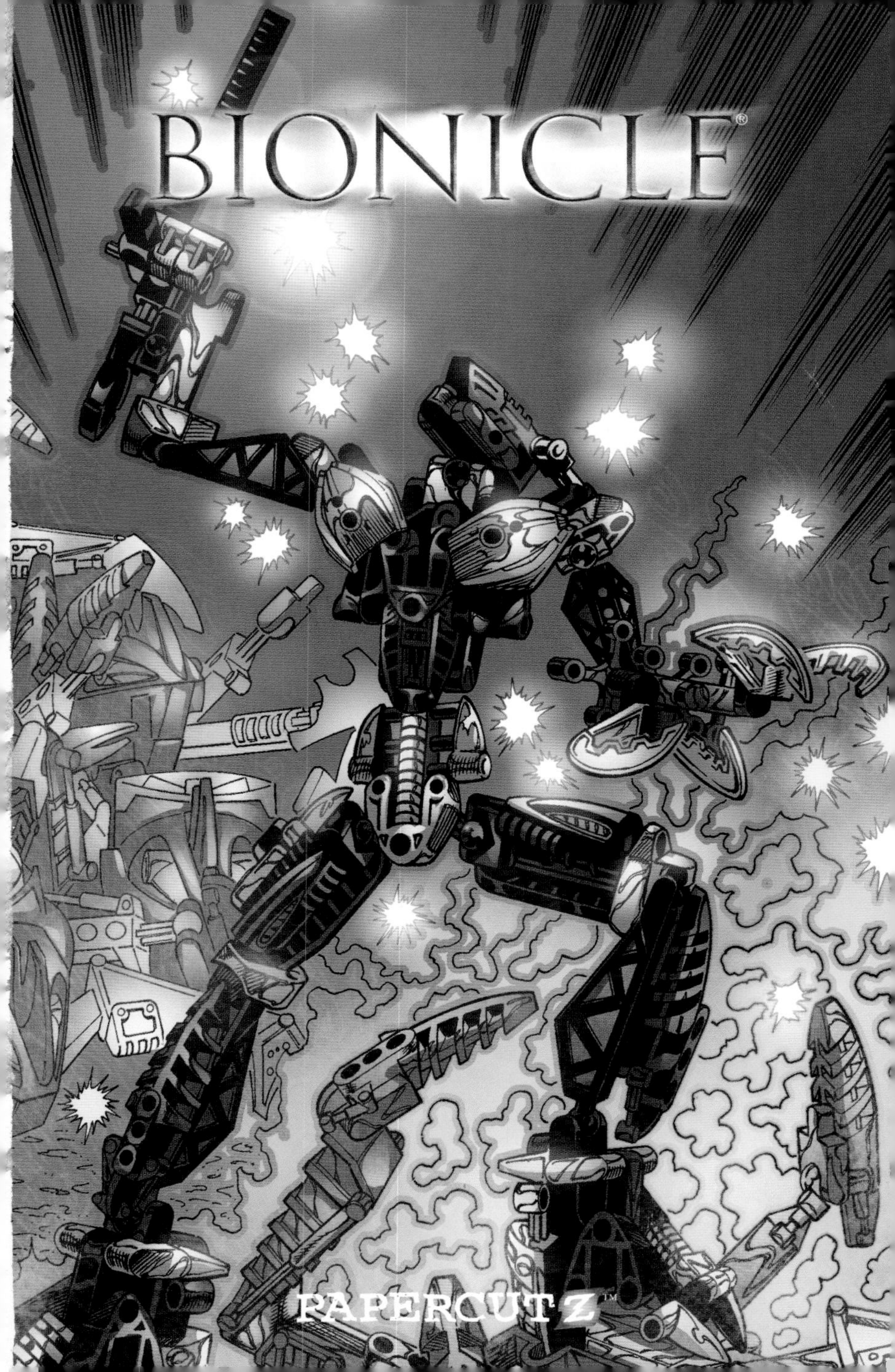
BIONICLE®
PAPERCUTZ™

BIONICLE® GRAPHIC NOVELS AVAILABLE FROM PAPERCUTZ

FULL-COLOR GRAPHIC NOVEL
BIONICLE
#1: RISE OF THE TOA NUVA
GREG FARSHTEY
RICHARD BENNETT
RANDY ELLIOTT
HOW IT ALL BEGAN...
PAPERCUTZ
LEGO

Graphic Novel #1
"The Rise of the Toa Nuva"

FULL-COLOR GRAPHIC NOVEL
BIONICLE
#2: CHALLENGE OF THE RAKSHI
GREG FARSHTEY
RANDY ELLIOTT
PAPERCUTZ
LEGO

Graphic Novel #2
"Challenge of the Rahkshi"

FULL-COLOR GRAPHIC NOVEL
BIONICLE
#3: CITY OF LEGENDS
GREG FARSHTEY
RANDY ELLIOTT
PAPERCUTZ
LEGO

Graphic Novel #3
"City of Legends"

FULL-COLOR GRAPHIC NOVEL
BIONICLE
#4: TRIAL BY FIRE
GREG FARSHTEY
RANDY ELLIOTT
PAPERCUTZ
LEGO

Graphic Novel #4
"Trial by Fire"

FULL-COLOR GRAPHIC NOVEL
BIONICLE
#5: The Battle of Voya Nui
GREG FARSHTEY
STUART SAYGER
PAPERCUTZ
LEGO

Coming in May:
Graphic Novel #5
"The Battle of Voya Nui"

$7.95 each paperback, $12.95 each in hardcover. Please add $4.00 for postage and handling for the first book, add $1.00 for each additional book. Please make check payable to NBM Publishing. Send to: Papercutz, 40 Exchange Place, Suite 1308, New York, NY 10005 • 1-800-886-1223 • www.papercutz.com

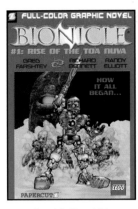

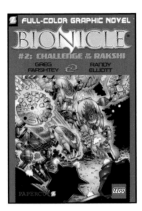

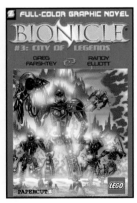

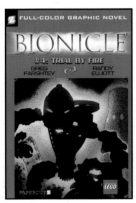

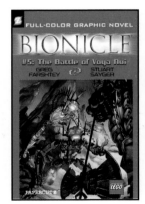

BIONICLE®

#4 Trial by Fire

GREG FARSHTEY
WRITER

RANDY ELLIOTT

PAPERCUTZ™
NEW YORK

Trial by Fire

GREG FARSHTEY – Writer
RANDY ELLIOTT— Artist
TOBY DUTKIEWICZ – Art Director/Design
PETER PANTAZIS — Colorist
KEN LOPEZ, NICK J. NAPOLITANO – Letterers
JAYE GARDNER – Original Editor
JOHN McCARTHY – Production
MICHAEL PETRANEK – Editorial Assistant
JIM SALICRUP
Editor-in-Chief

ISBN 10: 1-59707-132-3 paperback edition
ISBN 13: 978-1-59707-132-1 paperback edition
ISBN 10: 1-59707-133-1 hardcover edition
ISBN 13: 978-1-59707-133-8 hardcover edition
LEGO, the LEGO logo and BIONICLE are trademarks of the LEGO Group.
Manufactured and distributed by Papercutz under license from the LEGO Group.
© 2003, 2009 The LEGO Group. All rights reserved.
Originally published as comicbooks by DC Comics as BIONICLE #22-27.
Editorial matter © 2009 Papercutz.
Printed in China.
Distributed by Macmillan.
10 9 8 7 6 5 4 3 2 1

TRIAL BY FIRE
CHAPTER ONE

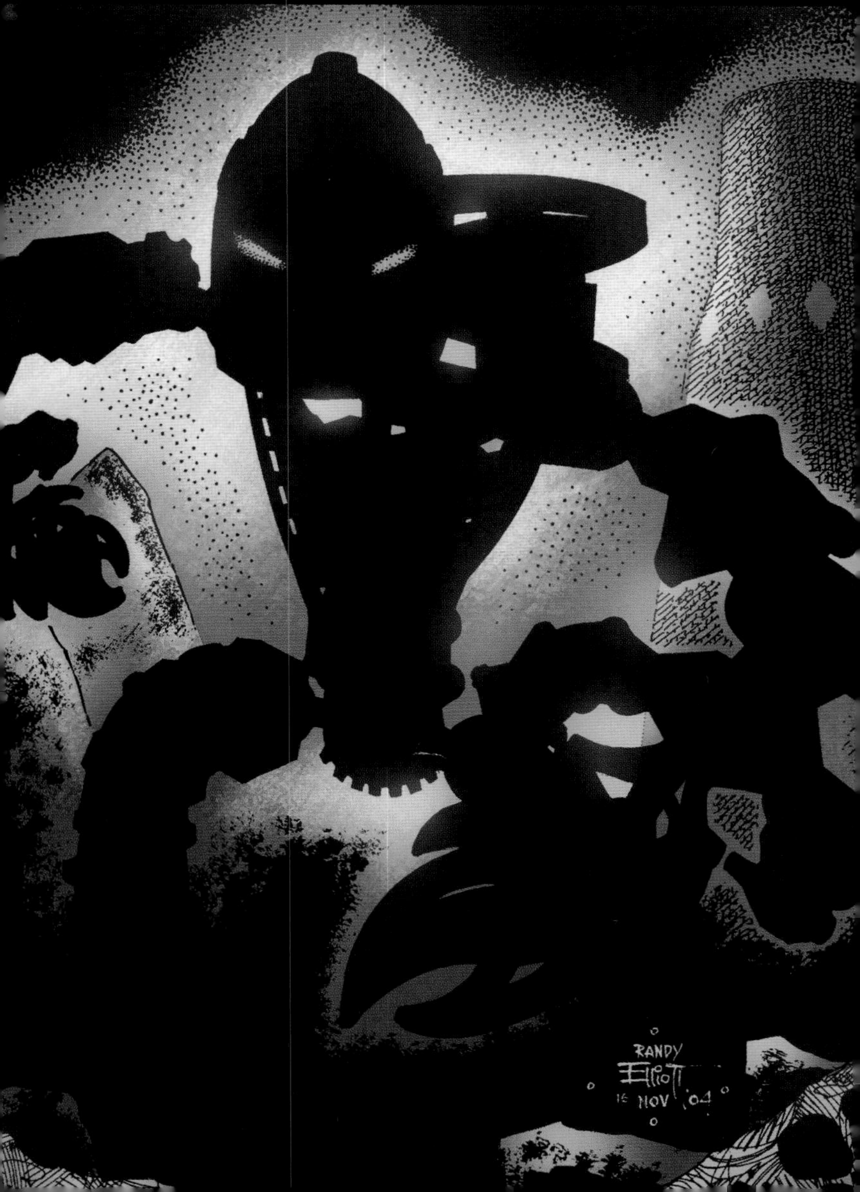
RANDY
ELLIOTT
16 NOV '04

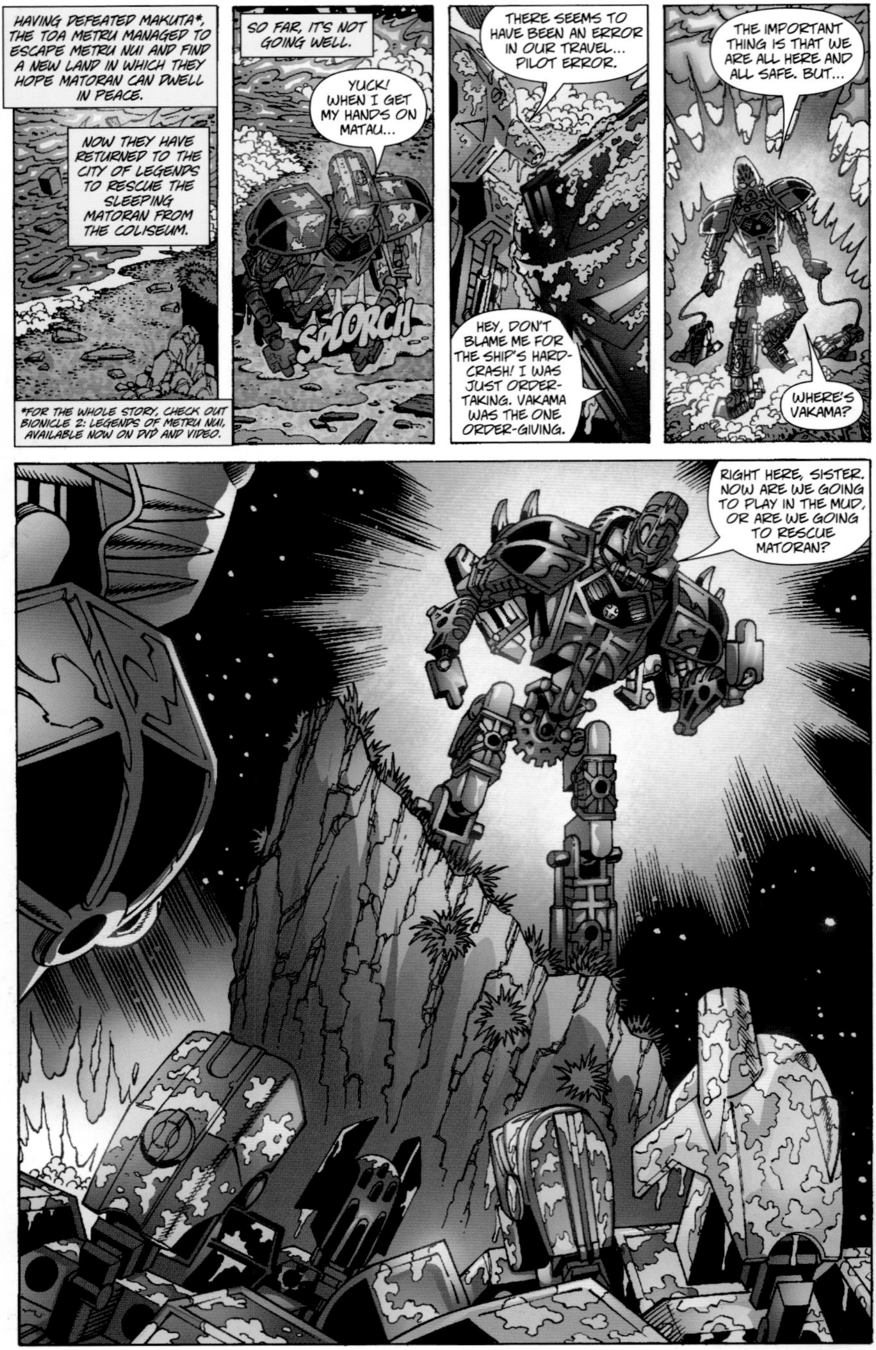
HAVING DEFEATED MAKUTA*, THE TOA METRU MANAGED TO ESCAPE METRU NUI AND FIND A NEW LAND IN WHICH THEY HOPE MATORAN CAN DWELL IN PEACE.
NOW THEY HAVE RETURNED TO THE CITY OF LEGENDS TO RESCUE THE SLEEPING MATORAN FROM THE COLISEUM.
*FOR THE WHOLE STORY, CHECK OUT BIONICLE 2: LEGENDS OF METRU NUI, AVAILABLE NOW ON DVD AND VIDEO.
SO FAR, IT'S NOT GOING WELL.
YUCK! WHEN I GET MY HANDS ON MATAU...
SPLORCH
THERE SEEMS TO HAVE BEEN AN ERROR IN OUR TRAVEL... PILOT ERROR.
HEY, DON'T BLAME ME FOR THE SHIP'S HARD-CRASH! I WAS JUST ORDER-TAKING. VAKAMA WAS THE ONE ORDER-GIVING.
THE IMPORTANT THING IS THAT WE ARE ALL HERE AND ALL SAFE. BUT...
WHERE'S VAKAMA?
RIGHT HERE, SISTER. NOW ARE WE GOING TO PLAY IN THE MUD, OR ARE WE GOING TO RESCUE MATORAN?

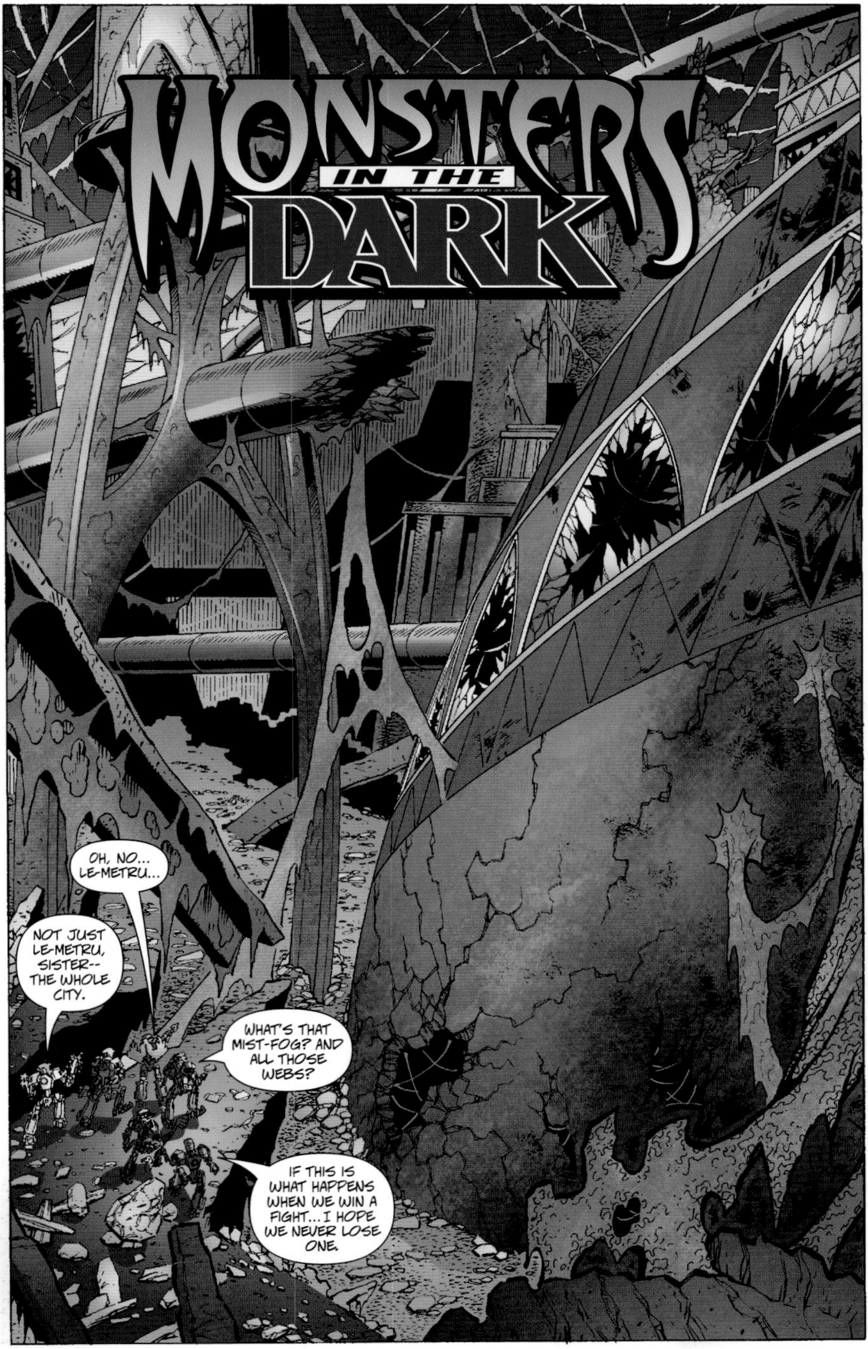
MONSTERS IN THE DARK
OH, NO... LE-METRU...
NOT JUST LE-METRU, SISTER-- THE WHOLE CITY.
WHAT'S THAT MIST-FOG? AND ALL THOSE WEBS?
IF THIS IS WHAT HAPPENS WHEN WE WIN A FIGHT... I HOPE WE NEVER LOSE ONE.

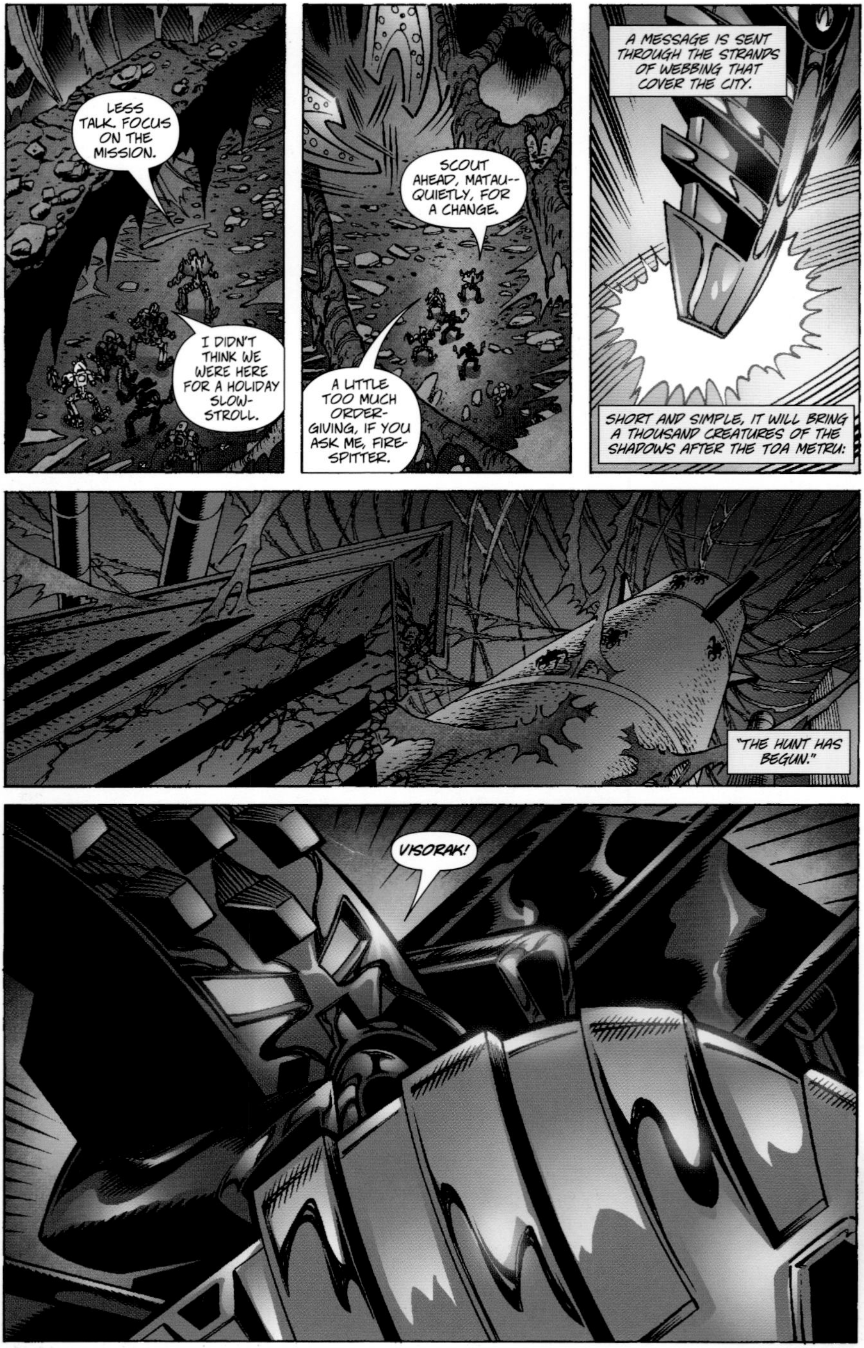
LESS TALK. FOCUS ON THE MISSION.
I DIDN'T THINK WE WERE HERE FOR A HOLIDAY SLOW-STROLL.
SCOUT AHEAD, MATAU--QUIETLY, FOR A CHANGE.
A LITTLE TOO MUCH ORDER-GIVING, IF YOU ASK ME, FIRE-SPITTER.
A MESSAGE IS SENT THROUGH THE STRANDS OF WEBBING THAT COVER THE CITY.
SHORT AND SIMPLE, IT WILL BRING A THOUSAND CREATURES OF THE SHADOWS AFTER THE TOA METRU:
"THE HUNT HAS BEGUN."
VISORAK!

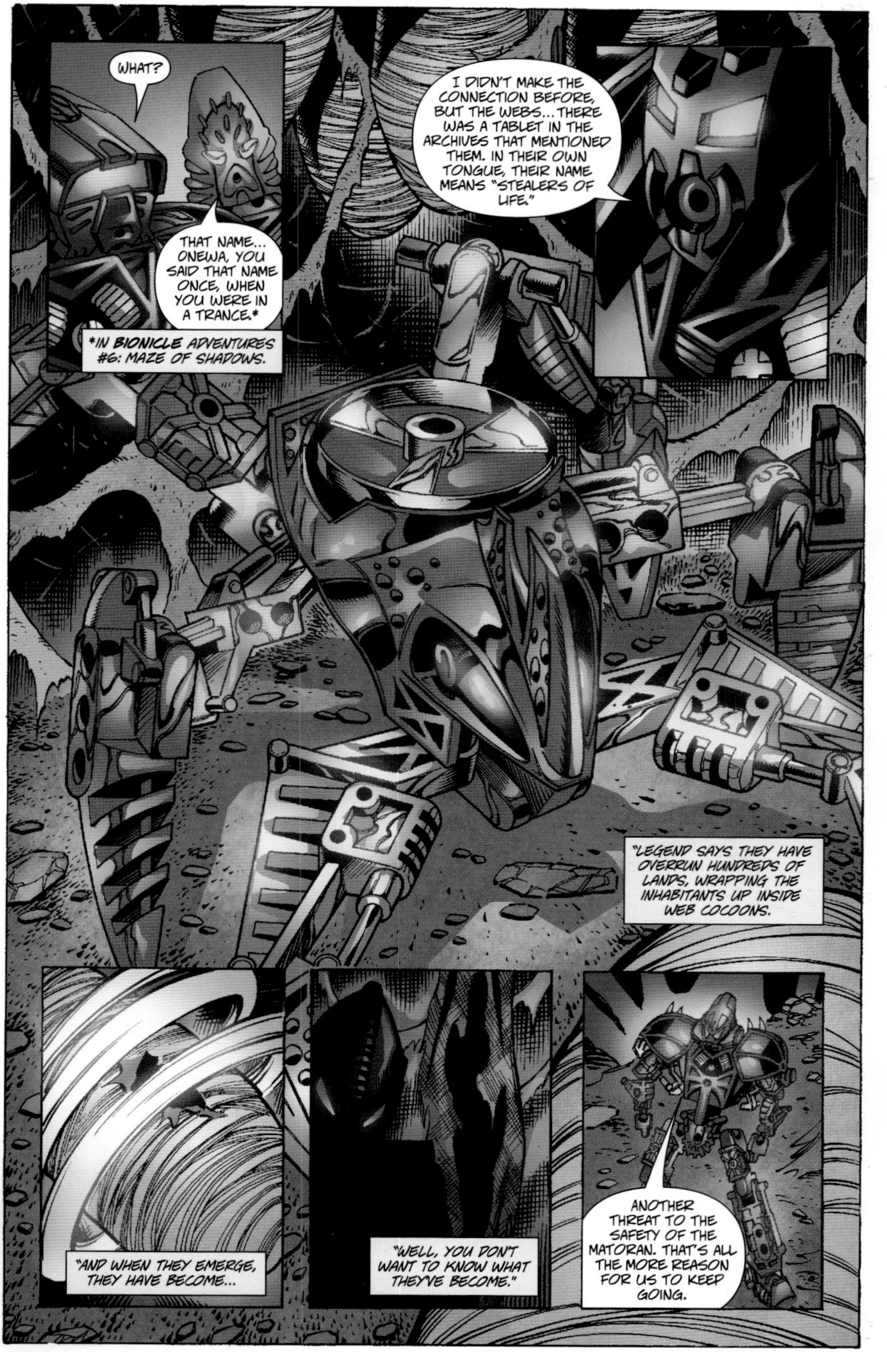
WHAT?
THAT NAME... ONEWA, YOU SAID THAT NAME ONCE, WHEN YOU WERE IN A TRANCE.*
*IN BIONICLE ADVENTURES #6: MAZE OF SHADOWS.
I DIDN'T MAKE THE CONNECTION BEFORE, BUT THE WEBS... THERE WAS A TABLET IN THE ARCHIVES THAT MENTIONED THEM. IN THEIR OWN TONGUE, THEIR NAME MEANS "STEALERS OF LIFE."
"LEGEND SAYS THEY HAVE OVERRUN HUNDREDS OF LANDS, WRAPPING THE INHABITANTS UP INSIDE WEB COCOONS.
"AND WHEN THEY EMERGE, THEY HAVE BECOME...
"WELL, YOU DON'T WANT TO KNOW WHAT THEY'VE BECOME."
ANOTHER THREAT TO THE SAFETY OF THE MATORAN. THAT'S ALL THE MORE REASON FOR US TO KEEP GOING.

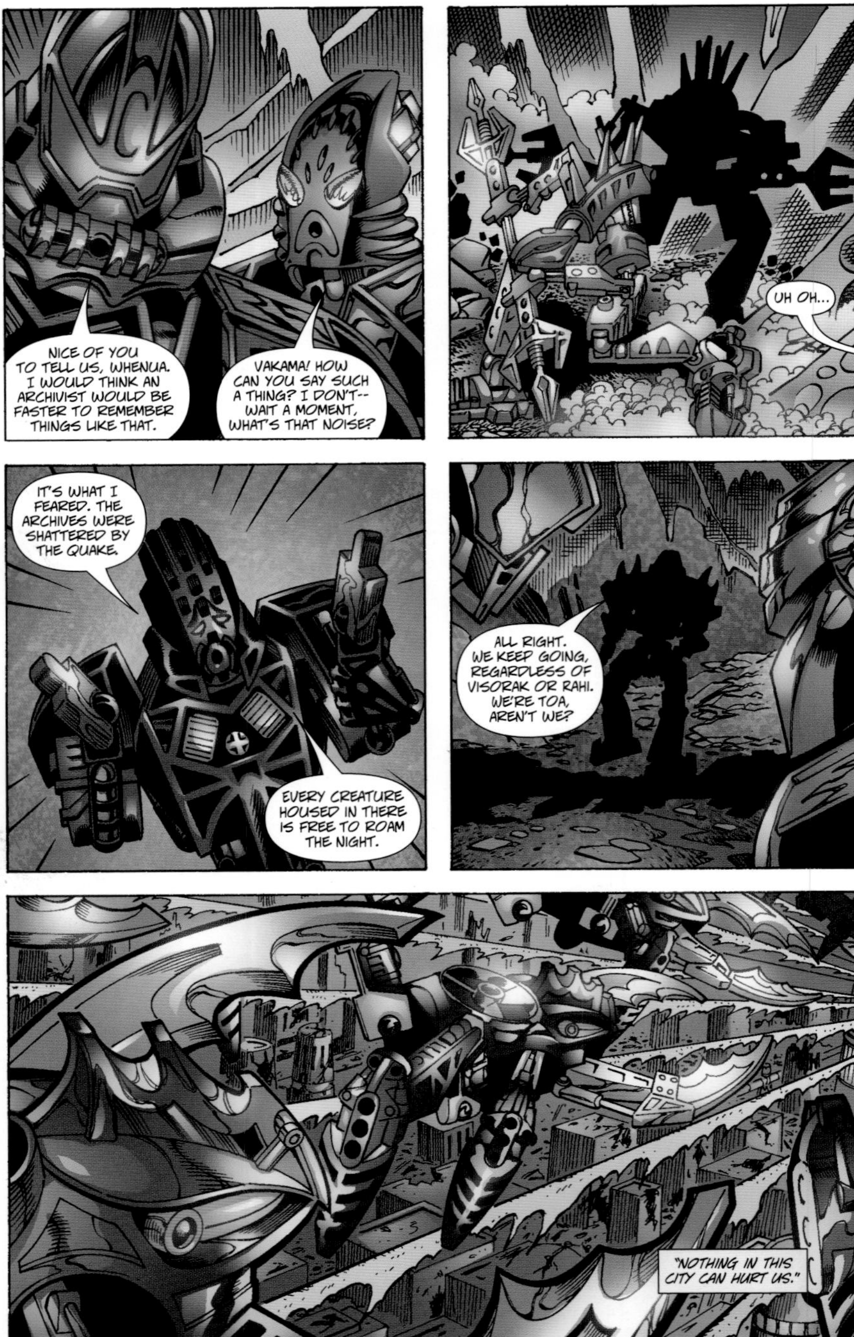
NICE OF YOU TO TELL US, WHENUA. I WOULD THINK AN ARCHIVIST WOULD BE FASTER TO REMEMBER THINGS LIKE THAT.
VAKAMA! HOW CAN YOU SAY SUCH A THING? I DON'T-- WAIT A MOMENT, WHAT'S THAT NOISE?
UH OH...
IT'S WHAT I FEARED. THE ARCHIVES WERE SHATTERED BY THE QUAKE.
EVERY CREATURE HOUSED IN THERE IS FREE TO ROAM THE NIGHT.
ALL RIGHT. WE KEEP GOING, REGARDLESS OF VISORAK OR RAHI. WE'RE TOA, AREN'T WE?
"NOTHING IN THIS CITY CAN HURT US."

LATER...

SEE? I TOLD YOU WE WOULD MAKE IT HERE WITHOUT ANY PROBLEM.

SURE, IT WAS ONE BIG HAPPY-WALK...

* FOR FULL DETAILS CHECK OUT **BIONICLE** ADVENTURES 7: WEB OF THE VISORAK.

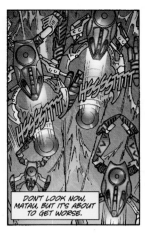

HSSSSTTT!

HSSSSTTT!

HSSSSTTT!

DON'T LOOK NOW, MATAU, BUT IT'S ABOUT TO GET WORSE.

THE VISORAK SPINNERS STRIKE THEIR TARGETS.

UNNNGGHH!

INSTANTLY PARALYZED, THE TOA FALL!

SENSING FINAL VICTORY, THE VISORAK KEELERAK CLOSE IN ON THE HELPLESS TOA.

THE HUNT HAS ENDED IN THE ONLY WAY IT COULD. BUT THE NIGHTMARE IS JUST BEGINNING...

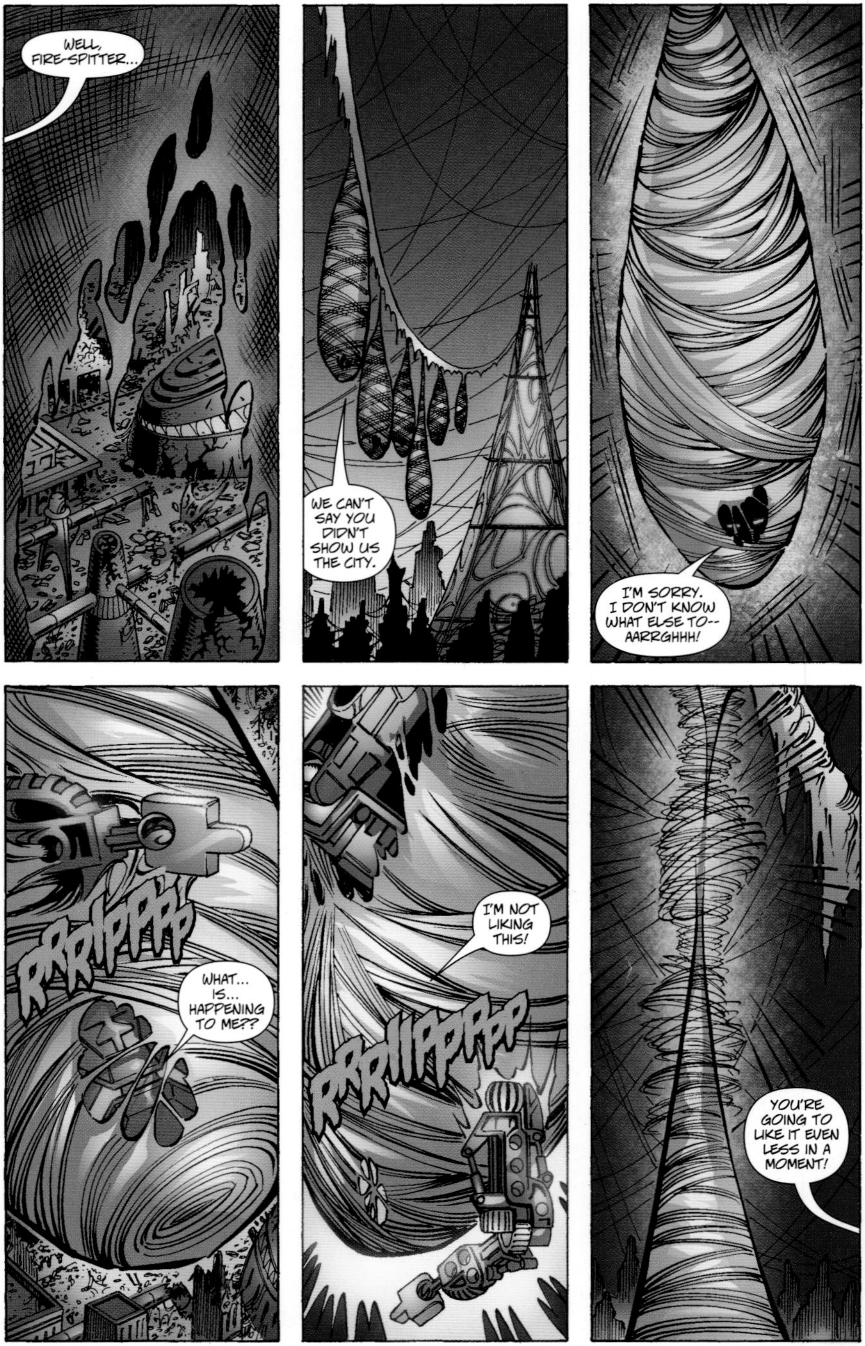
WELL, FIRE-SPITTER...
WE CAN'T SAY YOU DIDN'T SHOW US THE CITY.
I'M SORRY. I DON'T KNOW WHAT ELSE TO-- AARRGHHH!
RRRIPPPP
WHAT... IS... HAPPENING TO ME??
I'M NOT LIKING THIS!
RRRIIPPPP
YOU'RE GOING TO LIKE IT EVEN LESS IN A MOMENT!

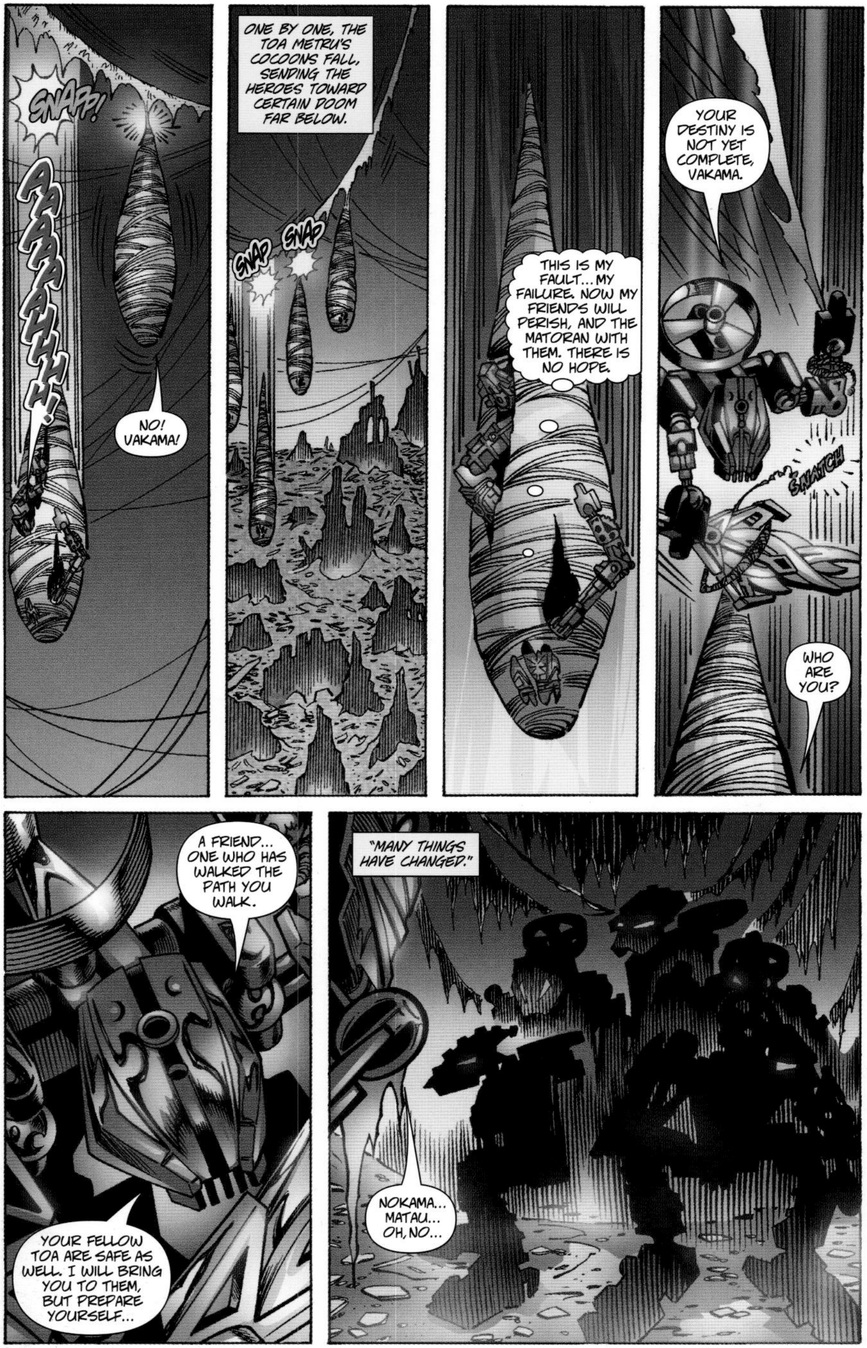
SNAPP!
AAAAAAHHHH!
NO! VAKAMA!
ONE BY ONE, THE TOA METRU'S COCOONS FALL, SENDING THE HEROES TOWARD CERTAIN DOOM FAR BELOW.
SNAP
SNAP
THIS IS MY FAULT... MY FAILURE. NOW MY FRIENDS WILL PERISH, AND THE MATORAN WITH THEM. THERE IS NO HOPE.
YOUR DESTINY IS NOT YET COMPLETE, VAKAMA.
SNATCH
WHO ARE YOU?
A FRIEND... ONE WHO HAS WALKED THE PATH YOU WALK.
YOUR FELLOW TOA ARE SAFE AS WELL. I WILL BRING YOU TO THEM, BUT PREPARE YOURSELF...
"MANY THINGS HAVE CHANGED."
NOKAMA... MATAU... OH, NO...

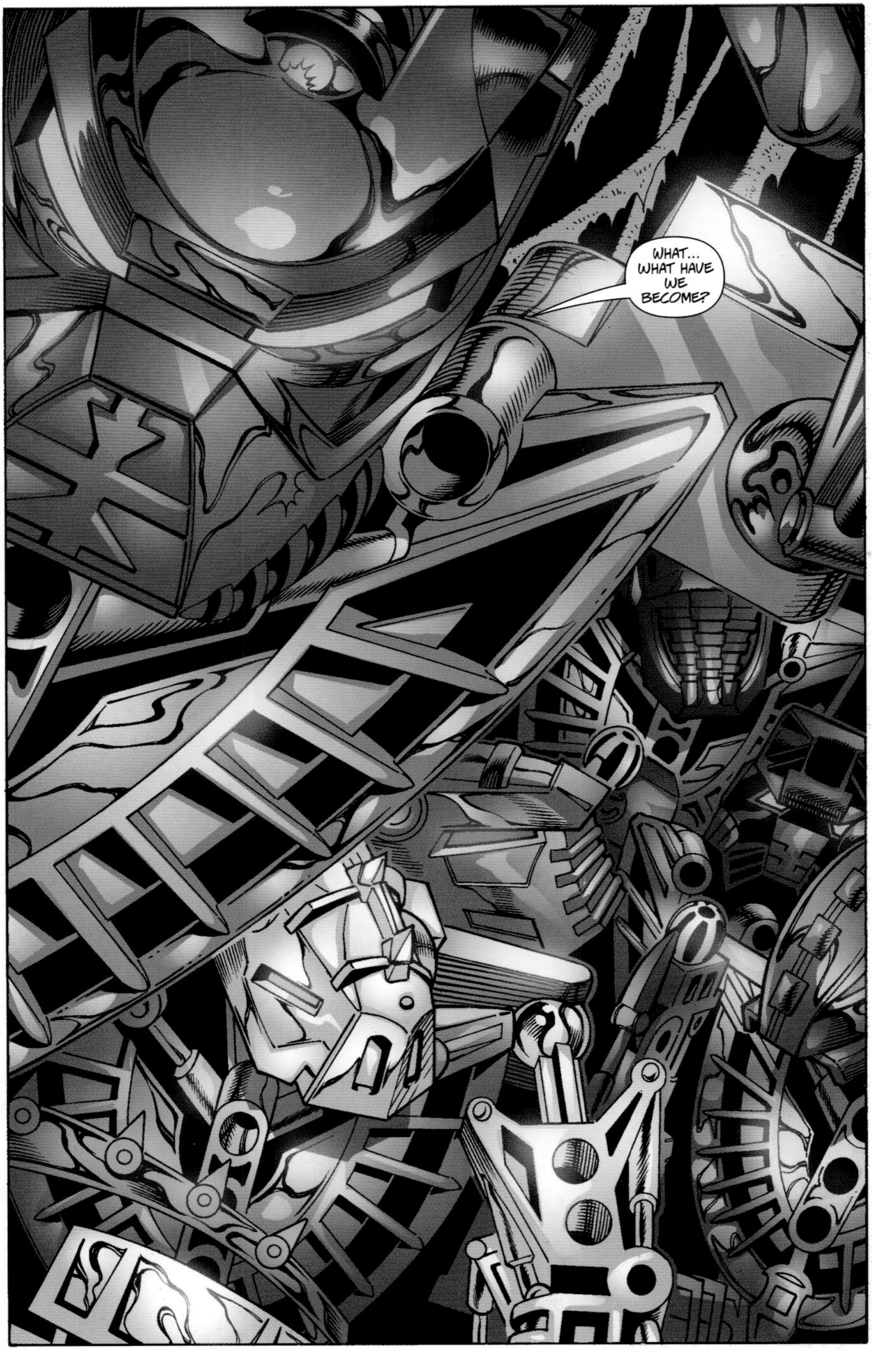
WHAT... WHAT HAVE WE BECOME?

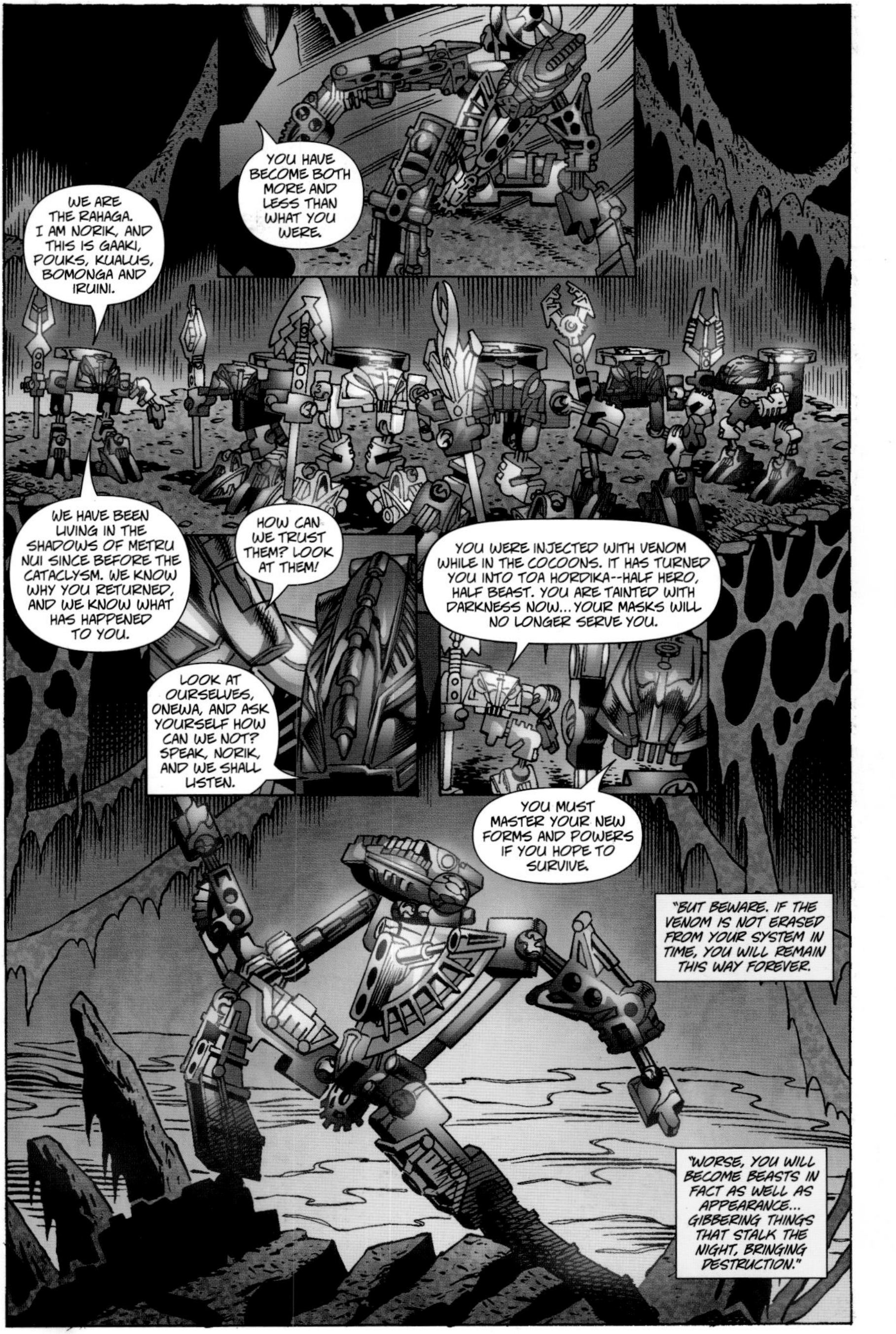
YOU HAVE BECOME BOTH MORE AND LESS THAN WHAT YOU WERE.
WE ARE THE RAHAGA. I AM NORIK, AND THIS IS GAAKI, POUKS, KUALUS, BOMONGA AND IRUINI.
WE HAVE BEEN LIVING IN THE SHADOWS OF METRU NUI SINCE BEFORE THE CATACLYSM. WE KNOW WHY YOU RETURNED, AND WE KNOW WHAT HAS HAPPENED TO YOU.
HOW CAN WE TRUST THEM? LOOK AT THEM!
LOOK AT OURSELVES, ONEWA, AND ASK YOURSELF HOW CAN WE NOT? SPEAK, NORIK, AND WE SHALL LISTEN.
YOU WERE INJECTED WITH VENOM WHILE IN THE COCOONS. IT HAS TURNED YOU INTO TOA HORDIKA--HALF HERO, HALF BEAST. YOU ARE TAINTED WITH DARKNESS NOW... YOUR MASKS WILL NO LONGER SERVE YOU.
YOU MUST MASTER YOUR NEW FORMS AND POWERS IF YOU HOPE TO SURVIVE.
"BUT BEWARE. IF THE VENOM IS NOT ERASED FROM YOUR SYSTEM IN TIME, YOU WILL REMAIN THIS WAY FOREVER.
"WORSE, YOU WILL BECOME BEASTS IN FACT AS WELL AS APPEARANCE... GIBBERING THINGS THAT STALK THE NIGHT, BRINGING DESTRUCTION."

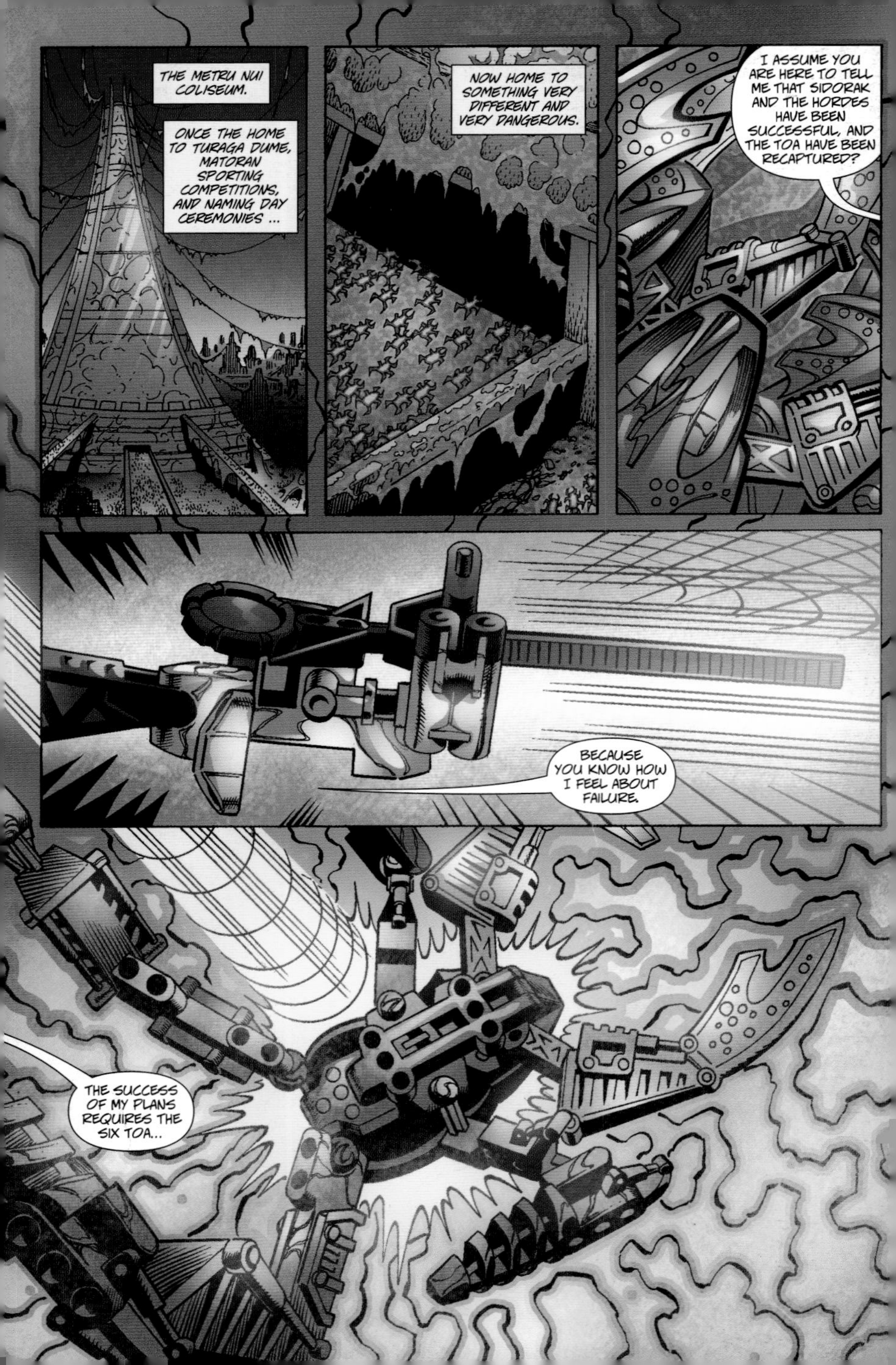
THE METRU NUI COLISEUM.
ONCE THE HOME TO TURAGA DUME, MATORAN SPORTING COMPETITIONS, AND NAMING DAY CEREMONIES ...
NOW HOME TO SOMETHING VERY DIFFERENT AND VERY DANGEROUS.
I ASSUME YOU ARE HERE TO TELL ME THAT SIDORAK AND THE HORDES HAVE BEEN SUCCESSFUL, AND THE TOA HAVE BEEN RECAPTURED?
BECAUSE YOU KNOW HOW I FEEL ABOUT FAILURE.
THE SUCCESS OF MY PLANS REQUIRES THE SIX TOA...

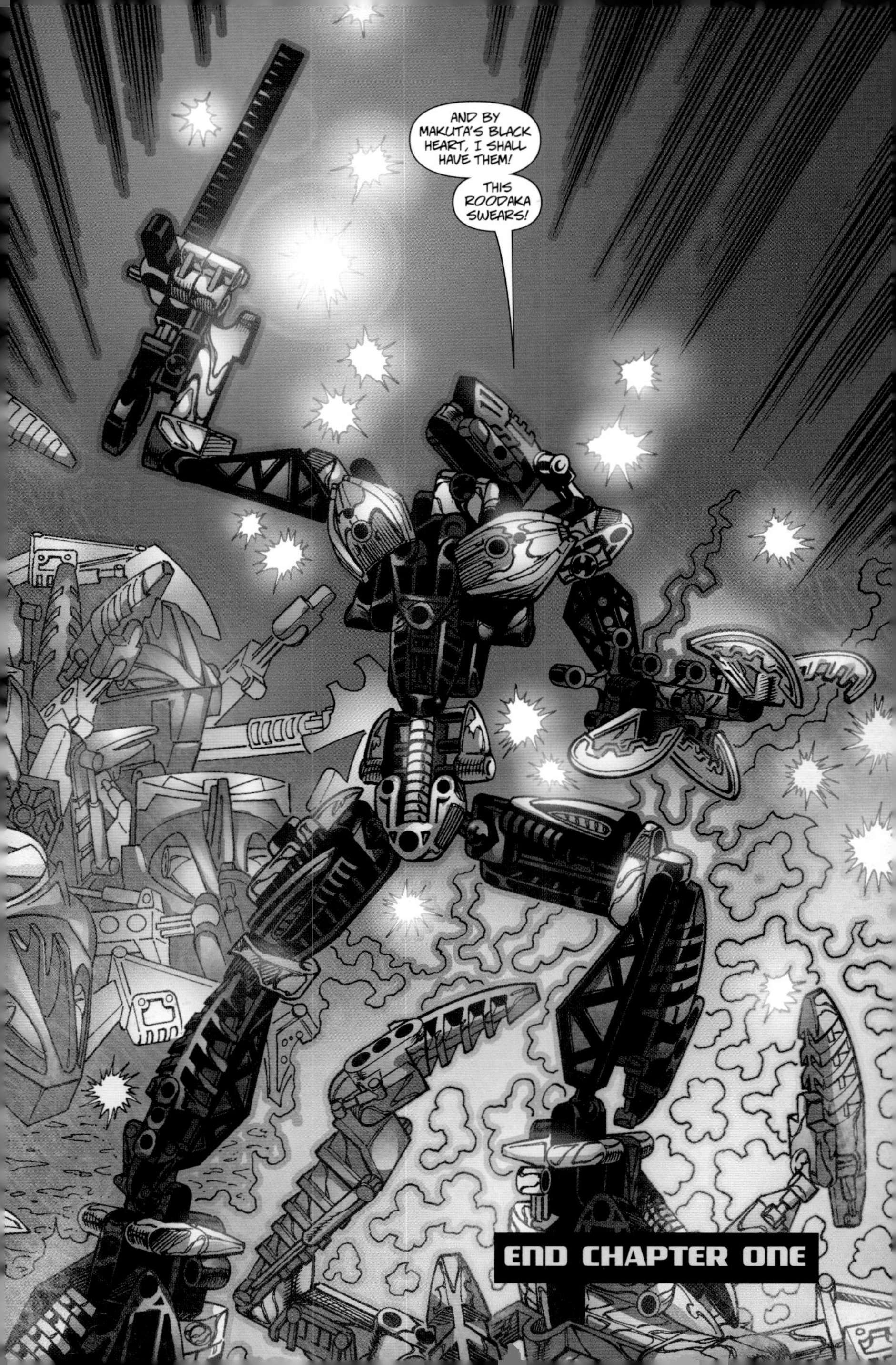
AND BY MAKUTA'S BLACK HEART, I SHALL HAVE THEM!
THIS ROODAKA SWEARS!
END CHAPTER ONE

TRIAL BY FIRE
CHAPTER TWO

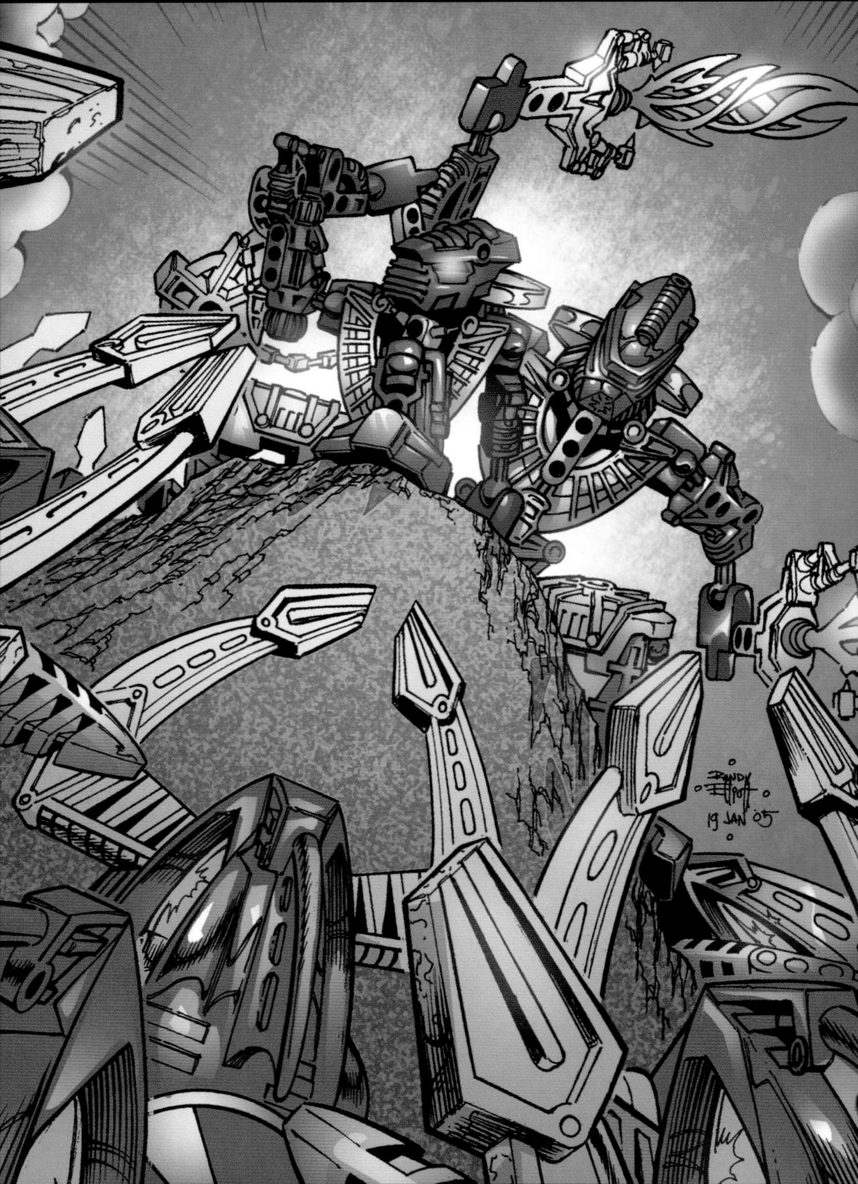
RANDY ELLIOTT
19 JAN '05

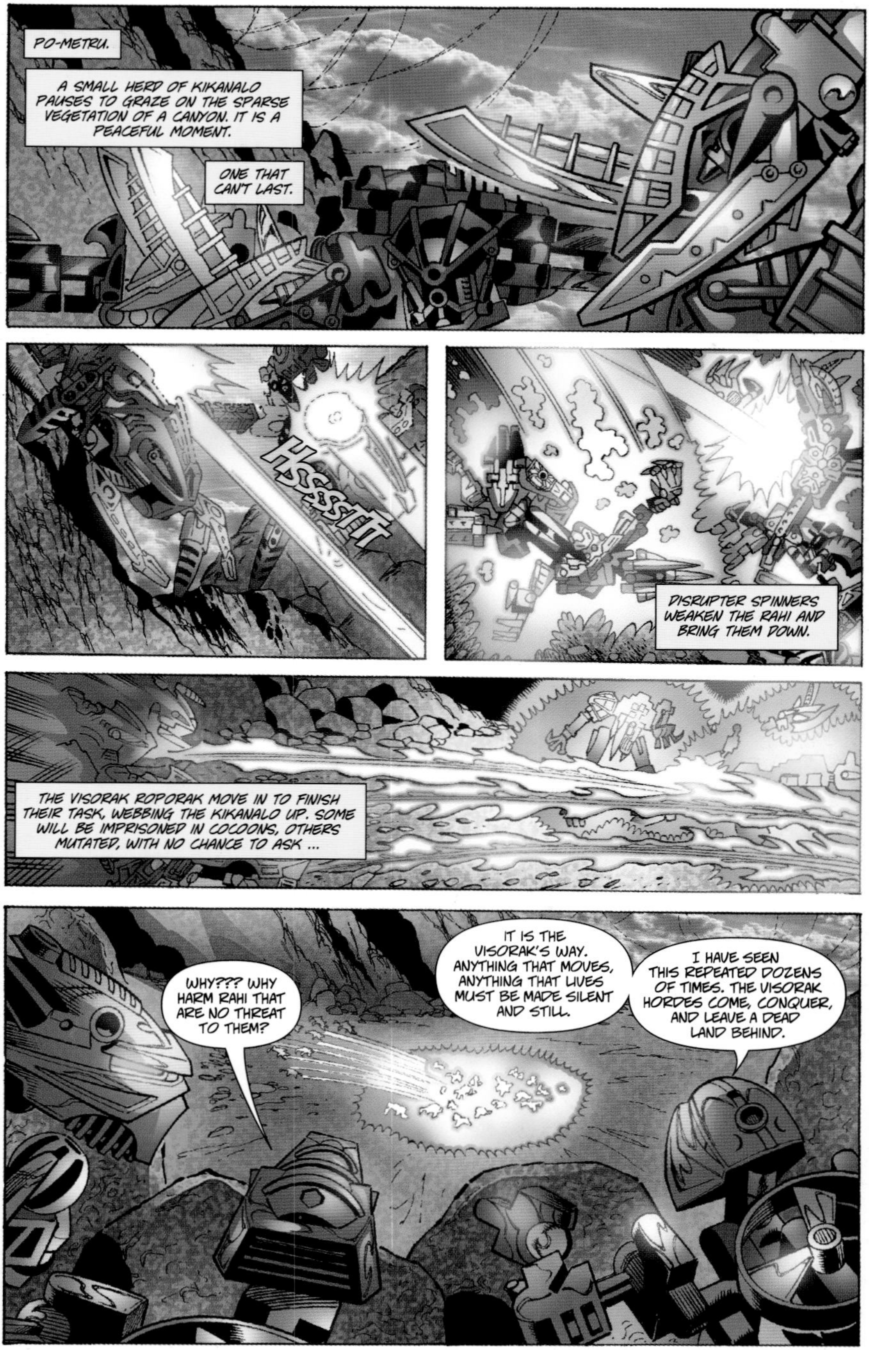

PO-METRU.
A SMALL HERD OF KIKANALO PAUSES TO GRAZE ON THE SPARSE VEGETATION OF A CANYON. IT IS A PEACEFUL MOMENT.
ONE THAT CAN'T LAST.
HSSSSTTT
DISRUPTER SPINNERS WEAKEN THE RAHI AND BRING THEM DOWN.
THE VISORAK ROPORAK MOVE IN TO FINISH THEIR TASK, WEBBING THE KIKANALO UP. SOME WILL BE IMPRISONED IN COCOONS, OTHERS MUTATED, WITH NO CHANCE TO ASK ...
WHY??? WHY HARM RAHI THAT ARE NO THREAT TO THEM?
IT IS THE VISORAK'S WAY. ANYTHING THAT MOVES, ANYTHING THAT LIVES MUST BE MADE SILENT AND STILL.
I HAVE SEEN THIS REPEATED DOZENS OF TIMES. THE VISORAK HORDES COME, CONQUER, AND LEAVE A DEAD LAND BEHIND.

NOT THIS TIME. NOT IN MY CITY.

VAKAMA! THIS WAS JUST MEANT TO BE A SCOUTING MISSION!

HE'S NOT LISTENING, RAHAGA. THEN AGAIN, WHEN DOES HE EVER?

YOU ARE THE ONE WHO SHOWED ME HOW TO CHARGE THIS RHOTUKA SPINNER WITH MY NEW TOOLS, NORIK.

NOW SHUT UP AND LET ME DO MY JOB!

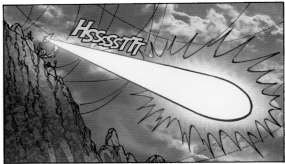

HSSSSTTT

VENGEANCE OF THE VISORAK

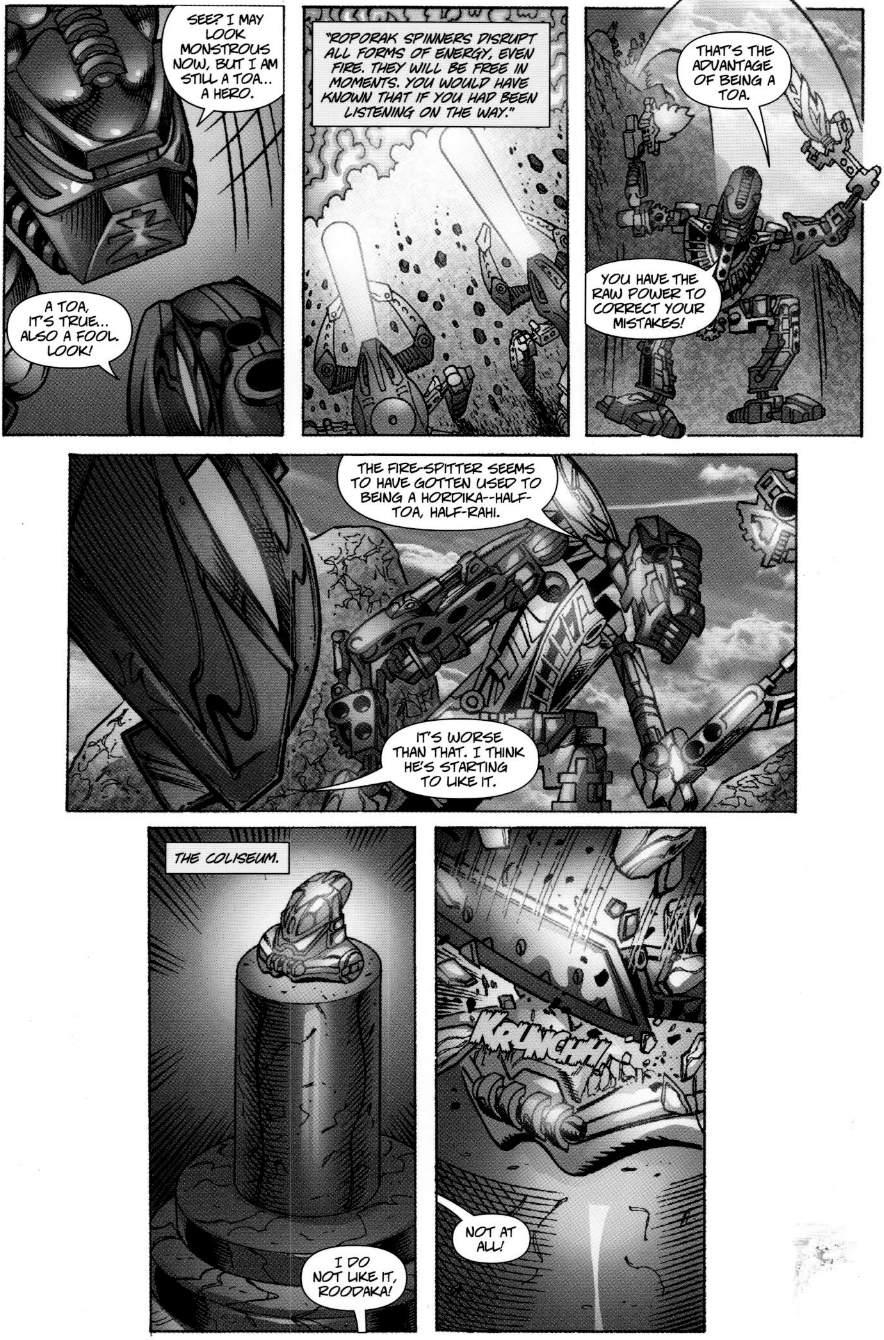

SEE? I MAY LOOK MONSTROUS NOW, BUT I AM STILL A TOA... A HERO.
A TOA, IT'S TRUE... ALSO A FOOL. LOOK!
"ROPORAK SPINNERS DISRUPT ALL FORMS OF ENERGY, EVEN FIRE. THEY WILL BE FREE IN MOMENTS. YOU WOULD HAVE KNOWN THAT IF YOU HAD BEEN LISTENING ON THE WAY."
THAT'S THE ADVANTAGE OF BEING A TOA.
YOU HAVE THE RAW POWER TO CORRECT YOUR MISTAKES!
THE FIRE-SPITTER SEEMS TO HAVE GOTTEN USED TO BEING A HORDIKA--HALF-TOA, HALF-RAHI.
IT'S WORSE THAN THAT. I THINK HE'S STARTING TO LIKE IT.
THE COLISEUM.
I DO NOT LIKE IT, ROODAKA!
KRUNCHH
NOT AT ALL!

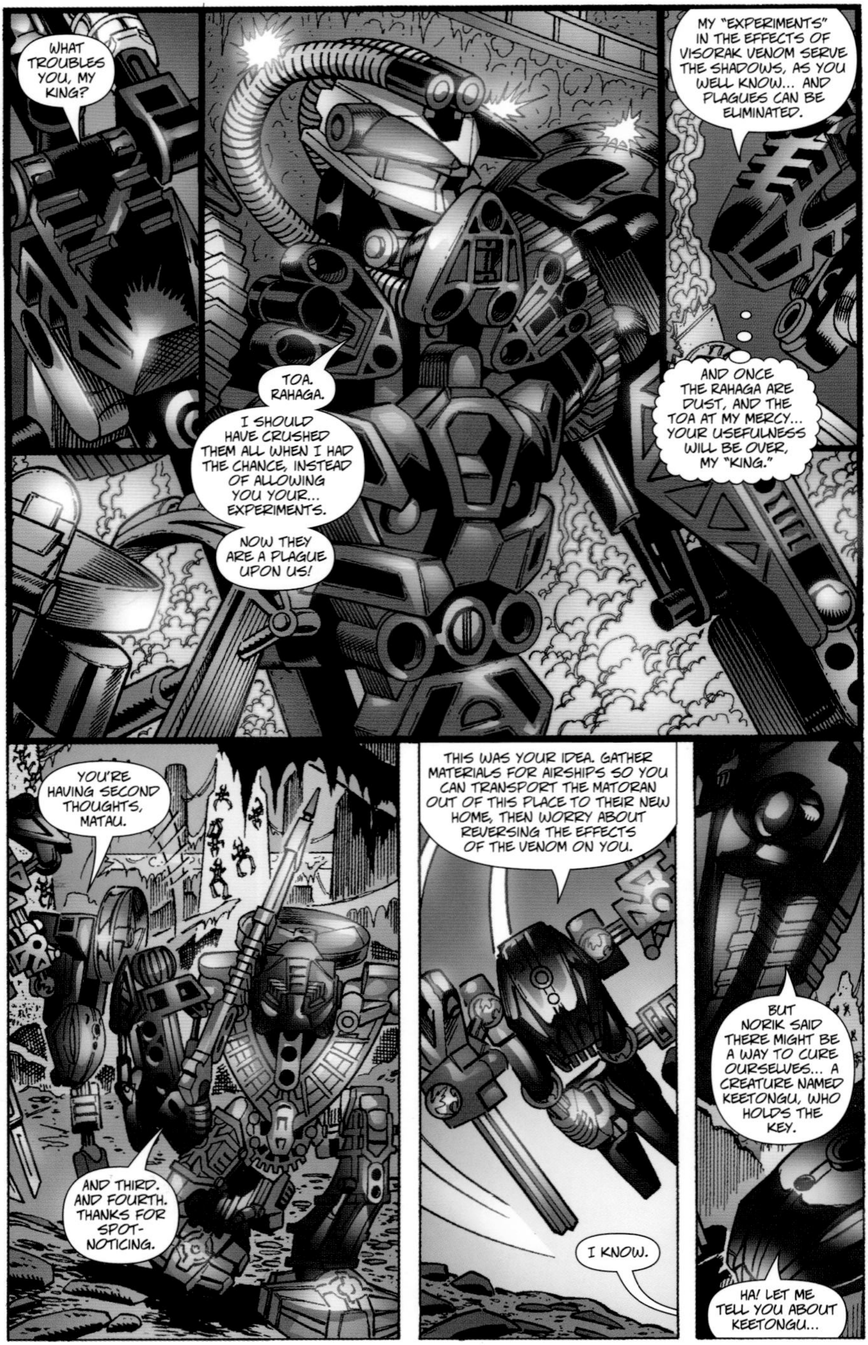
WHAT TROUBLES YOU, MY KING?
TOA. RAHAGA.
I SHOULD HAVE CRUSHED THEM ALL WHEN I HAD THE CHANCE, INSTEAD OF ALLOWING YOU YOUR... EXPERIMENTS.
NOW THEY ARE A PLAGUE UPON US!
MY "EXPERIMENTS" IN THE EFFECTS OF VISORAK VENOM SERVE THE SHADOWS, AS YOU WELL KNOW... AND PLAGUES CAN BE ELIMINATED.
AND ONCE THE RAHAGA ARE DUST, AND THE TOA AT MY MERCY... YOUR USEFULNESS WILL BE OVER, MY "KING."
YOU'RE HAVING SECOND THOUGHTS, MATAU.
AND THIRD. AND FOURTH. THANKS FOR SPOT-NOTICING.
THIS WAS YOUR IDEA. GATHER MATERIALS FOR AIRSHIPS SO YOU CAN TRANSPORT THE MATORAN OUT OF THIS PLACE TO THEIR NEW HOME, THEN WORRY ABOUT REVERSING THE EFFECTS OF THE VENOM ON YOU.
I KNOW.
BUT NORIK SAID THERE MIGHT BE A WAY TO CURE OURSELVES... A CREATURE NAMED KEETONGU, WHO HOLDS THE KEY.
HA! LET ME TELL YOU ABOUT KEETONGU...

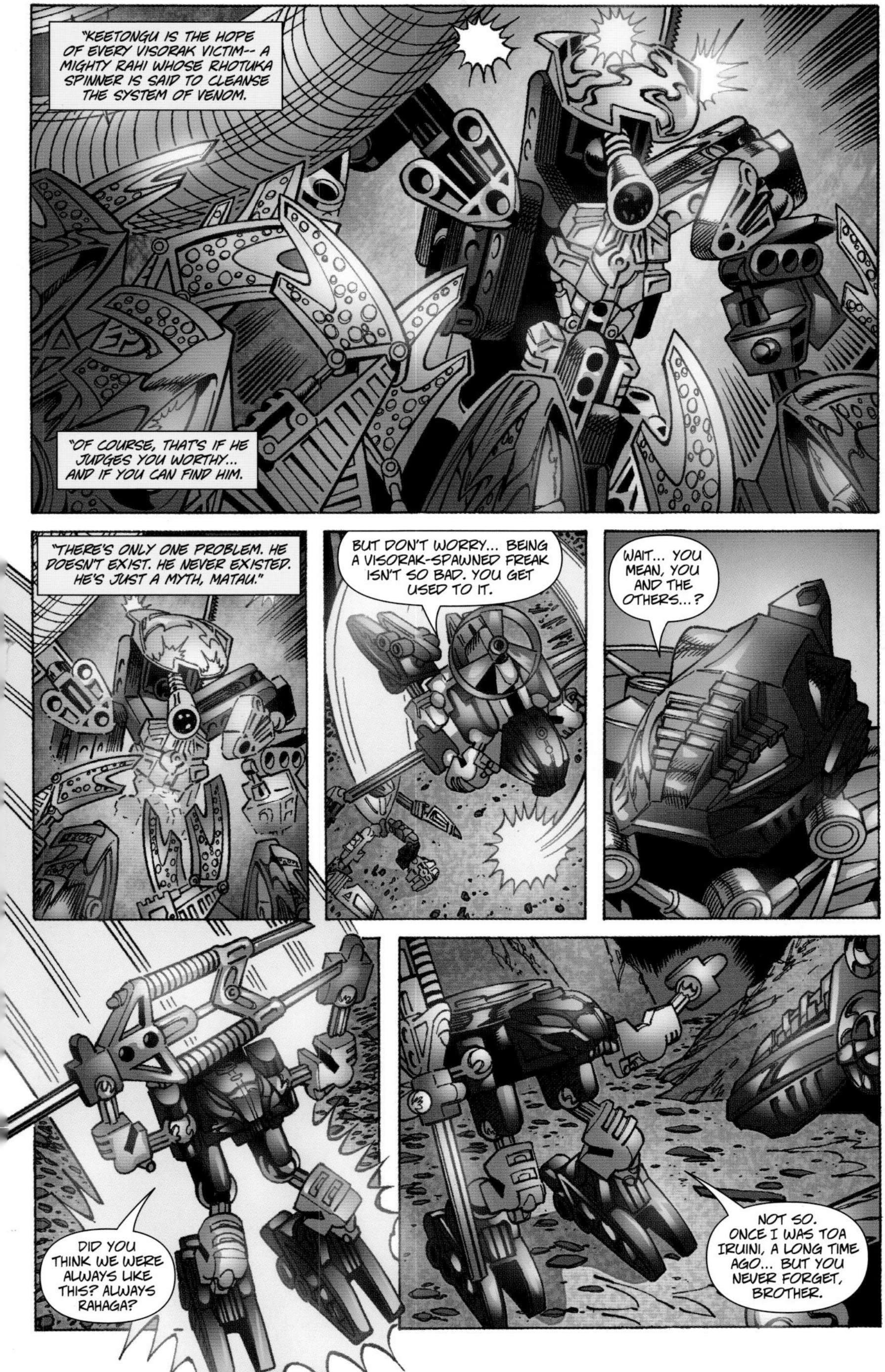
"KEETONGU IS THE HOPE OF EVERY VISORAK VICTIM-- A MIGHTY RAHI WHOSE RHOTUKA SPINNER IS SAID TO CLEANSE THE SYSTEM OF VENOM.
"OF COURSE, THAT'S IF HE JUDGES YOU WORTHY... AND IF YOU CAN FIND HIM.
"THERE'S ONLY ONE PROBLEM. HE DOESN'T EXIST. HE NEVER EXISTED. HE'S JUST A MYTH, MATAU."
BUT DON'T WORRY... BEING A VISORAK-SPAWNED FREAK ISN'T SO BAD. YOU GET USED TO IT.
WAIT... YOU MEAN, YOU AND THE OTHERS...?
DID YOU THINK WE WERE ALWAYS LIKE THIS? ALWAYS RAHAGA?
NOT SO. ONCE I WAS TOA IRUINI, A LONG TIME AGO... BUT YOU NEVER FORGET, BROTHER.

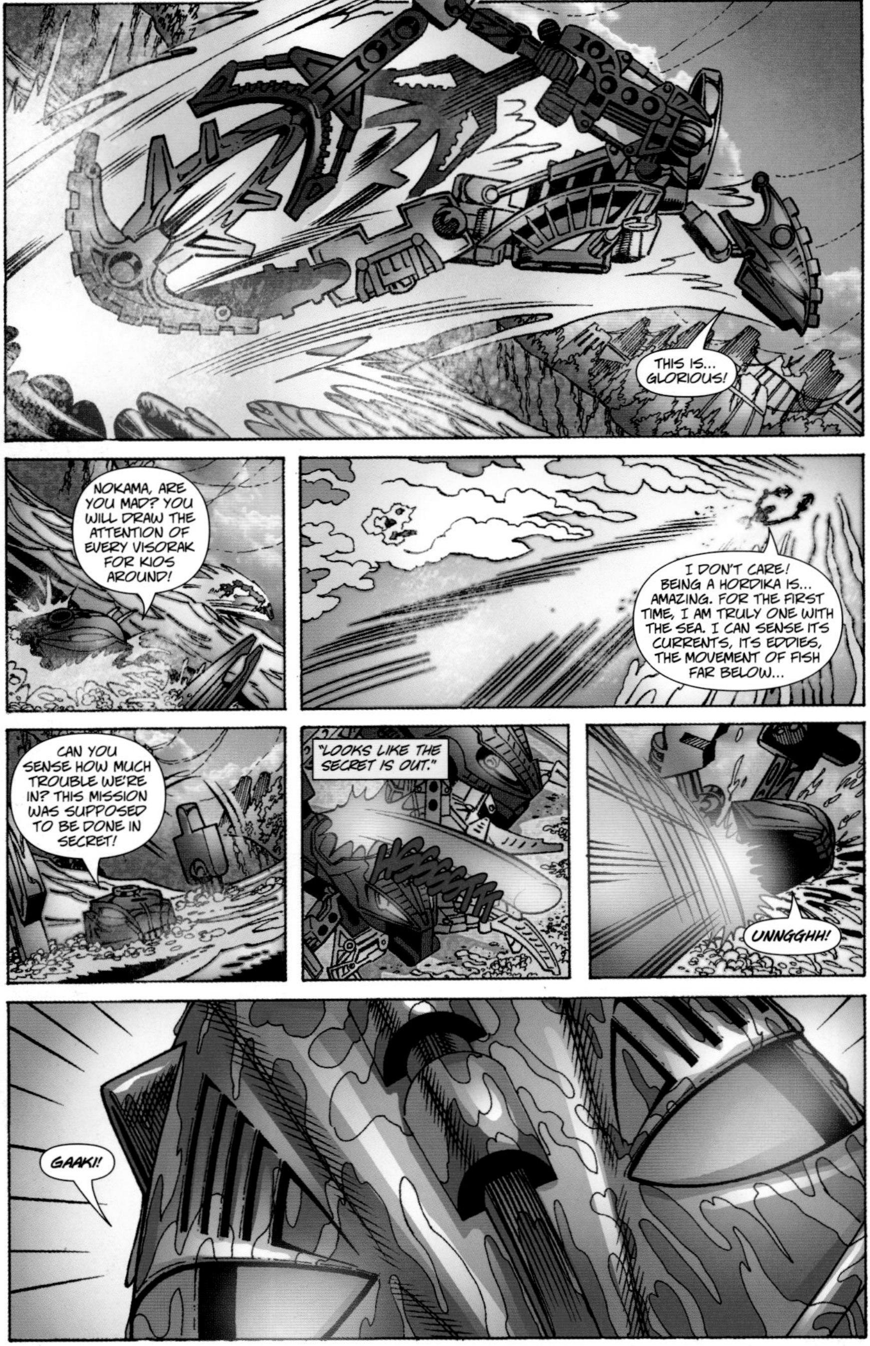
THIS IS... GLORIOUS!
NOKAMA, ARE YOU MAD? YOU WILL DRAW THE ATTENTION OF EVERY VISORAK FOR KIOS AROUND!
I DON'T CARE! BEING A HORDIKA IS... AMAZING. FOR THE FIRST TIME, I AM TRULY ONE WITH THE SEA. I CAN SENSE ITS CURRENTS, ITS EDDIES, THE MOVEMENT OF FISH FAR BELOW...
CAN YOU SENSE HOW MUCH TROUBLE WE'RE IN? THIS MISSION WAS SUPPOSED TO BE DONE IN SECRET!
"LOOKS LIKE THE SECRET IS OUT."
UNNGGHH!
GAAKI!

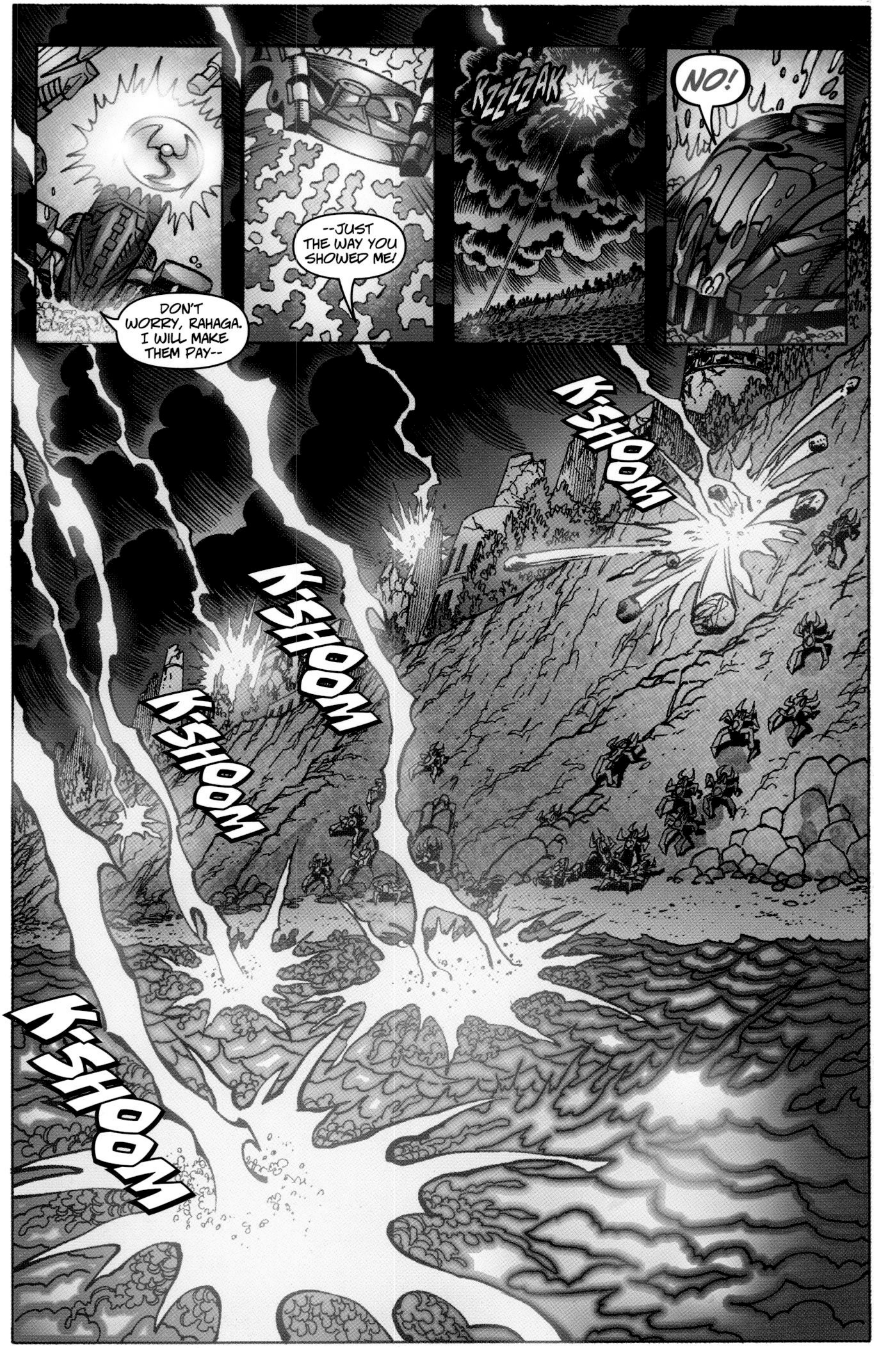
DON'T WORRY, RAHAGA. I WILL MAKE THEM PAY--
--JUST THE WAY YOU SHOWED ME!
KRZZZZAK
NO!
K-SHOOM
K-SHOOM
K-SHOOM
K-SHOOM

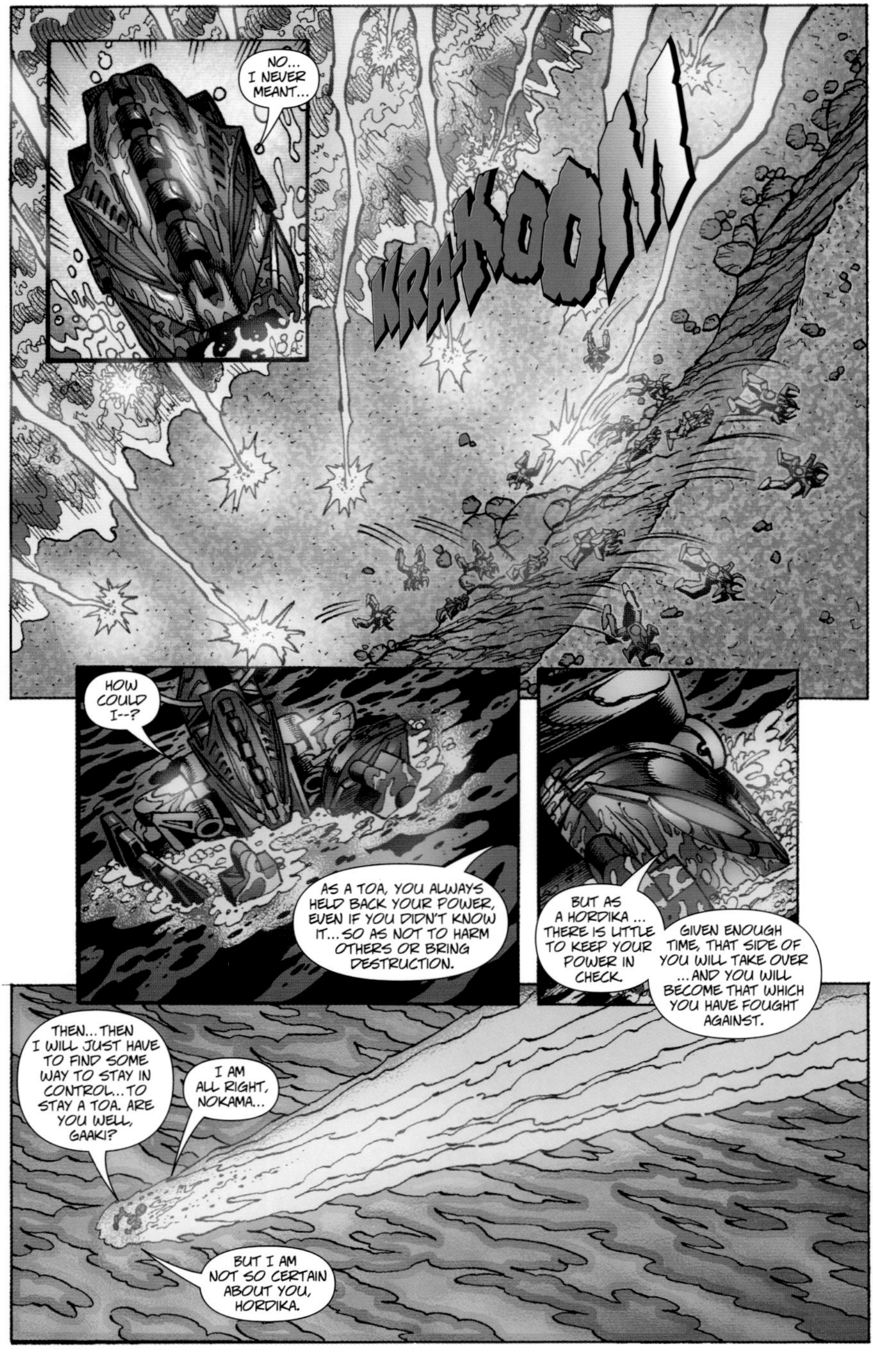
NO... I NEVER MEANT...
KRA-KOOM
HOW COULD I--?
AS A TOA, YOU ALWAYS HELD BACK YOUR POWER, EVEN IF YOU DIDN'T KNOW IT... SO AS NOT TO HARM OTHERS OR BRING DESTRUCTION.
BUT AS A HORDIKA ... THERE IS LITTLE TO KEEP YOUR POWER IN CHECK.
GIVEN ENOUGH TIME, THAT SIDE OF YOU WILL TAKE OVER ...AND YOU WILL BECOME THAT WHICH YOU HAVE FOUGHT AGAINST.
THEN... THEN I WILL JUST HAVE TO FIND SOME WAY TO STAY IN CONTROL... TO STAY A TOA. ARE YOU WELL, GAAKI?
I AM ALL RIGHT, NOKAMA...
BUT I AM NOT SO CERTAIN ABOUT YOU, HORDIKA.

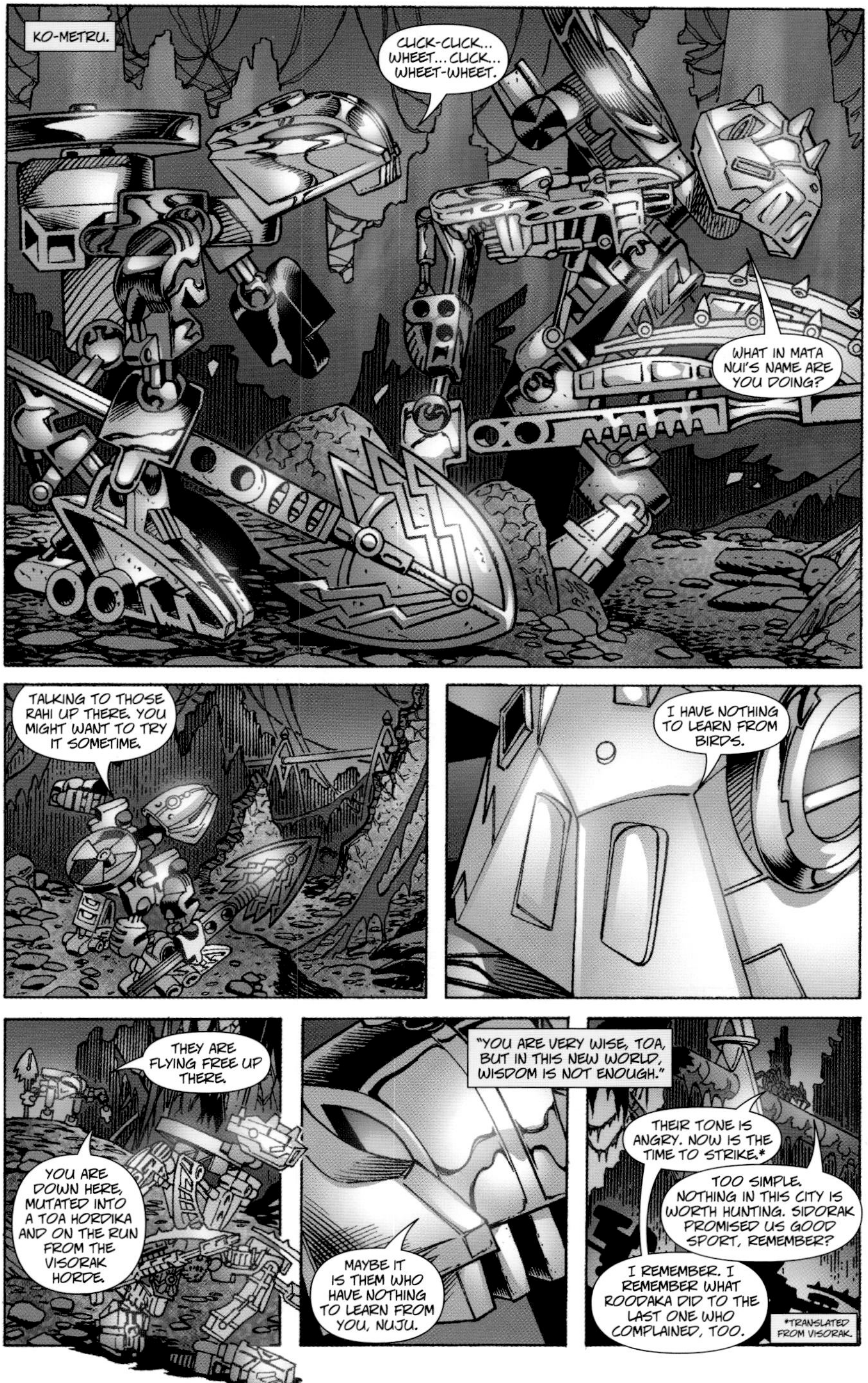
KO-METRU.
CLICK-CLICK... WHEET... CLICK... WHEET-WHEET.
WHAT IN MATA NUI'S NAME ARE YOU DOING?
TALKING TO THOSE RAHI UP THERE. YOU MIGHT WANT TO TRY IT SOMETIME.
I HAVE NOTHING TO LEARN FROM BIRDS.
THEY ARE FLYING FREE UP THERE.
YOU ARE DOWN HERE, MUTATED INTO A TOA HORDIKA AND ON THE RUN FROM THE VISORAK HORDE.
"YOU ARE VERY WISE, TOA, BUT IN THIS NEW WORLD, WISDOM IS NOT ENOUGH."
MAYBE IT IS THEM WHO HAVE NOTHING TO LEARN FROM YOU, NUJU.
THEIR TONE IS ANGRY. NOW IS THE TIME TO STRIKE.*
TOO SIMPLE. NOTHING IN THIS CITY IS WORTH HUNTING. SIDORAK PROMISED US GOOD SPORT, REMEMBER?
I REMEMBER. I REMEMBER WHAT ROODAKA DID TO THE LAST ONE WHO COMPLAINED, TOO.
*TRANSLATED FROM VISORAK.

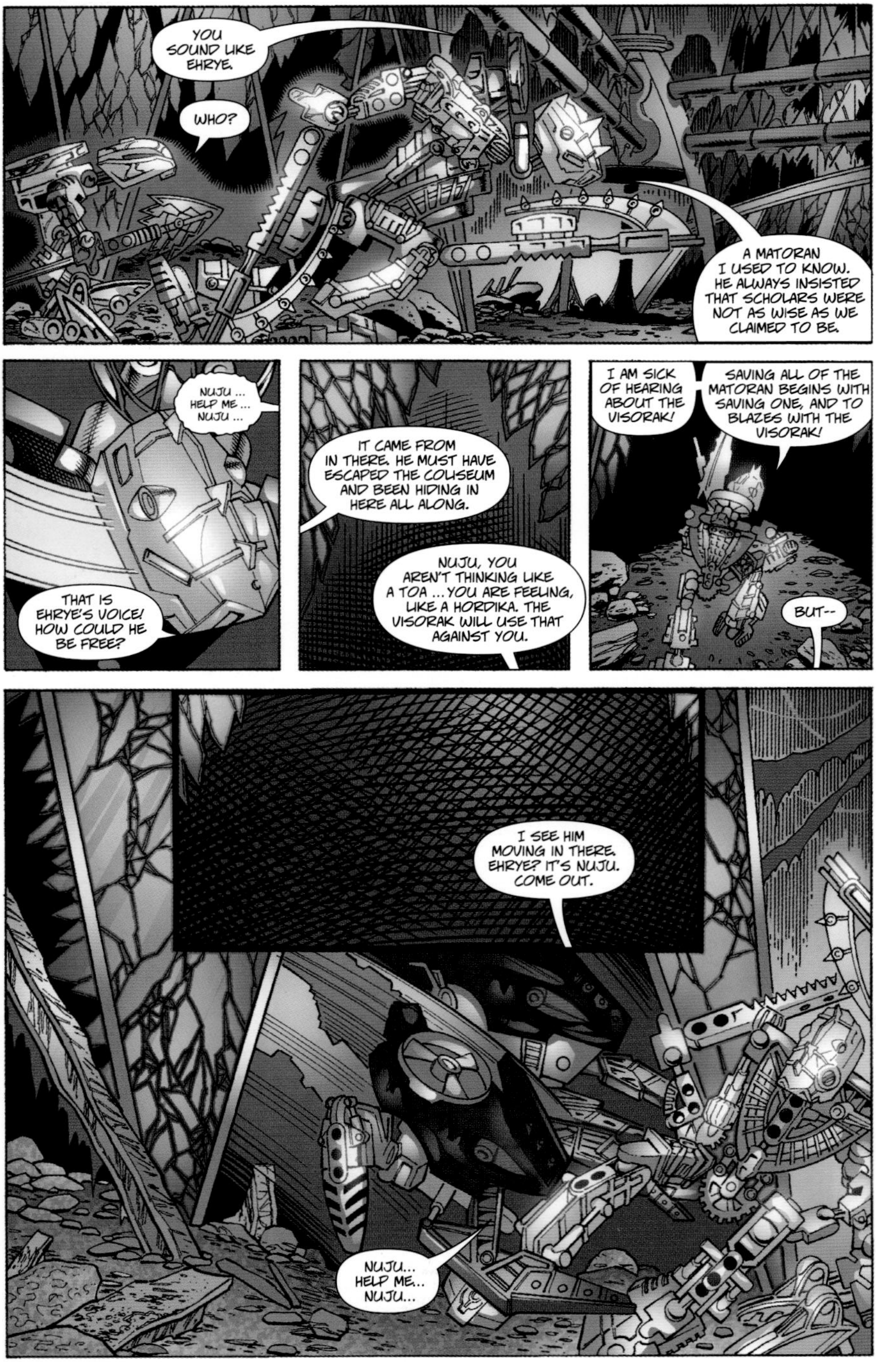
YOU SOUND LIKE EHRYE.
WHO?
A MATORAN I USED TO KNOW. HE ALWAYS INSISTED THAT SCHOLARS WERE NOT AS WISE AS WE CLAIMED TO BE.
NUJU ... HELP ME ... NUJU ...
THAT IS EHRYE'S VOICE! HOW COULD HE BE FREE?
IT CAME FROM IN THERE. HE MUST HAVE ESCAPED THE COLISEUM AND BEEN HIDING IN HERE ALL ALONG.
NUJU, YOU AREN'T THINKING LIKE A TOA ... YOU ARE FEELING, LIKE A HORDIKA. THE VISORAK WILL USE THAT AGAINST YOU.
I AM SICK OF HEARING ABOUT THE VISORAK!
SAVING ALL OF THE MATORAN BEGINS WITH SAVING ONE, AND TO BLAZES WITH THE VISORAK!
BUT--
I SEE HIM MOVING IN THERE. EHRYE? IT'S NUJU. COME OUT.
NUJU... HELP ME... NUJU...

OOHNORAK CAN IMITATE THE VOICES OF THOSE YOU TRUST, STOLEN FROM YOUR VERY THOUGHTS. I TRIED TO WARN YOU!

NEXT TIME, TRY HARDER!

I ENDURED YOUR VENOM, CREATURE... AND YOUR WEBS... BUT ONE THING I WILL NOT ENDURE--

--IS YOUR BREATH!

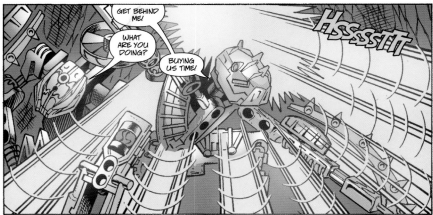

GET BEHIND ME!

WHAT ARE YOU DOING?

BUYING US TIME!

HSSSSSFT

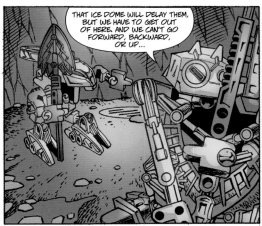

THAT ICE DOME WILL DELAY THEM, BUT WE HAVE TO GET OUT OF HERE AND WE CAN'T GO FORWARD, BACKWARD, OR UP...

...SO WE GO DOWN.

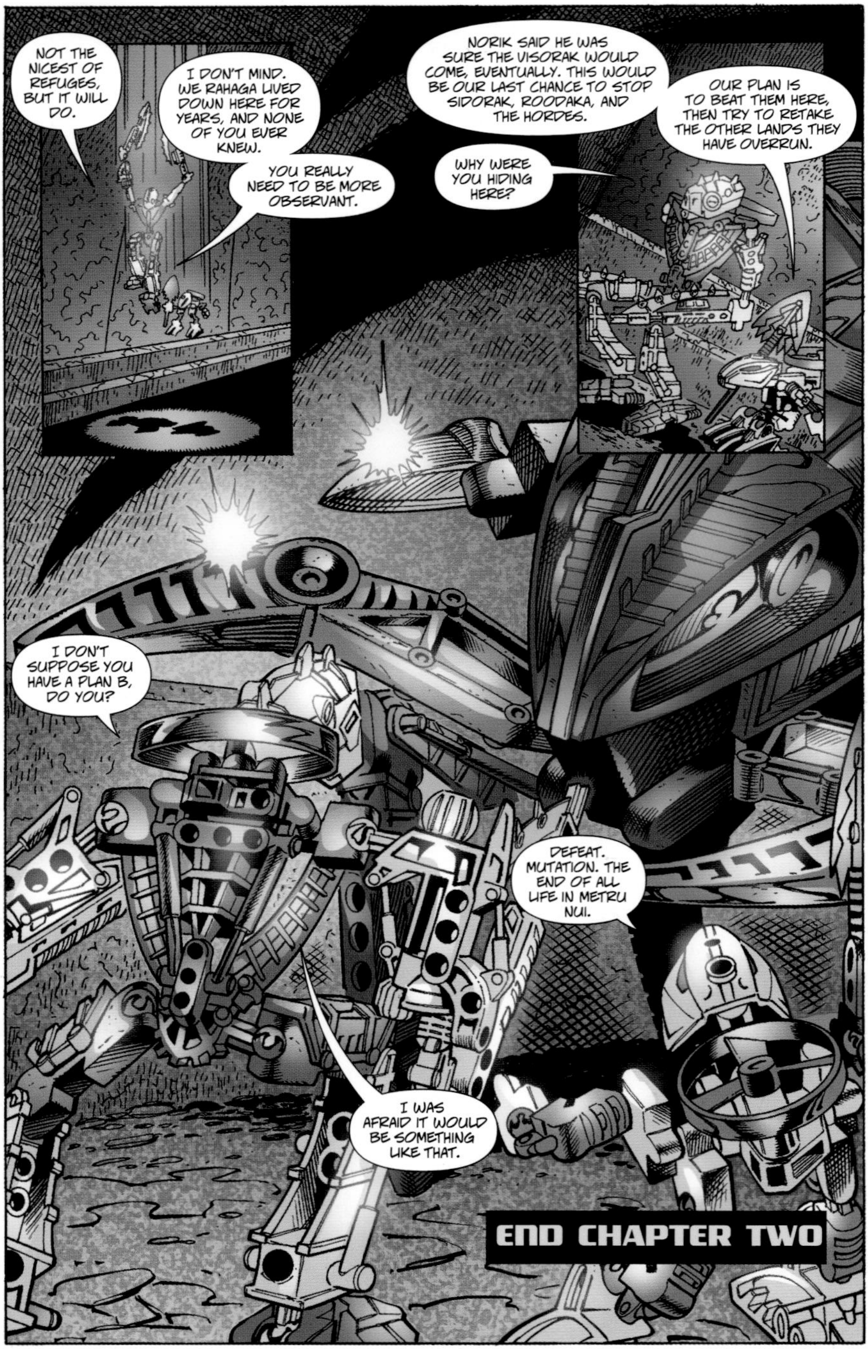
NOT THE NICEST OF REFUGES, BUT IT WILL DO.
I DON'T MIND. WE RAHAGA LIVED DOWN HERE FOR YEARS, AND NONE OF YOU EVER KNEW.
YOU REALLY NEED TO BE MORE OBSERVANT.
WHY WERE YOU HIDING HERE?
NORIK SAID HE WAS SURE THE VISORAK WOULD COME, EVENTUALLY. THIS WOULD BE OUR LAST CHANCE TO STOP SIDORAK, ROODAKA, AND THE HORDES.
OUR PLAN IS TO BEAT THEM HERE, THEN TRY TO RETAKE THE OTHER LANDS THEY HAVE OVERRUN.
I DON'T SUPPOSE YOU HAVE A PLAN B, DO YOU?
DEFEAT. MUTATION. THE END OF ALL LIFE IN METRU NUI.
I WAS AFRAID IT WOULD BE SOMETHING LIKE THAT.
END CHAPTER TWO

ince the events of **BIONICLE 2:** ***Legends of Metru Nui***. **Here is a quick guide to the earthquake ravaged "city of shadows"**

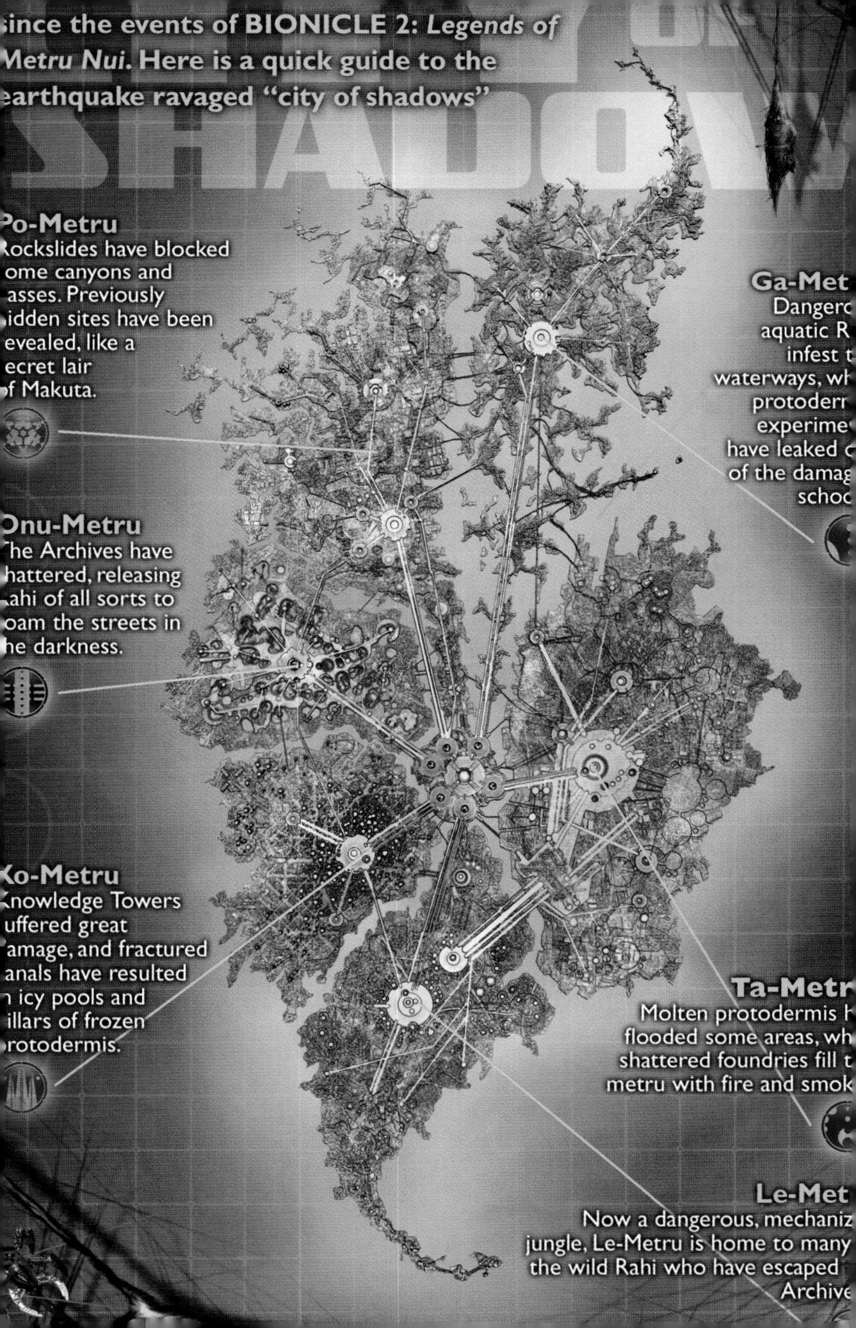

Po-Metru
Rockslides have blocked ome canyons and asses. Previously idden sites have been evealed, like a ecret lair f Makuta.

Onu-Metru
he Archives have hattered, releasing ahi of all sorts to oam the streets in he darkness.

Ko-Metru
nowledge Towers uffered great amage, and fractured anals have resulted n icy pools and illars of frozen rotodermis.

Ga-Met
Dangerc aquatic R infest t waterways, wh protoderr experime have leaked c of the damag schoc

Ta-Metr
Molten protodermis h flooded some areas, wh shattered foundries fill t metru with fire and smok

Le-Met
Now a dangerous, mechaniz jungle, Le-Metru is home to many the wild Rahi who have escaped Archive

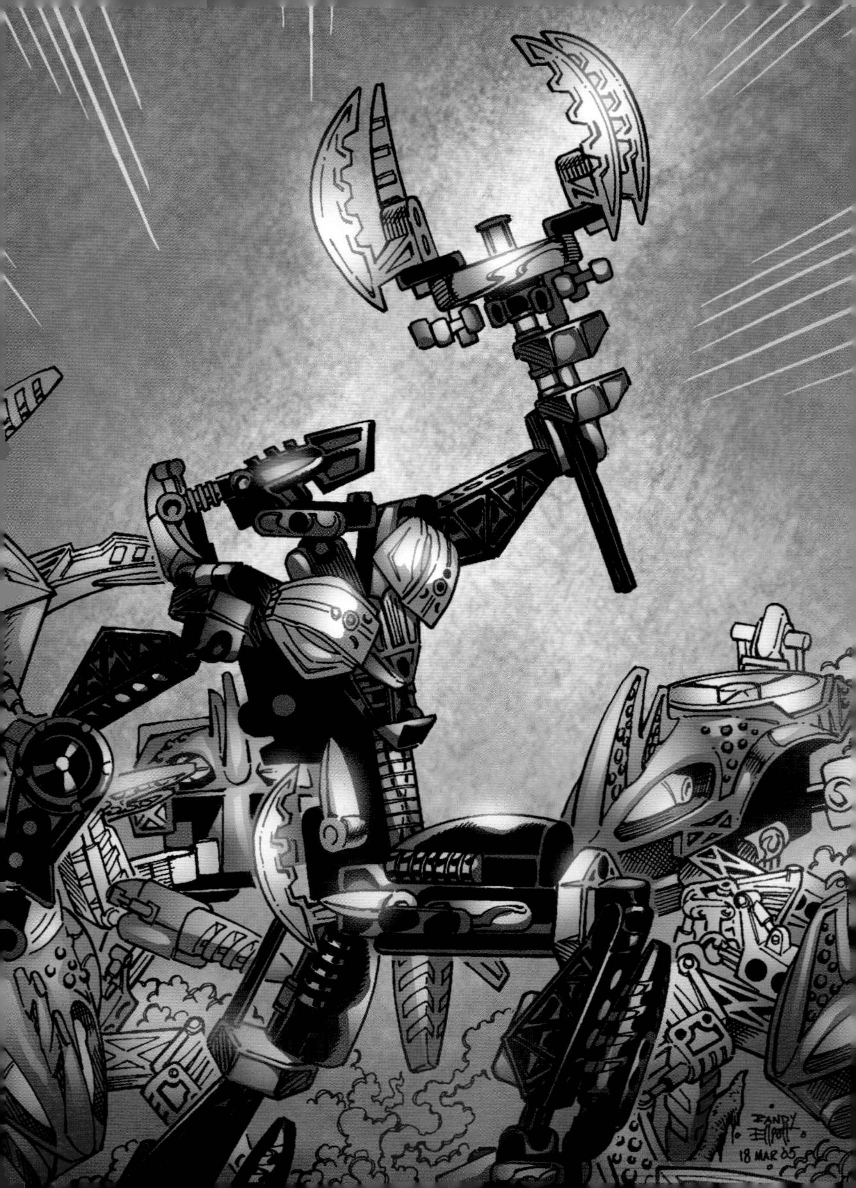
18 MAR 05

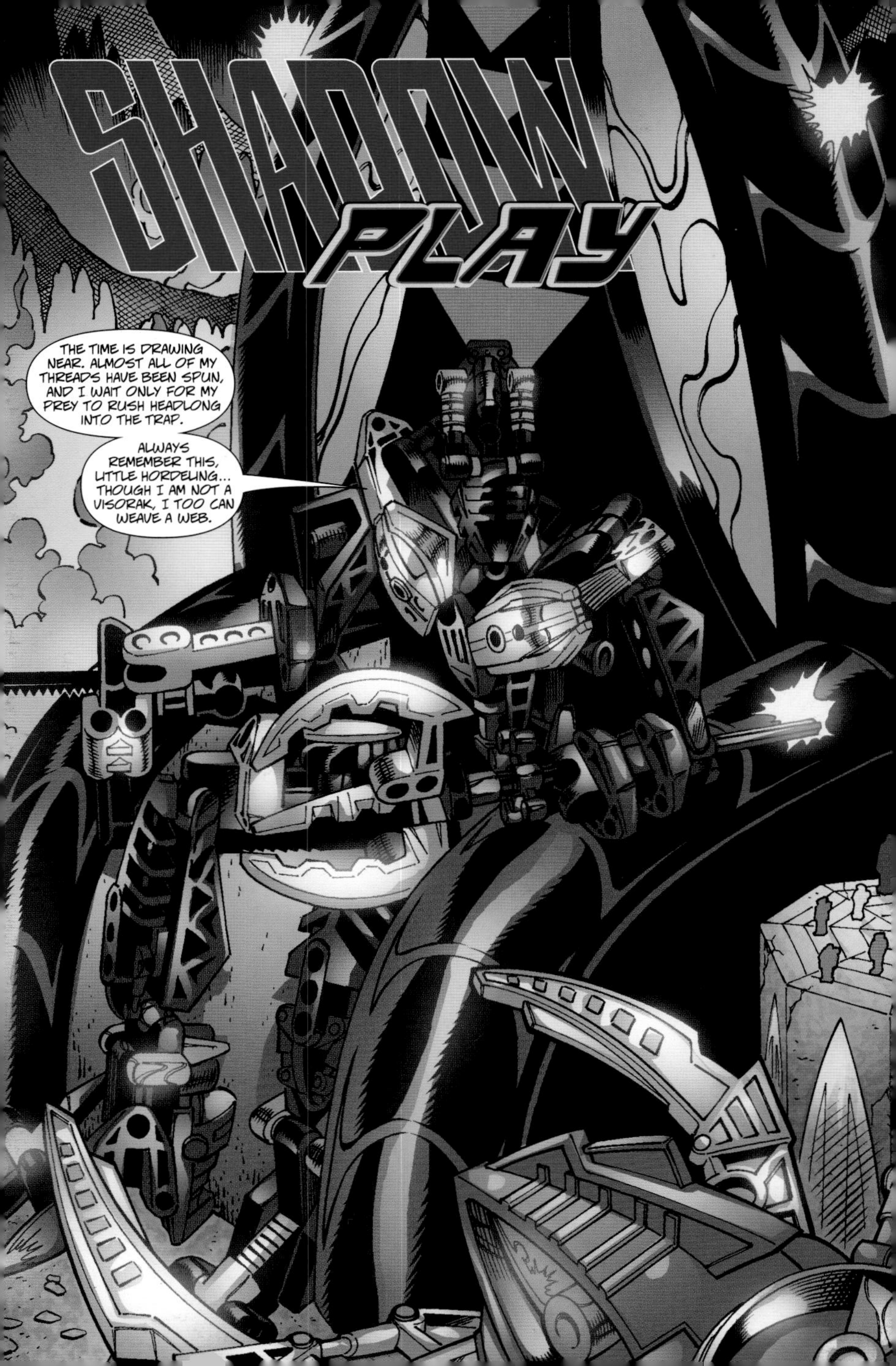
SHADOW PLAY
THE TIME IS DRAWING NEAR. ALMOST ALL OF MY THREADS HAVE BEEN SPUN, AND I WAIT ONLY FOR MY PREY TO RUSH HEADLONG INTO THE TRAP.
ALWAYS REMEMBER THIS, LITTLE HORDELING... THOUGH I AM NOT A VISORAK, I TOO CAN WEAVE A WEB.

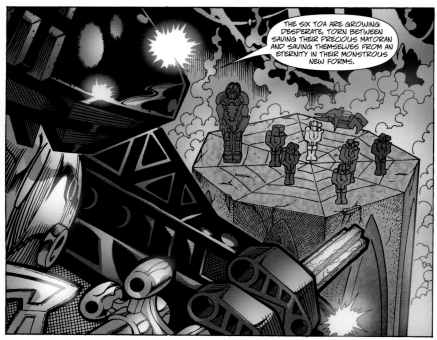

THE SIX TOA ARE GROWING DESPERATE, TORN BETWEEN SAVING THEIR PRECIOUS MATORAN AND SAVING THEMSELVES FROM AN ETERNITY IN THEIR MONSTROUS NEW FORMS.

DESPERATE TOA MAKE MISTAKES. AND IN THIS GAME, ONE MISTAKE IS ALL YOU ARE ALLOWED.

CRASH!

AH, SIDORAK, MY "KING"... SO SECURE IN YOUR POWER OVER THE HORDE. SO CONFIDENT IN OUR COMING ALLIANCE. SO CERTAIN OF VICTORY.

KRAKK

SO VERY, VERY FOOLISH.

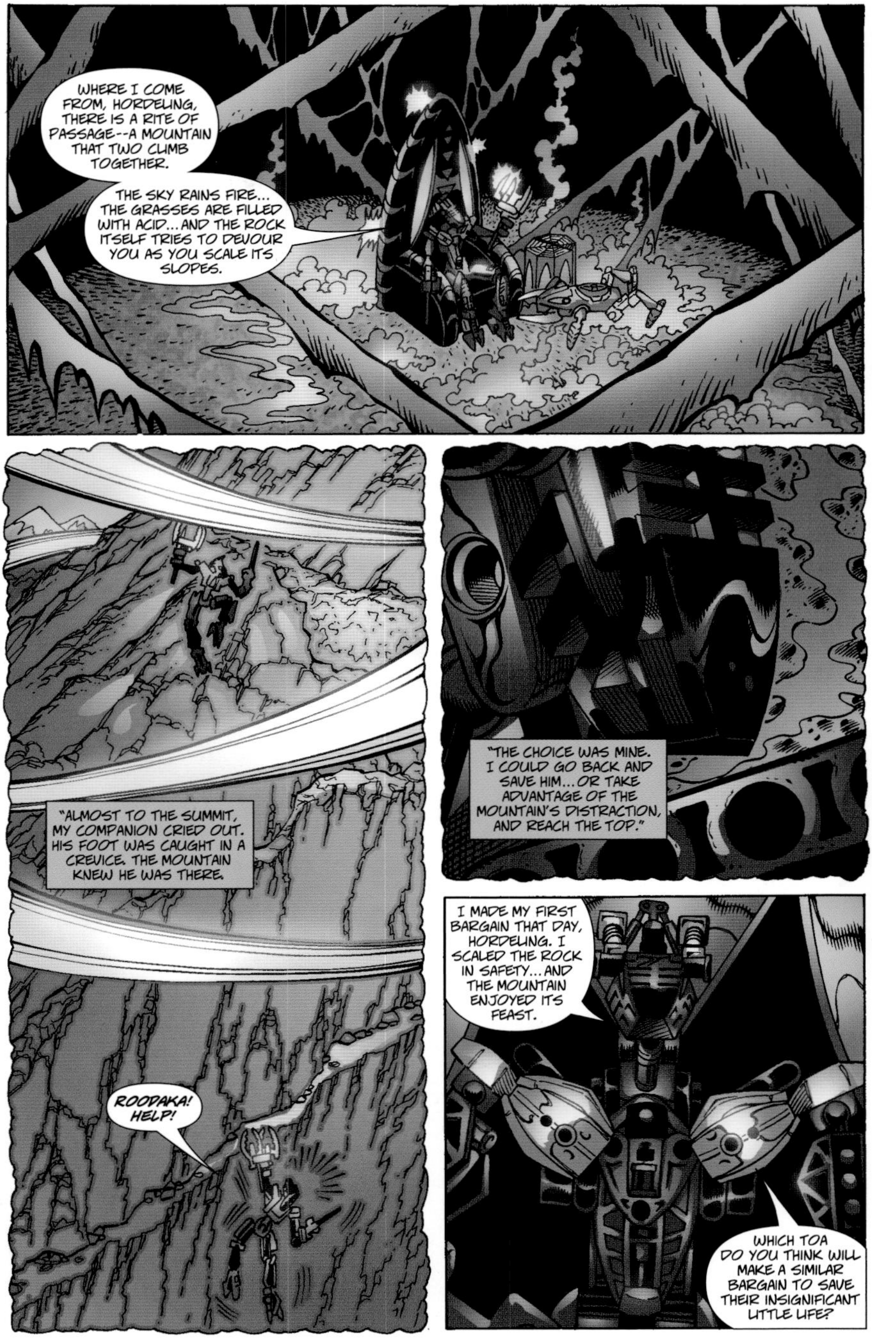

WHERE I COME FROM, HORDELING, THERE IS A RITE OF PASSAGE--A MOUNTAIN THAT TWO CLIMB TOGETHER.
THE SKY RAINS FIRE... THE GRASSES ARE FILLED WITH ACID...AND THE ROCK ITSELF TRIES TO DEVOUR YOU AS YOU SCALE ITS SLOPES.
"ALMOST TO THE SUMMIT, MY COMPANION CRIED OUT. HIS FOOT WAS CAUGHT IN A CREVICE. THE MOUNTAIN KNEW HE WAS THERE.
ROODAKA! HELP!
"THE CHOICE WAS MINE. I COULD GO BACK AND SAVE HIM...OR TAKE ADVANTAGE OF THE MOUNTAIN'S DISTRACTION, AND REACH THE TOP."
I MADE MY FIRST BARGAIN THAT DAY, HORDELING. I SCALED THE ROCK IN SAFETY...AND THE MOUNTAIN ENJOYED ITS FEAST.
WHICH TOA DO YOU THINK WILL MAKE A SIMILAR BARGAIN TO SAVE THEIR INSIGNIFICANT LITTLE LIFE?

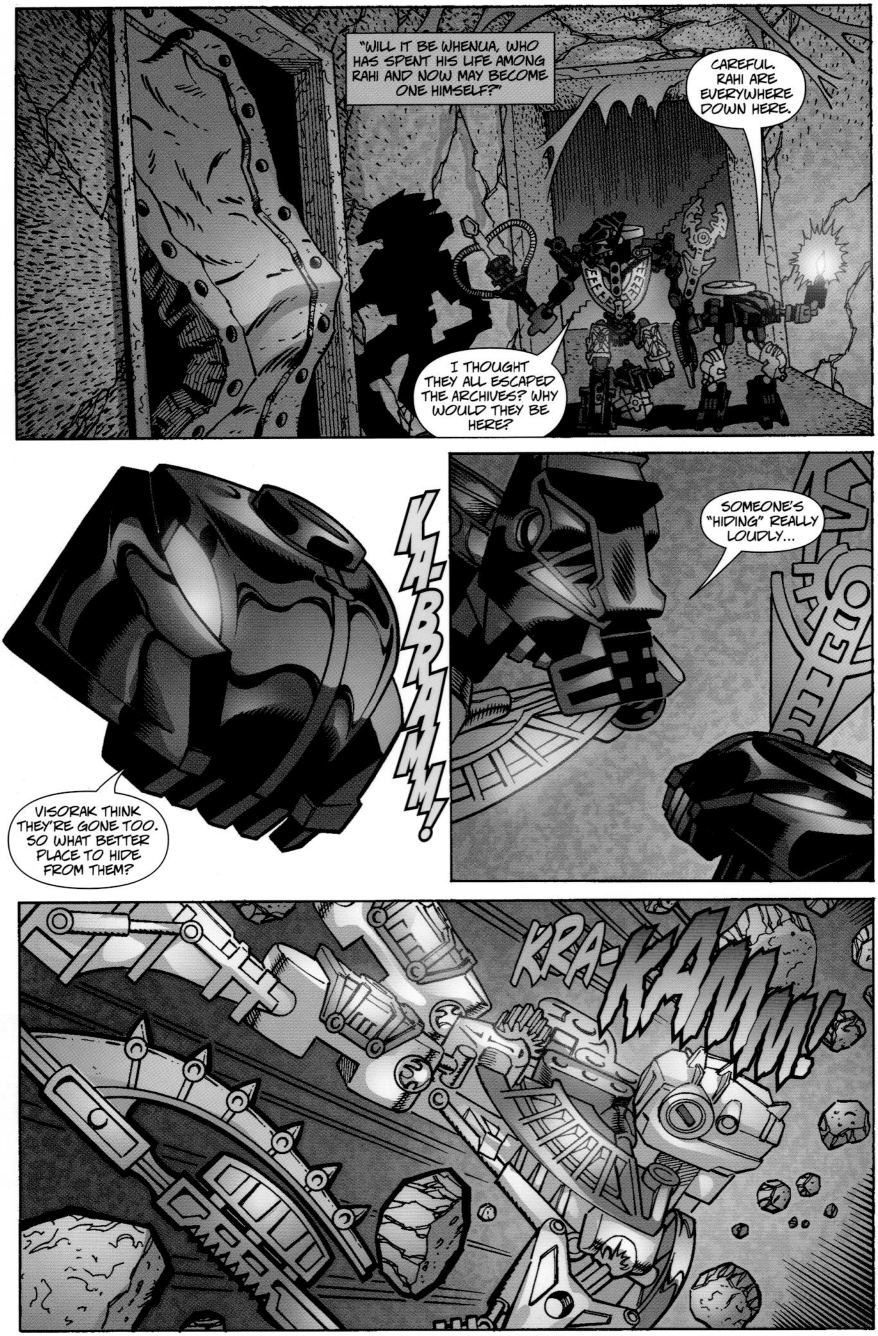
"WILL IT BE WHENUA, WHO HAS SPENT HIS LIFE AMONG RAHI AND NOW MAY BECOME ONE HIMSELF?"
CAREFUL. RAHI ARE EVERYWHERE DOWN HERE.
I THOUGHT THEY ALL ESCAPED THE ARCHIVES? WHY WOULD THEY BE HERE?
VISORAK THINK THEY'RE GONE TOO. SO WHAT BETTER PLACE TO HIDE FROM THEM?
KA-BRAMM!
SOMEONE'S "HIDING" REALLY LOUDLY...
KRA-KAMM!

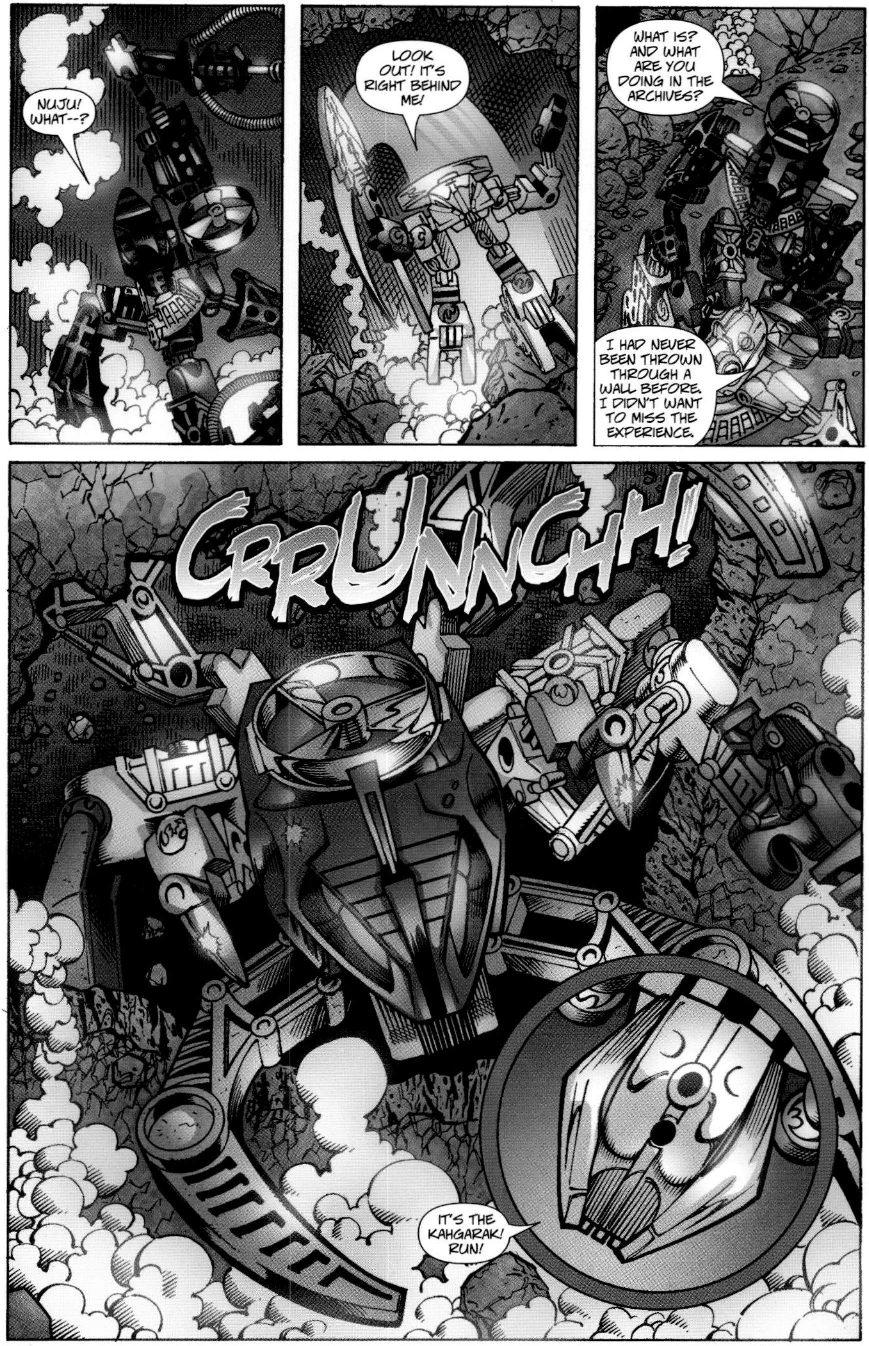
NUJU! WHAT--?
LOOK OUT! IT'S RIGHT BEHIND ME!
WHAT IS? AND WHAT ARE YOU DOING IN THE ARCHIVES?
I HAD NEVER BEEN THROWN THROUGH A WALL BEFORE. I DIDN'T WANT TO MISS THE EXPERIENCE.
CRRUNNCHH!
IT'S THE KAHGARAK! RUN!

I DIDN'T RUN AS A TOA. I WON'T AS... WHATEVER I AM NOW!

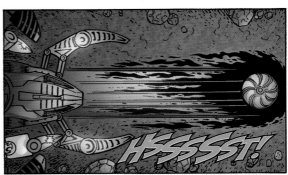

HSSSSST!

RHOTUKA SPINNERS ARE WHEELS OF ENERGY. LET'S SEE WHAT HAPPENS...

KRAAK!

...WHEN HIS HITS A MIRROR OF ICE.

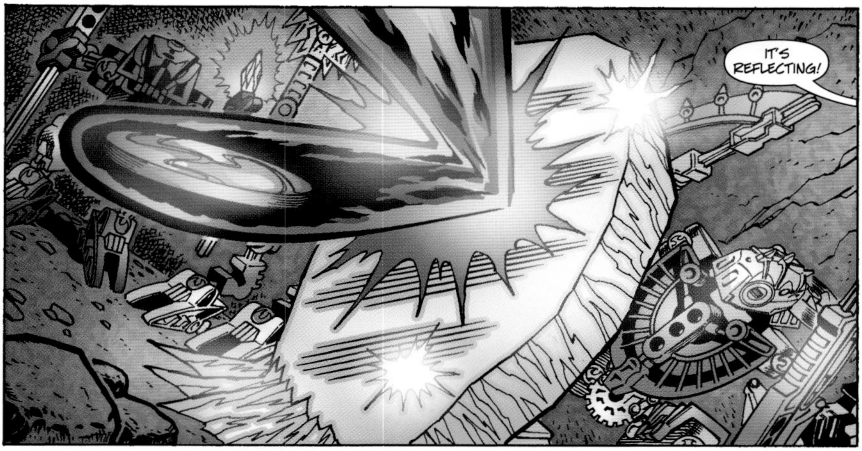
IT'S REFLECTING!

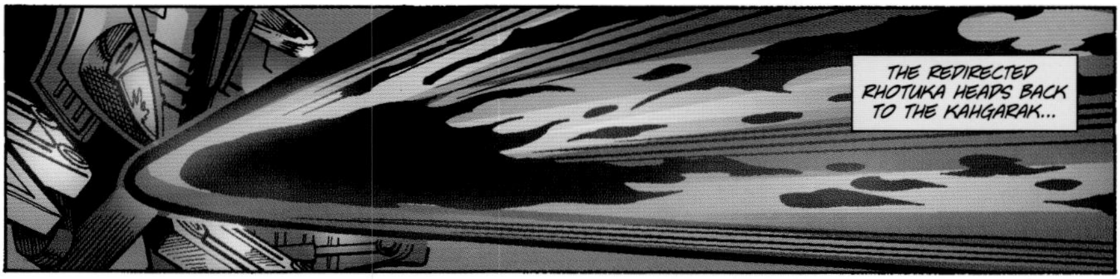
THE REDIRECTED RHOTUKA HEADS BACK TO THE KAHGARAK...

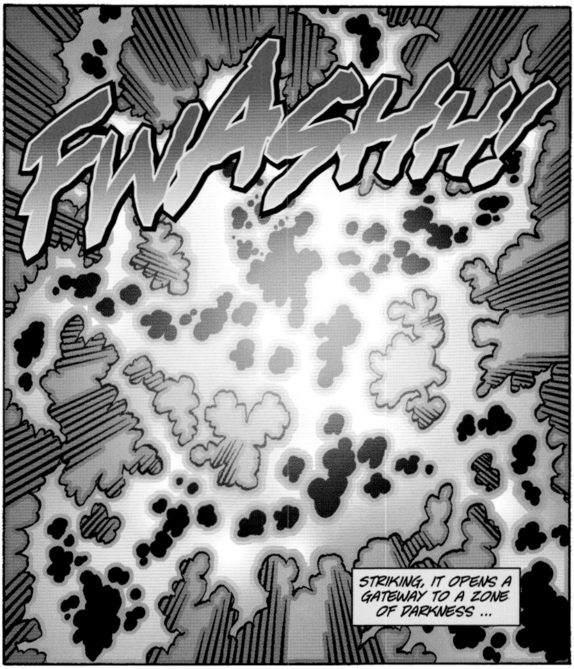
FWASHH!
STRIKING, IT OPENS A GATEWAY TO A ZONE OF DARKNESS ...

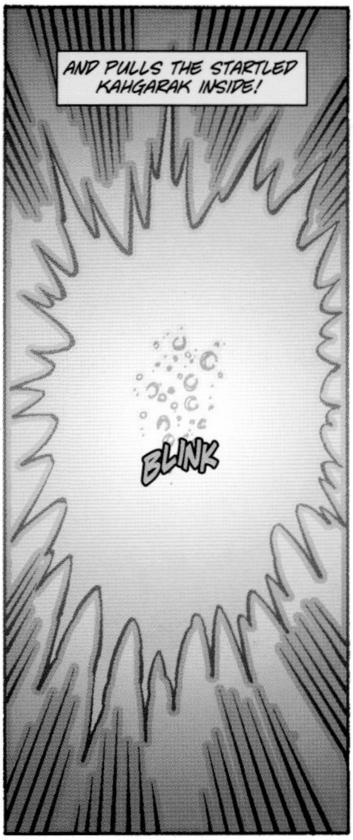
AND PULLS THE STARTLED KAHGARAK INSIDE!
BLINK

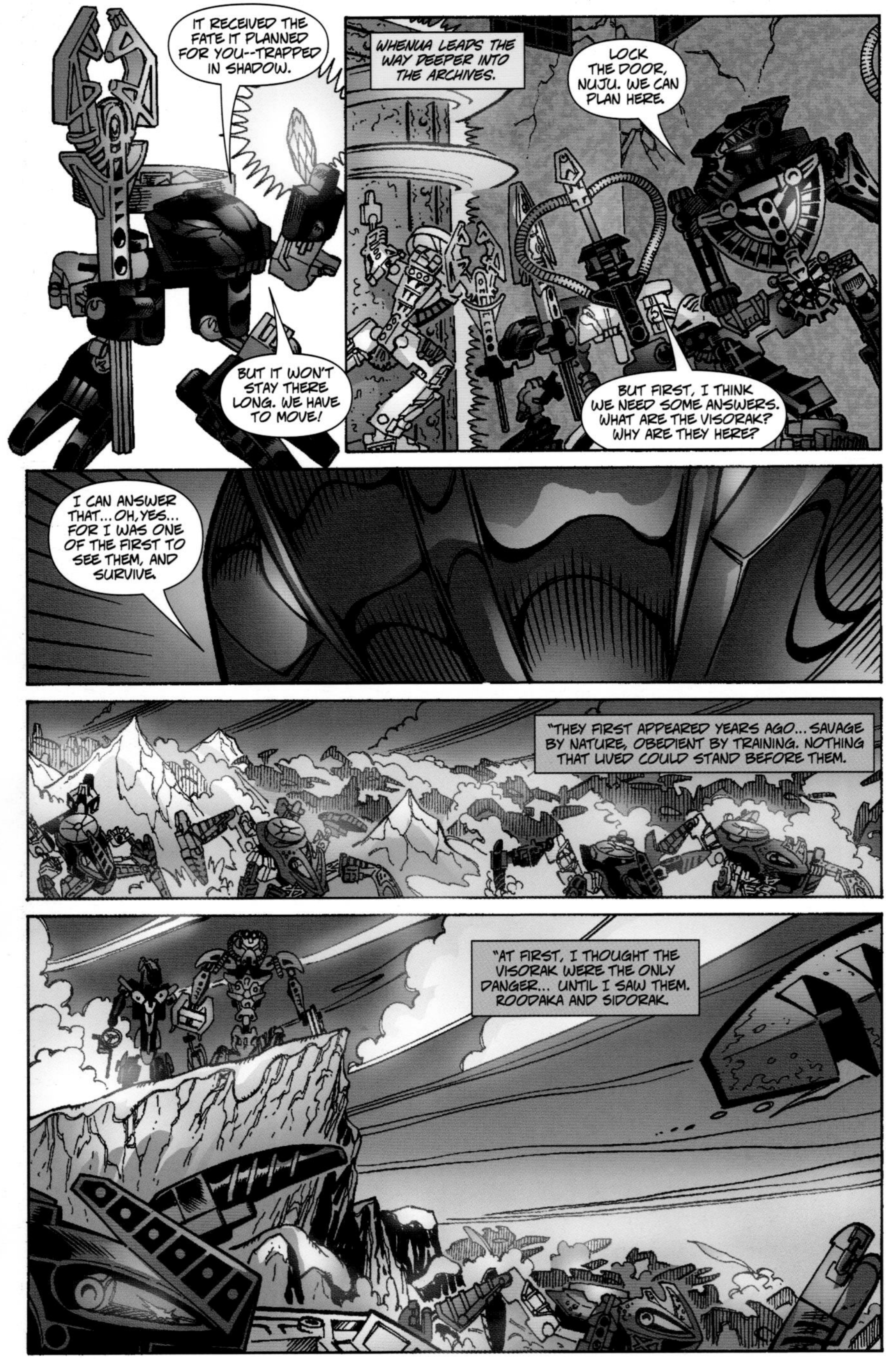
IT RECEIVED THE FATE IT PLANNED FOR YOU--TRAPPED IN SHADOW.
BUT IT WON'T STAY THERE LONG. WE HAVE TO MOVE!
WHENUA LEADS THE WAY DEEPER INTO THE ARCHIVES.
LOCK THE DOOR, NUJU. WE CAN PLAN HERE.
BUT FIRST, I THINK WE NEED SOME ANSWERS. WHAT ARE THE VISORAK? WHY ARE THEY HERE?
I CAN ANSWER THAT... OH, YES... FOR I WAS ONE OF THE FIRST TO SEE THEM, AND SURVIVE.
"THEY FIRST APPEARED YEARS AGO... SAVAGE BY NATURE, OBEDIENT BY TRAINING. NOTHING THAT LIVED COULD STAND BEFORE THEM.
"AT FIRST, I THOUGHT THE VISORAK WERE THE ONLY DANGER... UNTIL I SAW THEM. ROODAKA AND SIDORAK.

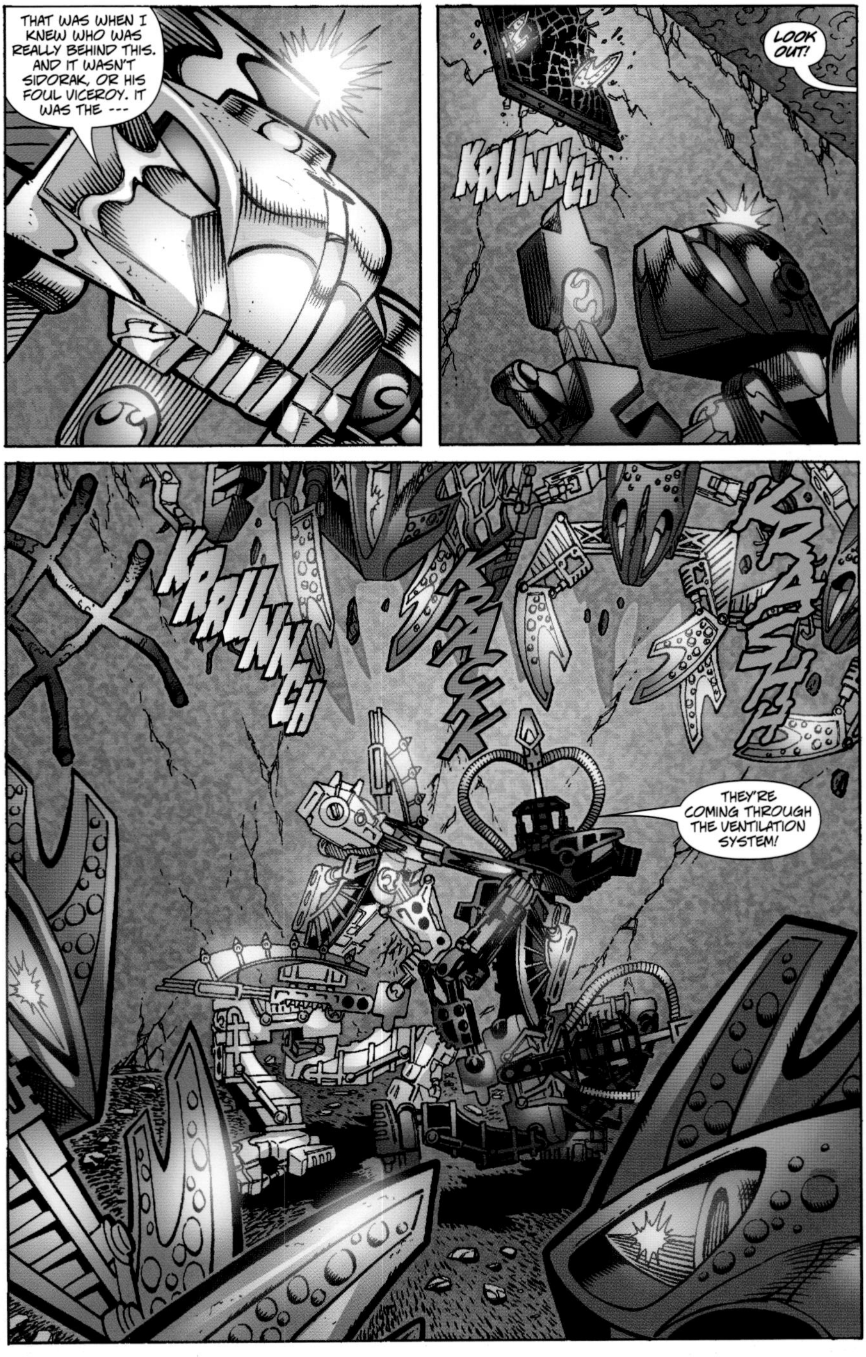
THAT WAS WHEN I KNEW WHO WAS REALLY BEHIND THIS. AND IT WASN'T SIDORAK, OR HIS FOUL VICEROY. IT WAS THE ---
LOOK OUT!
KRUNNCH
KRRUNNNCH
KRACK
KRASH
THEY'RE COMING THROUGH THE VENTILATION SYSTEM!

WHENUA, GET THAT DOOR OPEN! I'LL HOLD THEM OFF!

NO! NO, NO, NO...

THIS IS MY TERRITORY! MINE! YOU CAN'T BE HERE!

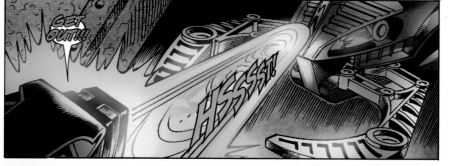

GET OUT!!!

NOW WHAT?!

RUMBLE

"IT'S WHENUA! HE'S GIVEN IN TO MADNESS!"

HSSSS!

HSSSS!

WHENUA, STOP IT! THE STRUCTURE CAN'T TAKE THE STRESS! YOU'LL BRING THE--

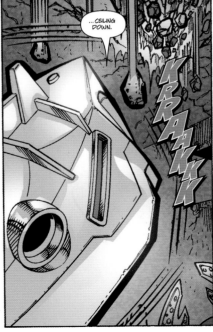

...CEILING DOWN.

KRRAAKK

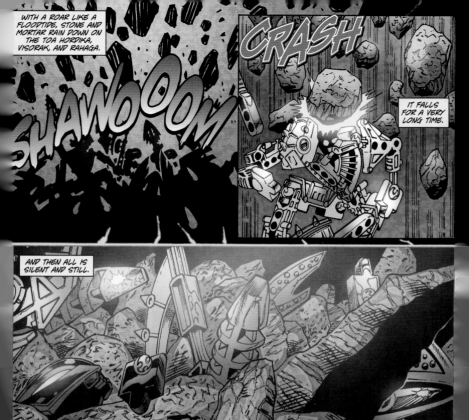

WITH A ROAR LIKE A FLOODTIDE, STONE AND MORTAR RAIN DOWN ON THE TOA HORDIKA, VISORAK, AND RAHAGA.

CRASH

SHAWOOOM!

IT FALLS FOR A VERY LONG TIME.

AND THEN ALL IS SILENT AND STILL.

END CHAPTER THREE

TRIAL BY FIRE
CHAPTER FOUR

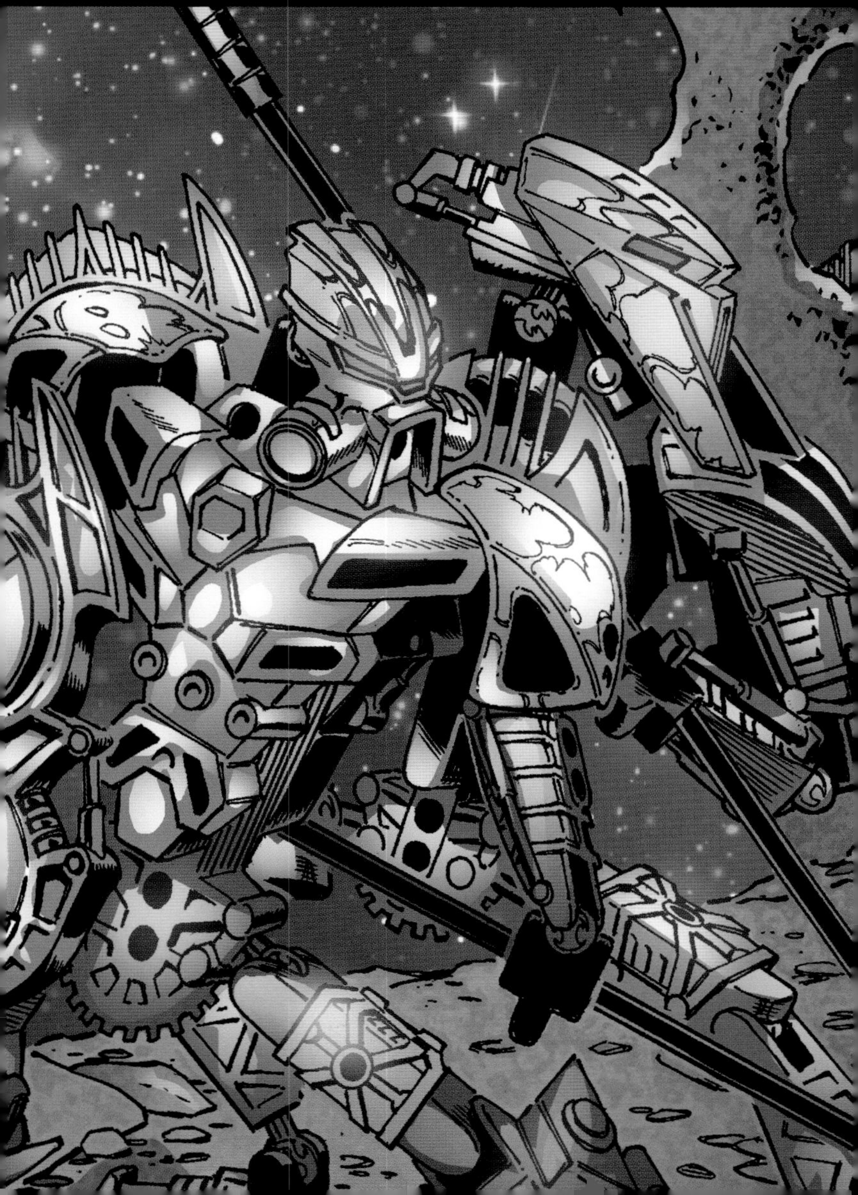

A FEW MOMENTS AGO, THIS CHAMBER WAS THE SCENE OF A FURIOUS BATTLE BETWEEN THE TOA HORDIKA, THEIR RAHAGA ALLIES, AND THE VISORAK.

NOW, IN THE AFTERMATH OF THAT DISASTROUS STRUGGLE, IT IS QUIET AS THE GRAVE.

BATTERED INTO UNCONSCIOUSNESS BY THE RUBBLE, KUALUS SLEEPS AND DREAMS...

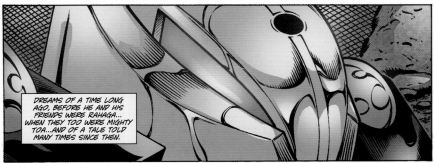

DREAMS OF A TIME LONG AGO, BEFORE HE AND HIS FRIENDS WERE RAHAGA... WHEN THEY TOO WERE MIGHTY TOA...AND OF A TALE TOLD MANY TIMES SINCE THEN.

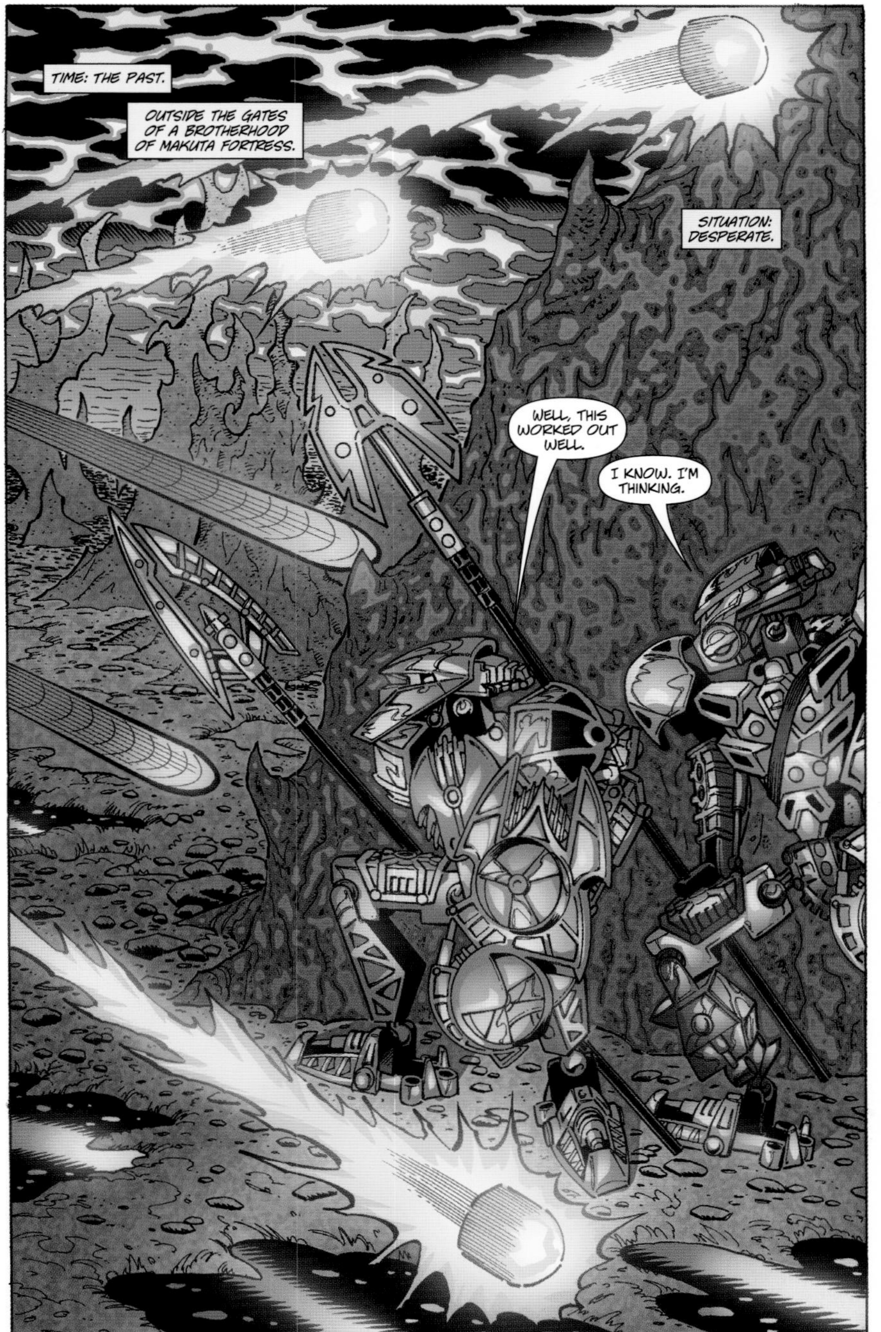
TIME: THE PAST.
OUTSIDE THE GATES OF A BROTHERHOOD OF MAKUTA FORTRESS.
SITUATION: DESPERATE.
WELL, THIS WORKED OUT WELL.
I KNOW. I'M THINKING.

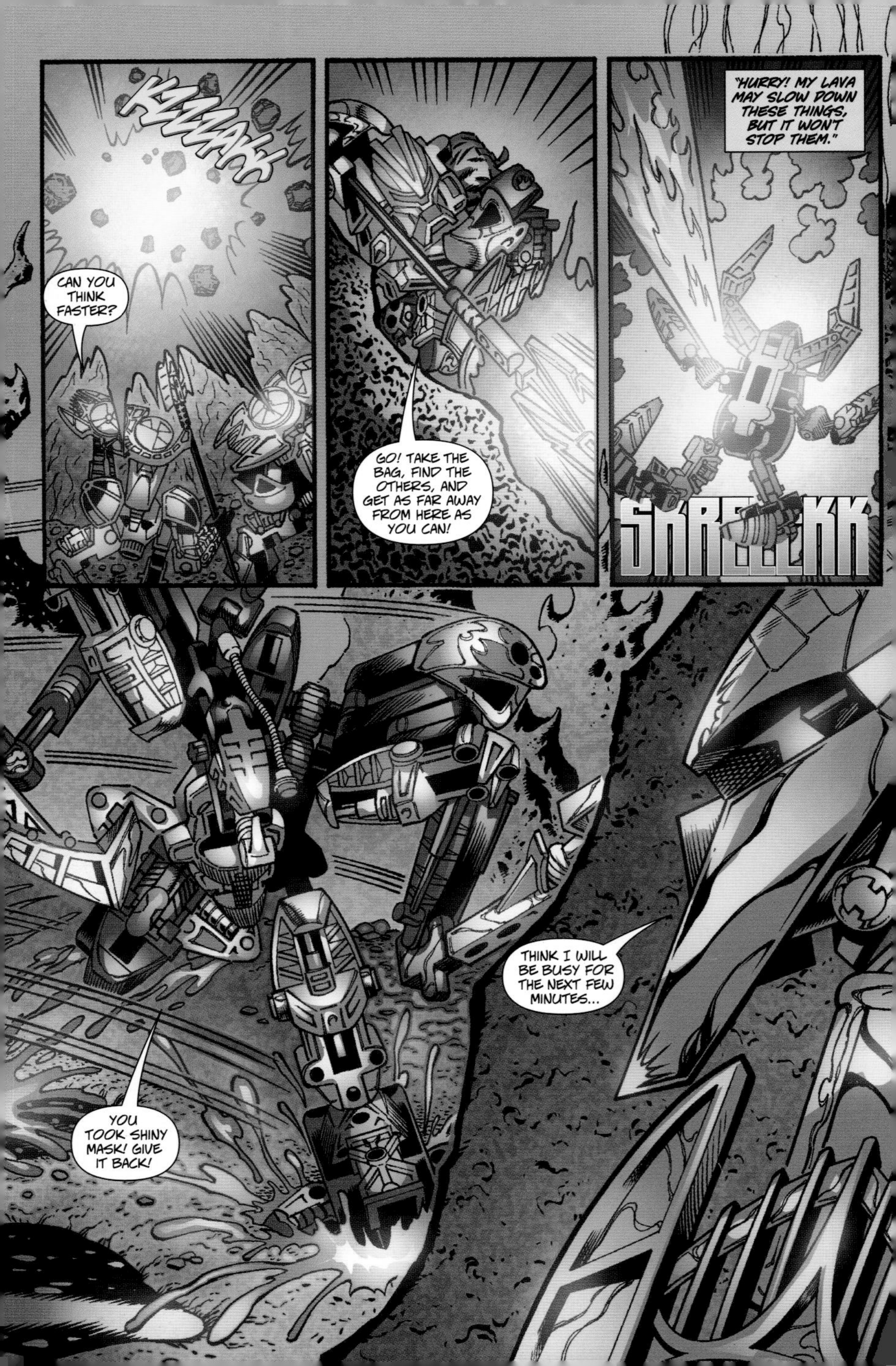
KZZZAKK
CAN YOU THINK FASTER?
GO! TAKE THE BAG, FIND THE OTHERS, AND GET AS FAR AWAY FROM HERE AS YOU CAN!
"HURRY! MY LAVA MAY SLOW DOWN THESE THINGS, BUT IT WON'T STOP THEM."
SKREEEKK
THINK I WILL BE BUSY FOR THE NEXT FEW MINUTES...
YOU TOOK SHINY MASK! GIVE IT BACK!

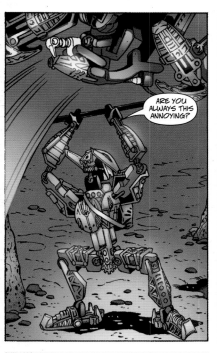

ARE YOU ALWAYS THIS ANNOYING?

WHEN YOU'RE QUITE THROUGH PLAYING 'DUMP THE DARK HUNTER,' IRUINI...

BE RIGHT-- ~*URK!*~ THERE!

WHAT--?

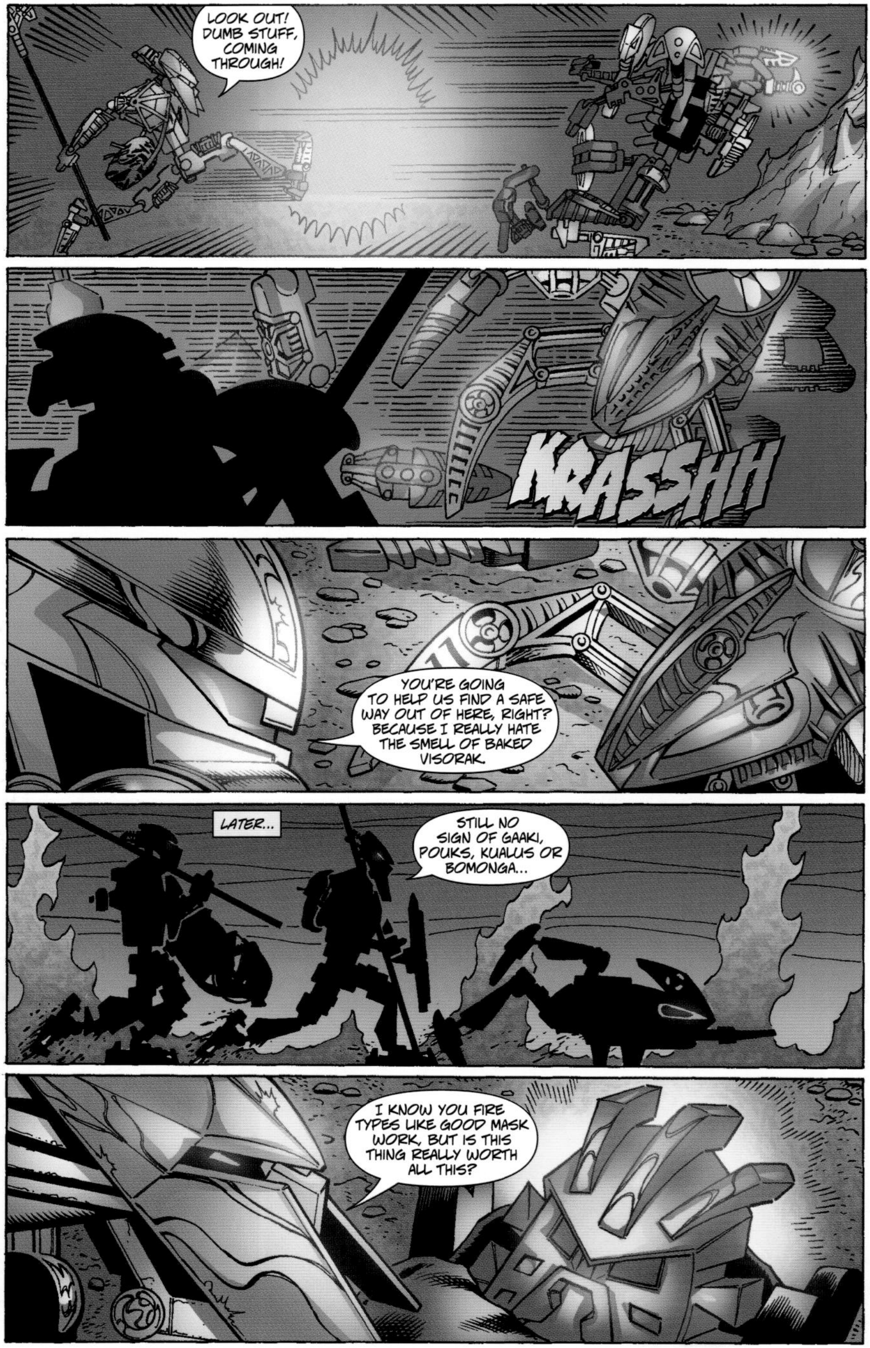
LOOK OUT! DUMB STUFF, COMING THROUGH!
KRASSHH
YOU'RE GOING TO HELP US FIND A SAFE WAY OUT OF HERE, RIGHT? BECAUSE I REALLY HATE THE SMELL OF BAKED VISORAK.
LATER...
STILL NO SIGN OF GAAKI, POUKS, KUALUS OR BOMONGA...
I KNOW YOU FIRE TYPES LIKE GOOD MASK WORK, BUT IS THIS THING REALLY WORTH ALL THIS?

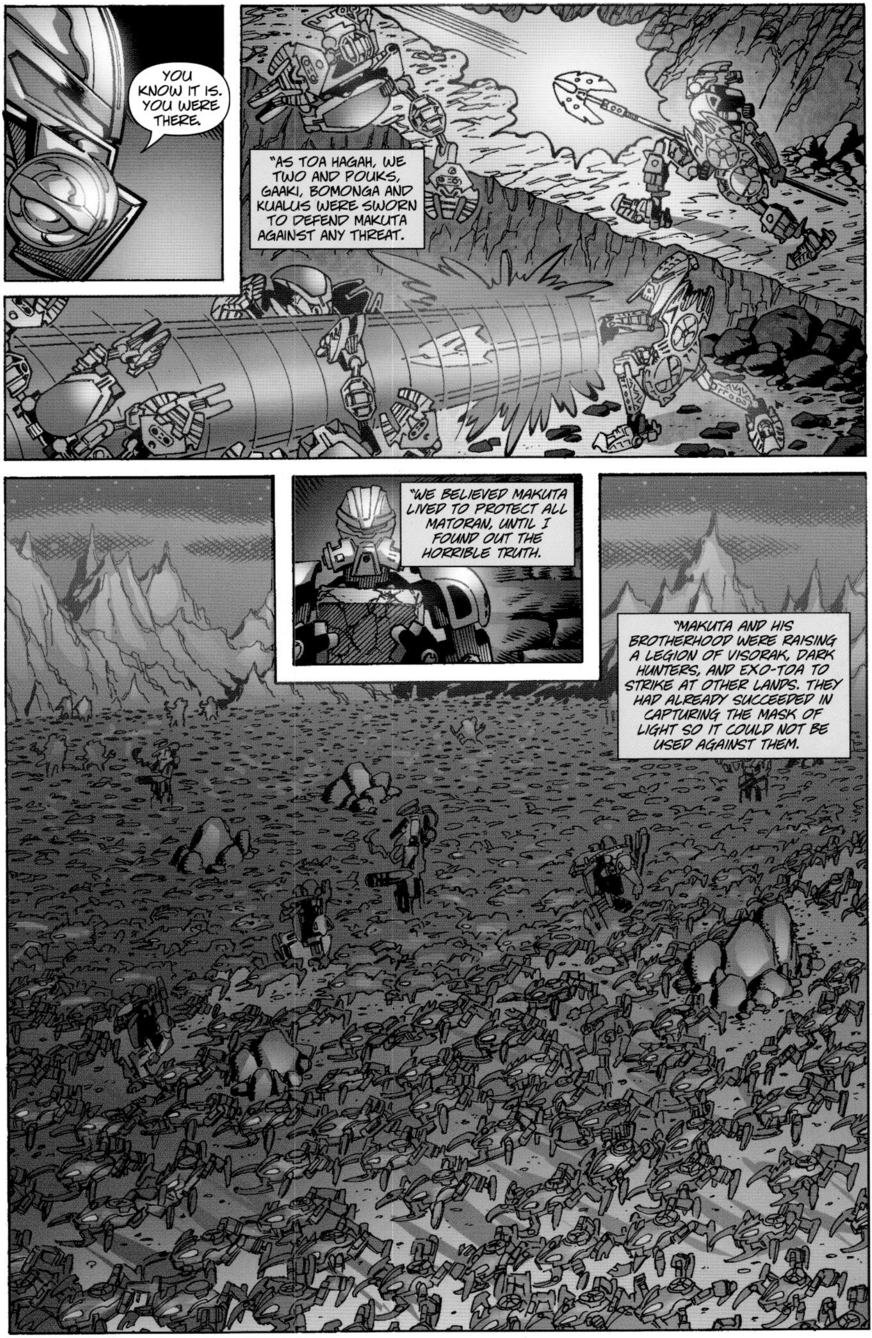
YOU KNOW IT IS. YOU WERE THERE.
"AS TOA HAGAH, WE TWO AND POUKS, GAAKI, BOMONGA AND KUALUS WERE SWORN TO DEFEND MAKUTA AGAINST ANY THREAT.
"WE BELIEVED MAKUTA LIVED TO PROTECT ALL MATORAN, UNTIL I FOUND OUT THE HORRIBLE TRUTH.
"MAKUTA AND HIS BROTHERHOOD WERE RAISING A LEGION OF VISORAK, DARK HUNTERS, AND EXO-TOA TO STRIKE AT OTHER LANDS. THEY HAD ALREADY SUCCEEDED IN CAPTURING THE MASK OF LIGHT SO IT COULD NOT BE USED AGAINST THEM.

"WE RAIDED THEIR FORTRESS, STOLE THE MASK BACK, AND MADE OUR ESCAPE."

HOLD IT! LOOK OVER THERE!

FOUR CAPTURED TOA TO "QUESTION"--HOW DELICIOUS.

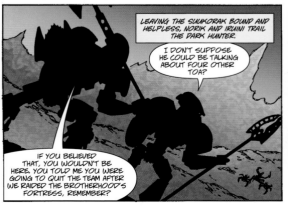

LEAVING THE SUUKORAK BOUND AND HELPLESS, NORIK AND IRUINI TRAIL THE DARK HUNTER.

I DON'T SUPPOSE HE COULD BE TALKING ABOUT FOUR OTHER TOA?

IF YOU BELIEVED THAT, YOU WOULDN'T BE HERE. YOU TOLD ME YOU WERE GOING TO QUIT THE TEAM AFTER WE RAIDED THE BROTHERHOOD'S FORTRESS, REMEMBER?

AND I WILL--AS SOON AS THE OTHERS ARE SAFE.

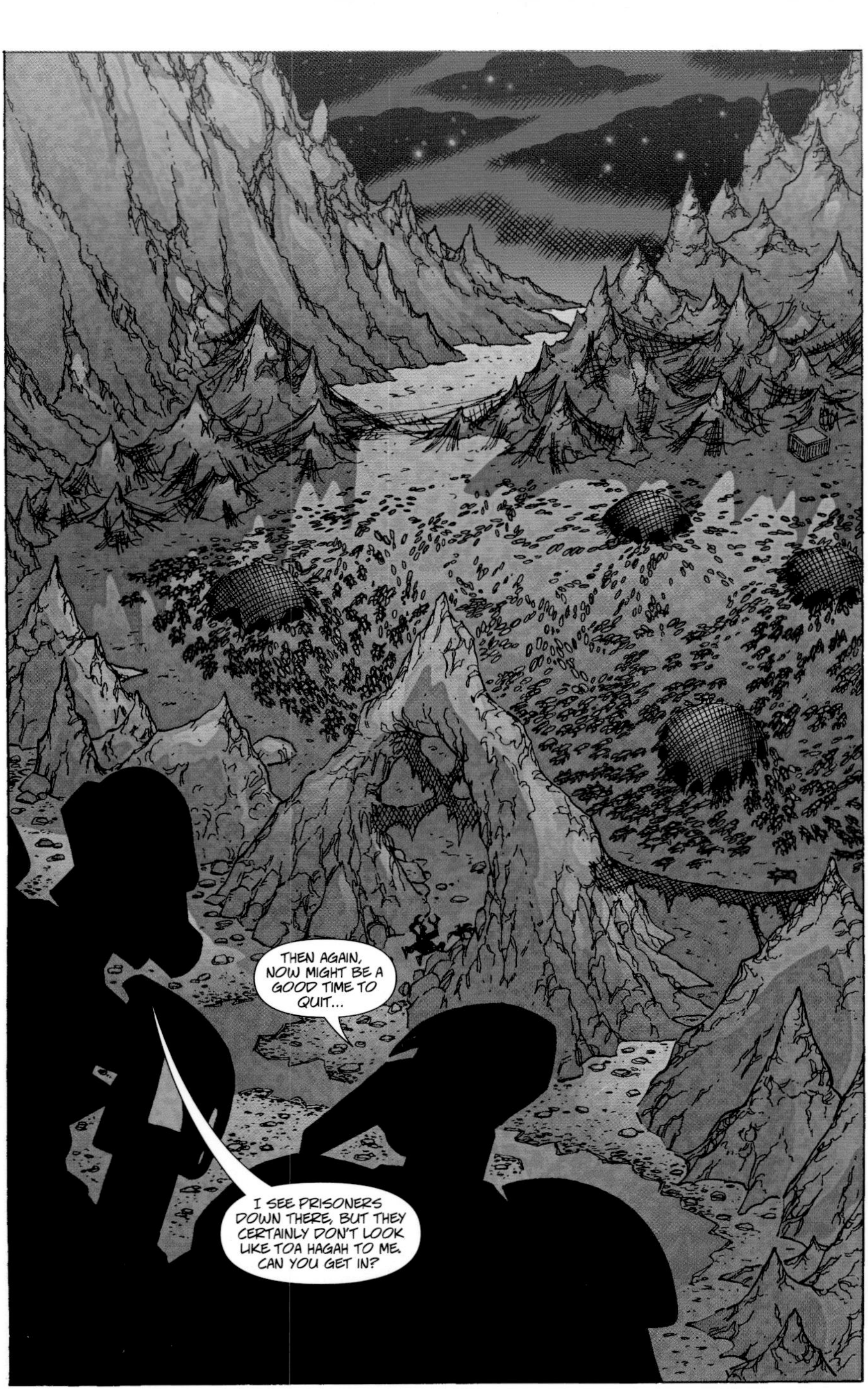
THEN AGAIN, NOW MIGHT BE A GOOD TIME TO QUIT...
I SEE PRISONERS DOWN THERE, BUT THEY CERTAINLY DON'T LOOK LIKE TOA HAGAH TO ME. CAN YOU GET IN?

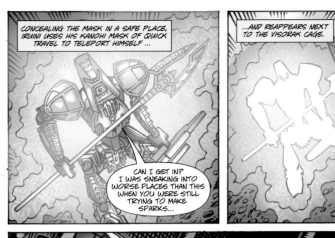

CONCEALING THE MASK IN A SAFE PLACE, IRUINI USES HIS KANOHI MASK OF QUICK TRAVEL TO TELEPORT HIMSELF...

CAN I GET IN? I WAS SNEAKING INTO WORSE PLACES THAN THIS WHEN YOU WERE STILL TRYING TO MAKE SPARKS...

...AND REAPPEARS NEXT TO THE VISORAK CAGE.

NOT SURE WHO YOU ARE, BUT I'M HERE TO GET YOU OUT. AND HAVE YOU SEEN FOUR TOA?

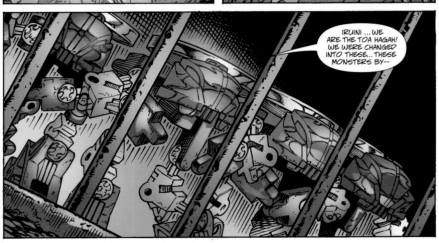

IRUINI...WE ARE THE TOA HAGAH! WE WERE CHANGED INTO THESE...THESE MONSTERS BY--

UNNGHH!

KRA-KAM

BY ME!

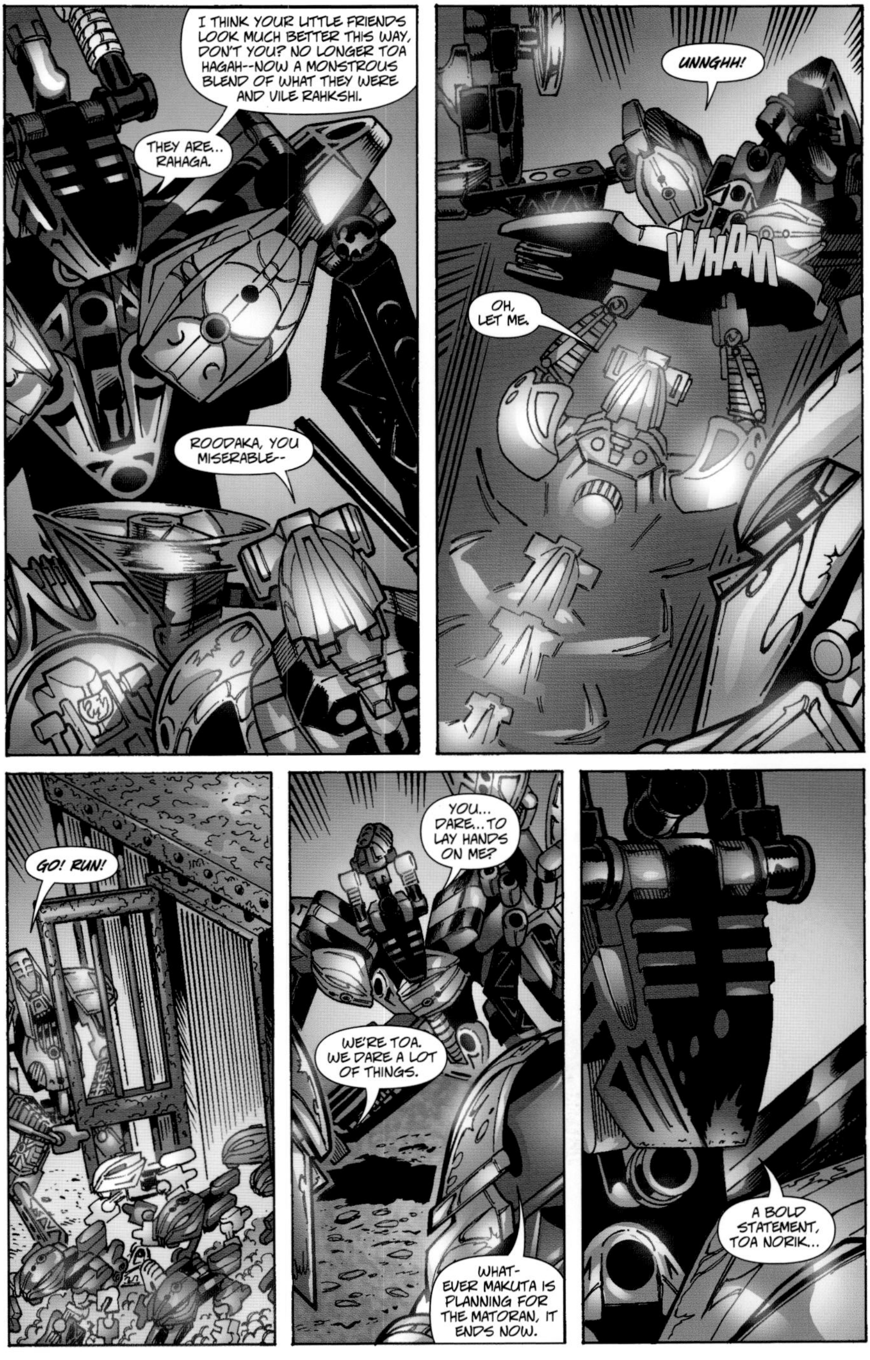
I THINK YOUR LITTLE FRIENDS LOOK MUCH BETTER THIS WAY, DON'T YOU? NO LONGER TOA HAGAH--NOW A MONSTROUS BLEND OF WHAT THEY WERE AND VILE RAHKSHI.
THEY ARE... RAHAGA.
ROODAKA, YOU MISERABLE--
UNNGHH!
WHAM
OH, LET ME.
GO! RUN!
YOU... DARE... TO LAY HANDS ON ME?
WE'RE TOA. WE DARE A LOT OF THINGS.
WHAT-EVER MAKUTA IS PLANNING FOR THE MATORAN, IT ENDS NOW.
A BOLD STATEMENT, TOA NORIK...

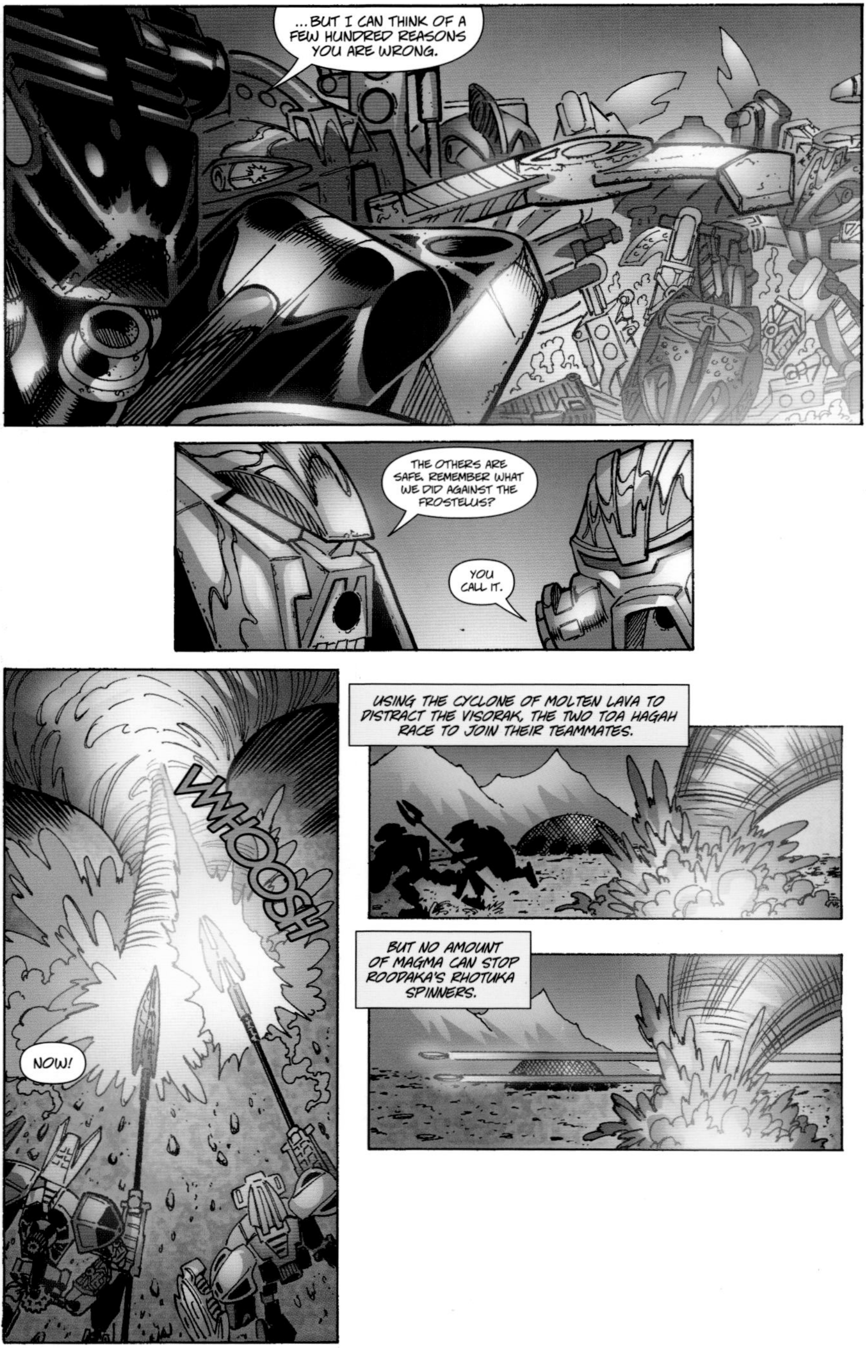
...BUT I CAN THINK OF A FEW HUNDRED REASONS YOU ARE WRONG.
THE OTHERS ARE SAFE. REMEMBER WHAT WE DID AGAINST THE FROSTELUS?
YOU CALL IT.
WHOOSH
NOW!
USING THE CYCLONE OF MOLTEN LAVA TO DISTRACT THE VISORAK, THE TWO TOA HAGAH RACE TO JOIN THEIR TEAMMATES.
BUT NO AMOUNT OF MAGMA CAN STOP ROODAKA'S RHOTUKA SPINNERS.

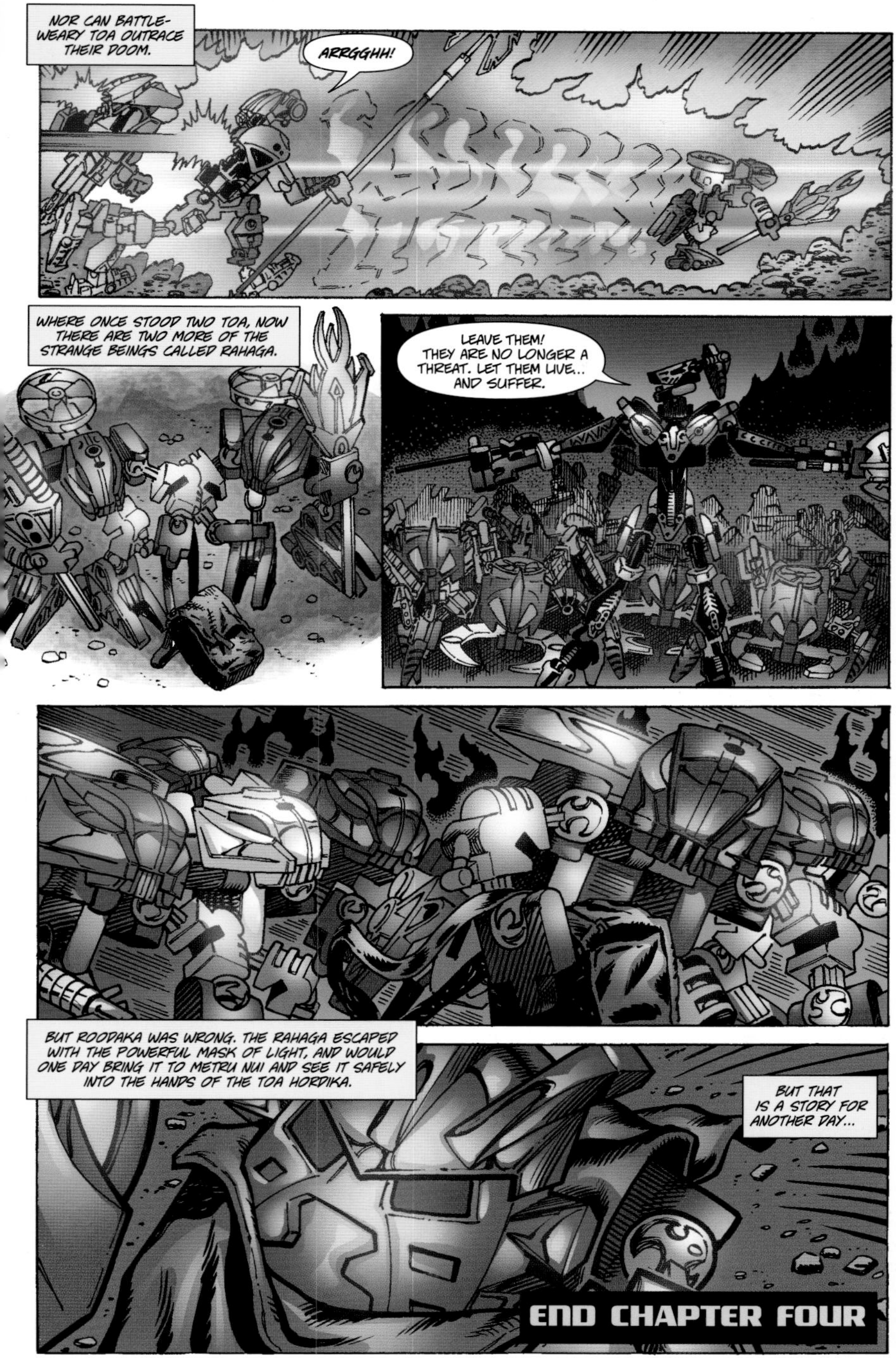
NOR CAN BATTLE-WEARY TOA OUTRACE THEIR DOOM.
ARRGGHH!
WHERE ONCE STOOD TWO TOA, NOW THERE ARE TWO MORE OF THE STRANGE BEINGS CALLED RAHAGA.
LEAVE THEM! THEY ARE NO LONGER A THREAT. LET THEM LIVE... AND SUFFER.
BUT ROODAKA WAS WRONG. THE RAHAGA ESCAPED WITH THE POWERFUL MASK OF LIGHT, AND WOULD ONE DAY BRING IT TO METRU NUI AND SEE IT SAFELY INTO THE HANDS OF THE TOA HORDIKA.
BUT THAT IS A STORY FOR ANOTHER DAY...
END CHAPTER FOUR

TRIAL BY FIRE
CHAPTER FIVE

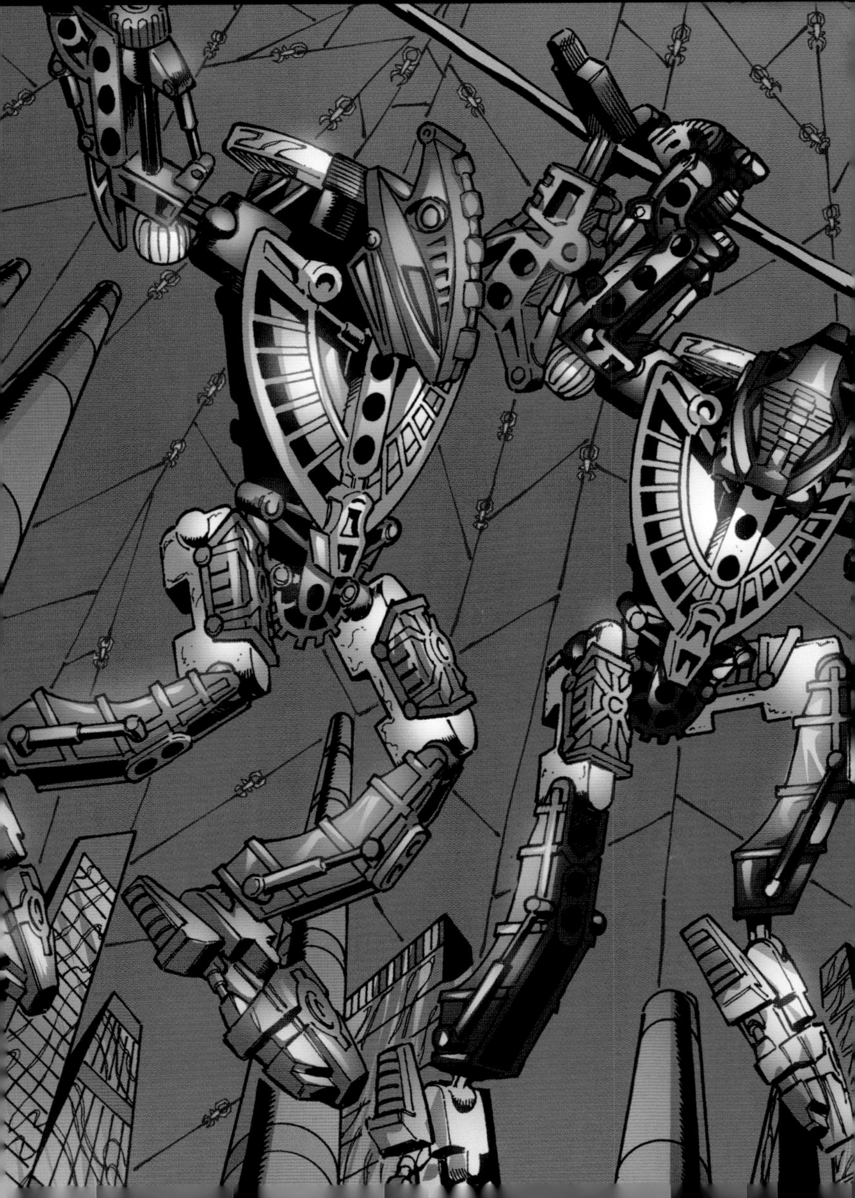

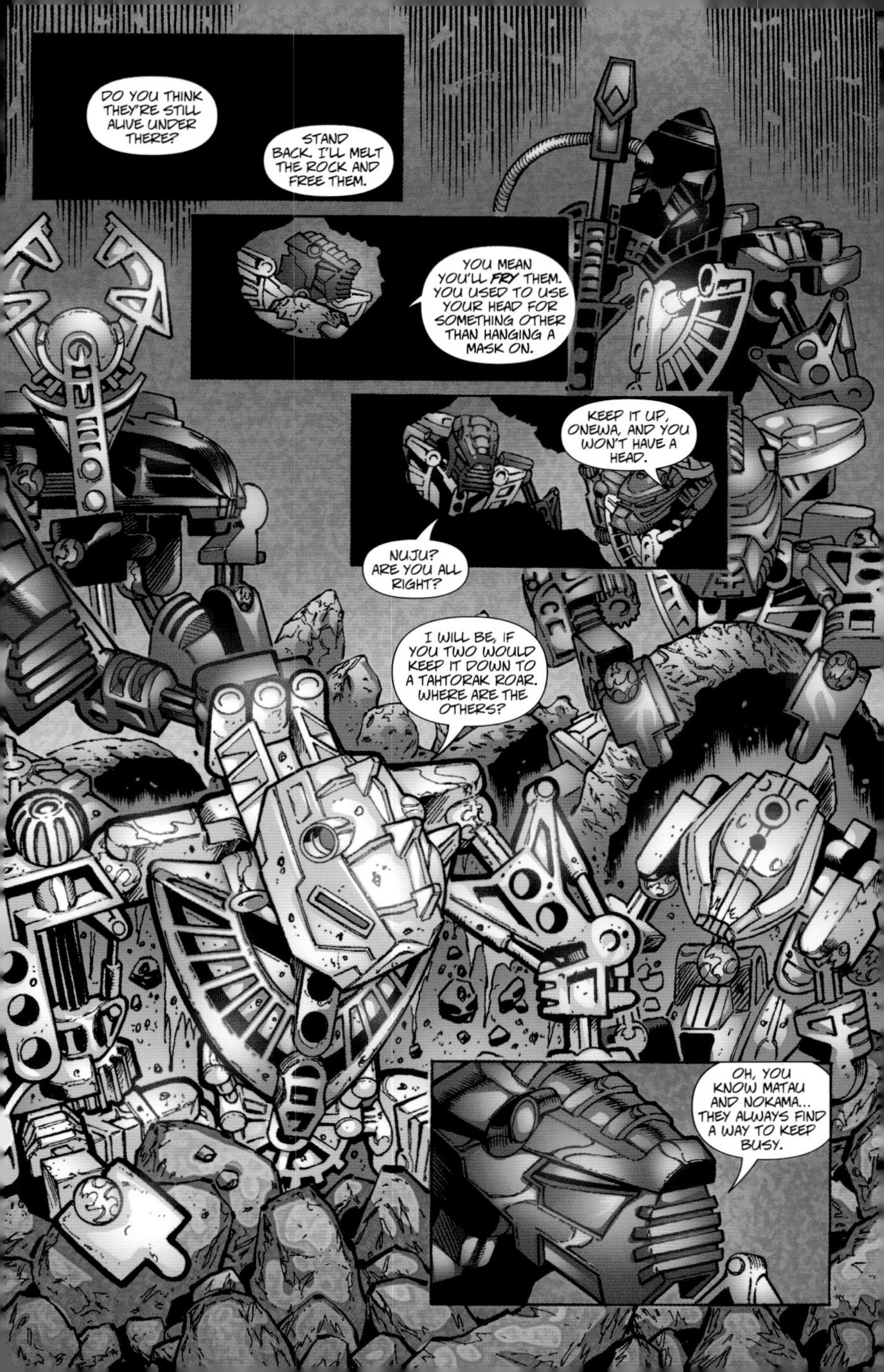

DO YOU THINK THEY'RE STILL ALIVE UNDER THERE?
STAND BACK. I'LL MELT THE ROCK AND FREE THEM.
YOU MEAN YOU'LL FRY THEM. YOU USED TO USE YOUR HEAD FOR SOMETHING OTHER THAN HANGING A MASK ON.
KEEP IT UP, ONEWA, AND YOU WON'T HAVE A HEAD.
NUJU? ARE YOU ALL RIGHT?
I WILL BE, IF YOU TWO WOULD KEEP IT DOWN TO A TAHTORAK ROAR. WHERE ARE THE OTHERS?
OH, YOU KNOW MATAU AND NOKAMA... THEY ALWAYS FIND A WAY TO KEEP BUSY.

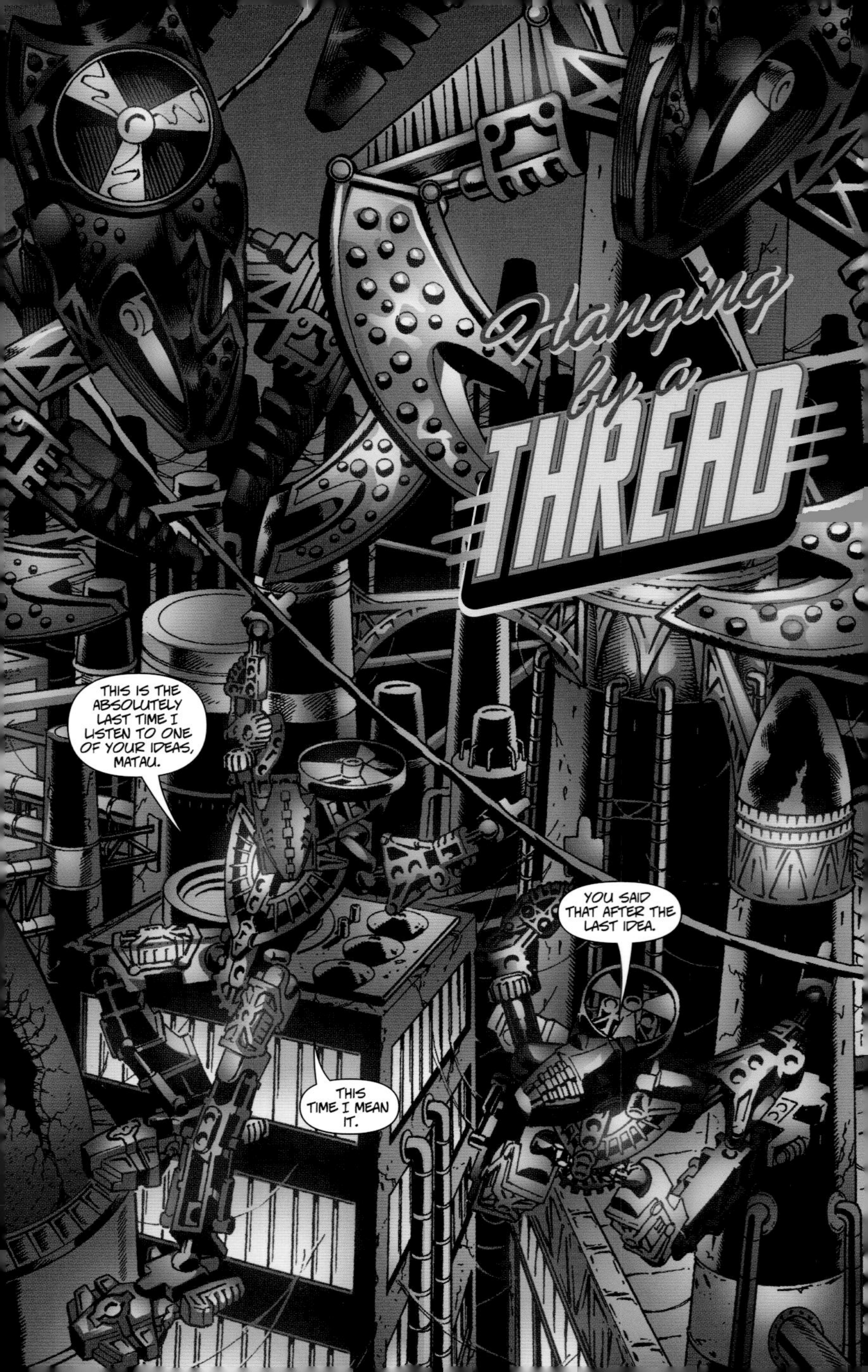
Hanging by a THREAD
THIS IS THE ABSOLUTELY LAST TIME I LISTEN TO ONE OF YOUR IDEAS, MATAU.
YOU SAID THAT AFTER THE LAST IDEA.
THIS TIME I MEAN IT.

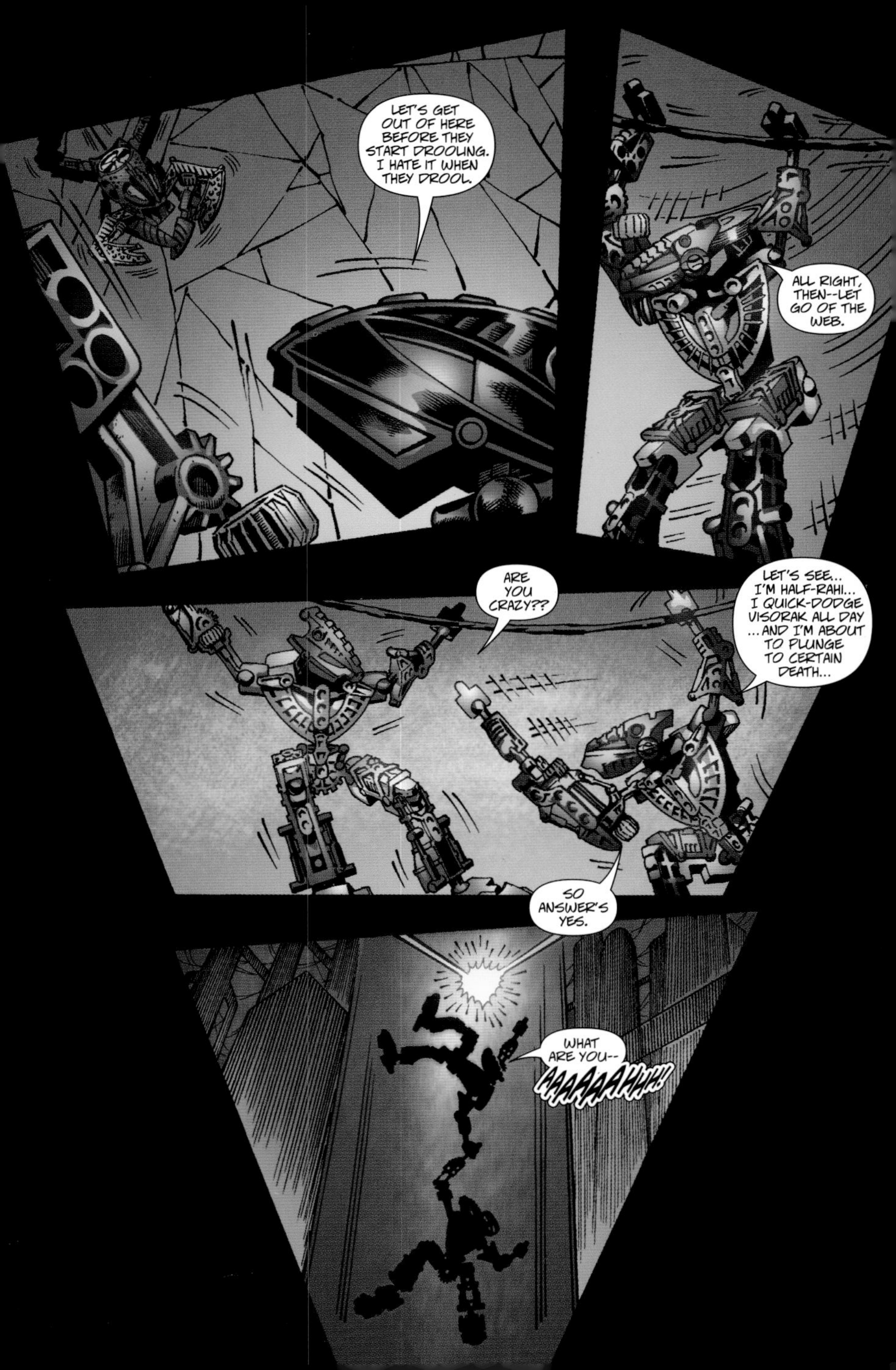
LET'S GET OUT OF HERE BEFORE THEY START DROOLING. I HATE IT WHEN THEY DROOL.
ALL RIGHT, THEN--LET GO OF THE WEB.
ARE YOU CRAZY??
LET'S SEE... I'M HALF-RAHI... I QUICK-DODGE VISORAK ALL DAY ...AND I'M ABOUT TO PLUNGE TO CERTAIN DEATH...
SO ANSWER'S YES.
WHAT ARE YOU--
AAAAAAAHH!!

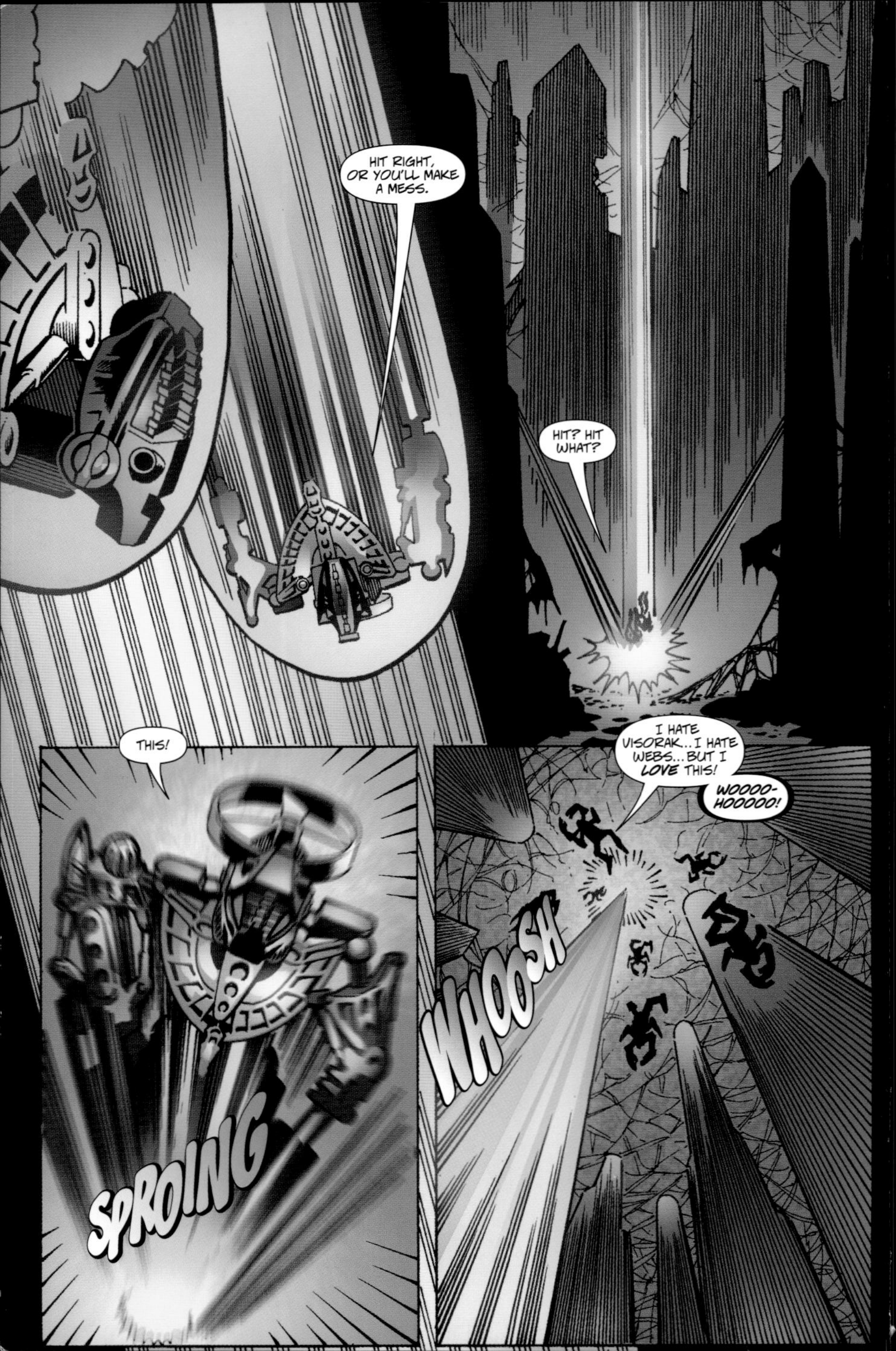
HIT RIGHT, OR YOU'LL MAKE A MESS.
HIT? HIT WHAT?
THIS!
SPROING
I HATE VISORAK... I HATE WEBS... BUT I LOVE THIS!
WOOOO-HOOOOO!
WHOOSH

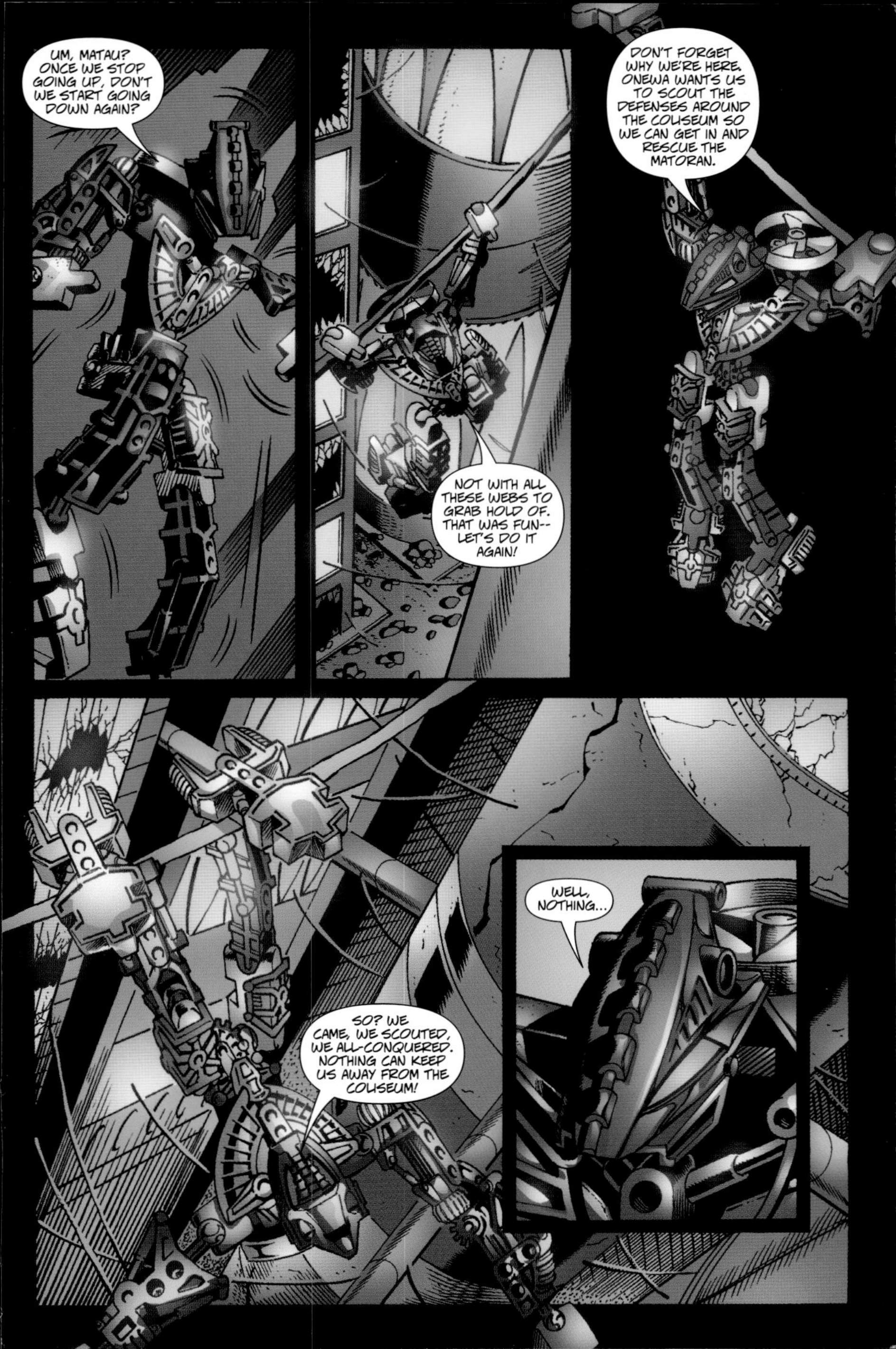
UM, MATAU? ONCE WE STOP GOING UP, DON'T WE START GOING DOWN AGAIN?
NOT WITH ALL THESE WEBS TO GRAB HOLD OF. THAT WAS FUN-- LET'S DO IT AGAIN!
DON'T FORGET WHY WE'RE HERE. ONEWA WANTS US TO SCOUT THE DEFENSES AROUND THE COLISEUM SO WE CAN GET IN AND RESCUE THE MATORAN.
SO? WE CAME, WE SCOUTED, WE ALL-CONQUERED. NOTHING CAN KEEP US AWAY FROM THE COLISEUM!
WELL, NOTHING...

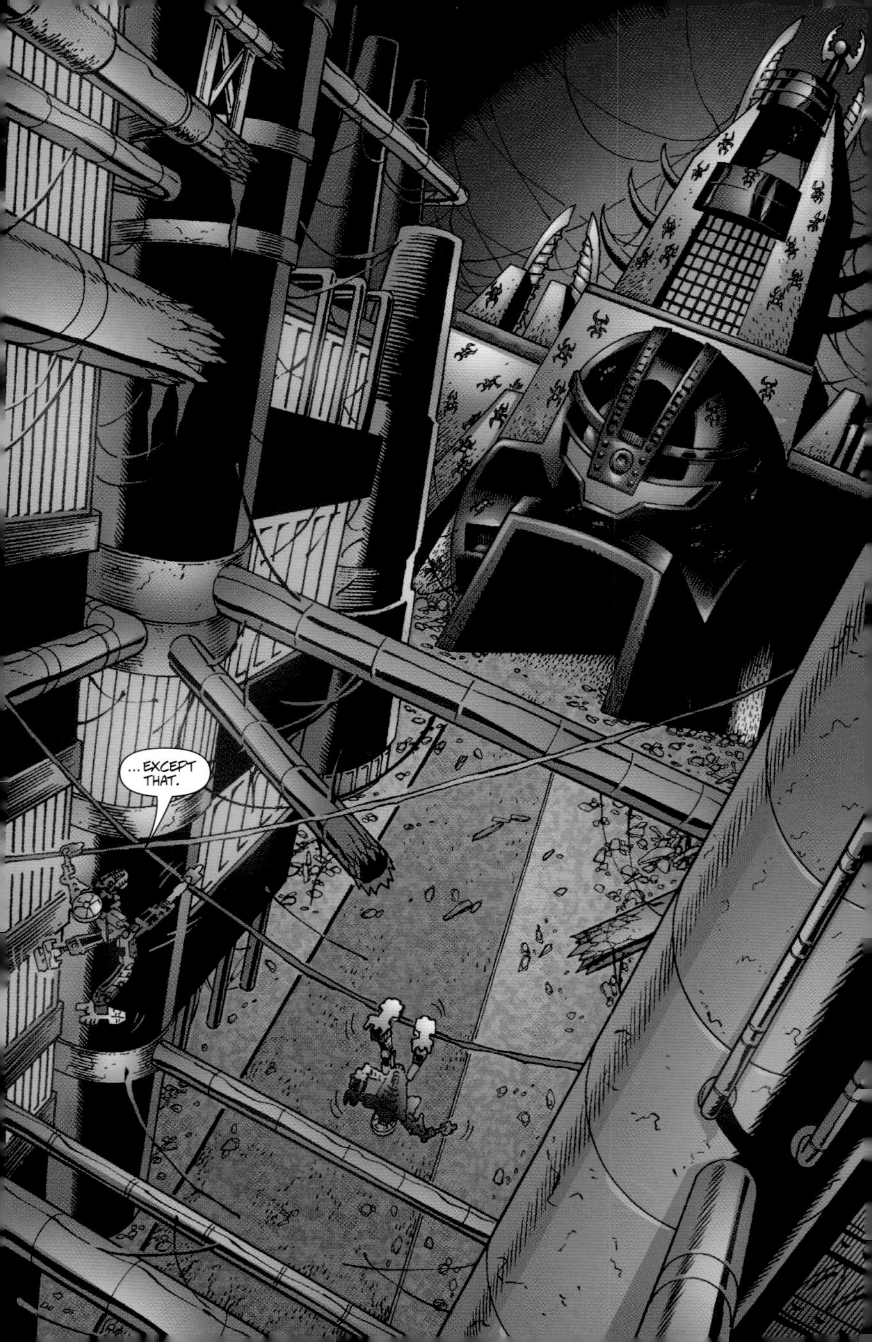
...EXCEPT THAT.

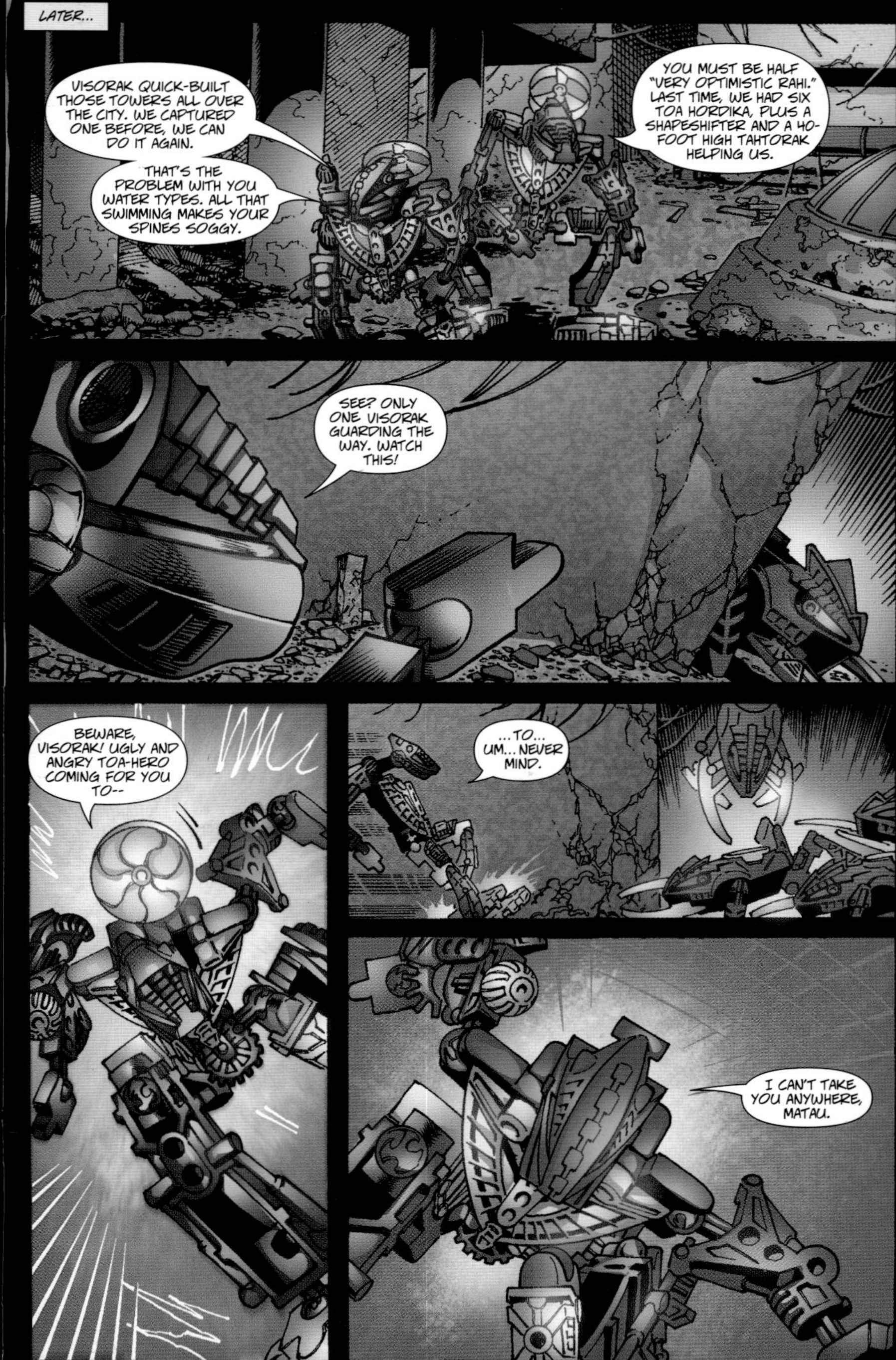
LATER...
VISORAK QUICK-BUILT THOSE TOWERS ALL OVER THE CITY. WE CAPTURED ONE BEFORE, WE CAN DO IT AGAIN.
THAT'S THE PROBLEM WITH YOU WATER TYPES. ALL THAT SWIMMING MAKES YOUR SPINES SOGGY.
YOU MUST BE HALF "VERY OPTIMISTIC RAHI." LAST TIME, WE HAD SIX TOA HORDIKA, PLUS A SHAPESHIFTER AND A 40-FOOT HIGH TAHTORAK HELPING US.
SEE? ONLY ONE VISORAK GUARDING THE WAY. WATCH THIS!
BEWARE, VISORAK! UGLY AND ANGRY TOA-HERO COMING FOR YOU TO--
...TO... UM... NEVER MIND.
I CAN'T TAKE YOU ANYWHERE, MATAU.

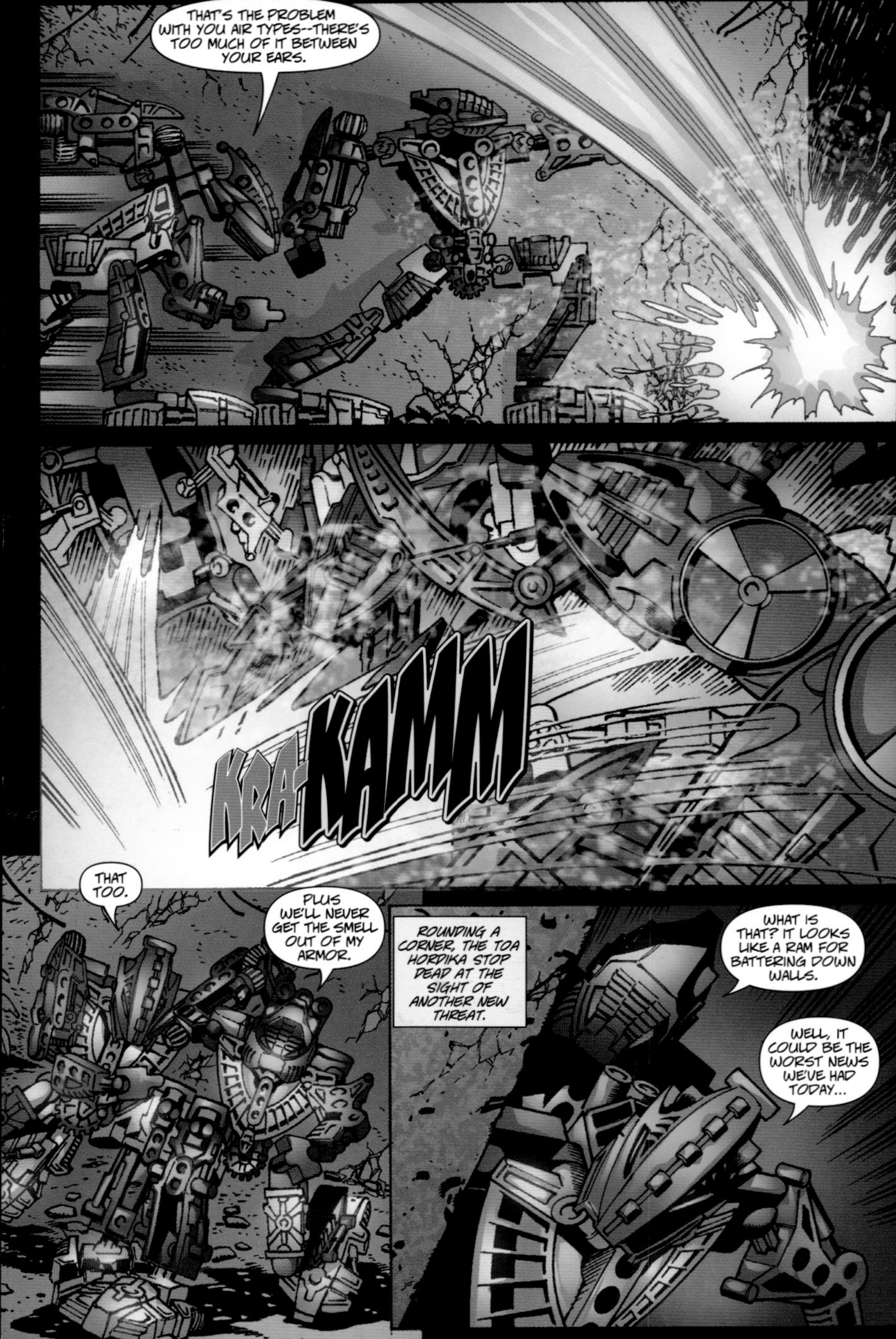
THAT'S THE PROBLEM WITH YOU AIR TYPES--THERE'S TOO MUCH OF IT BETWEEN YOUR EARS.
KRA-KAMM
THAT TOO.
PLUS WE'LL NEVER GET THE SMELL OUT OF MY ARMOR.
ROUNDING A CORNER, THE TOA HORDIKA STOP DEAD AT THE SIGHT OF ANOTHER NEW THREAT.
WHAT IS THAT? IT LOOKS LIKE A RAM FOR BATTERING DOWN WALLS.
WELL, IT COULD BE THE WORST NEWS WE'VE HAD TODAY...

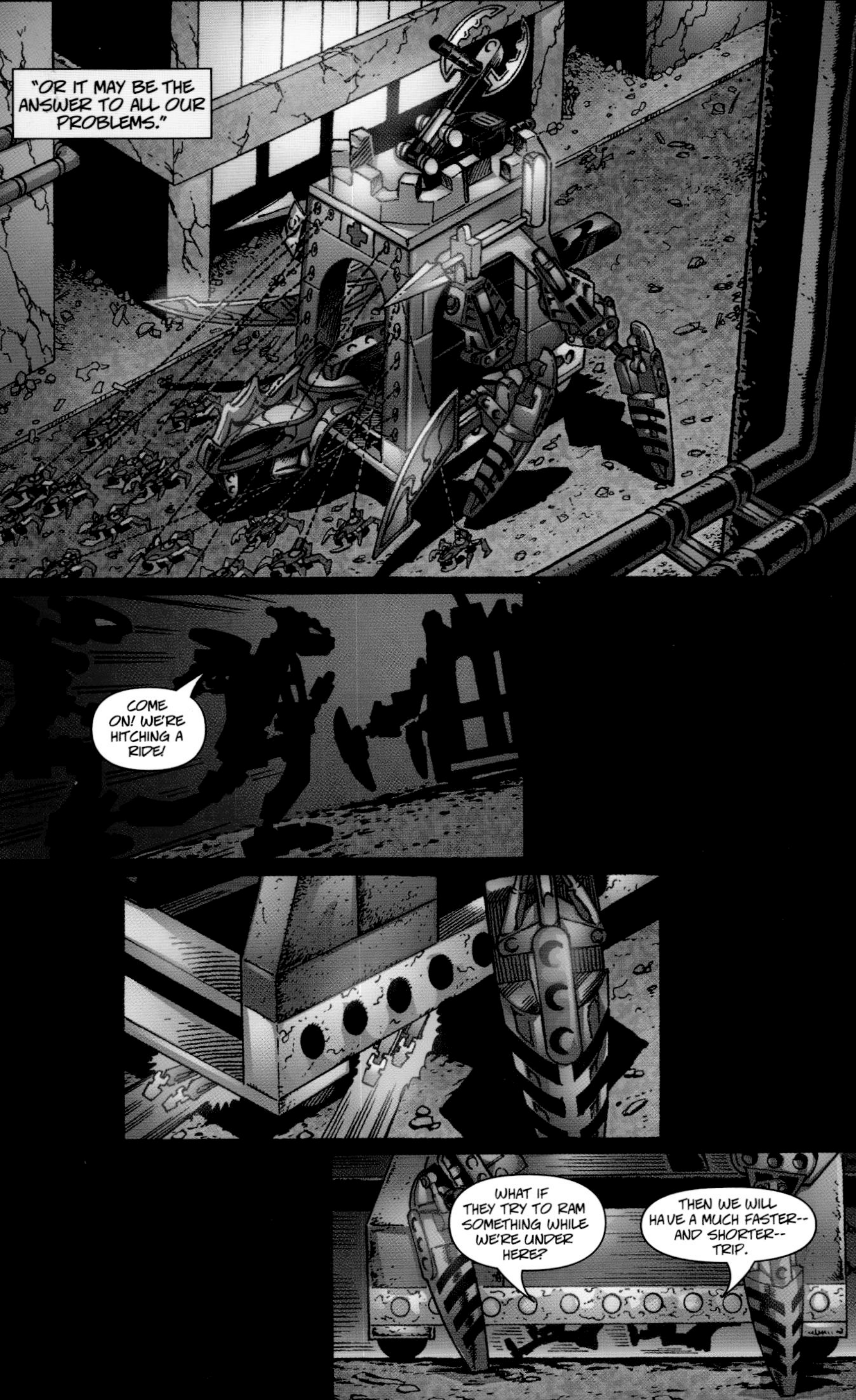
"OR IT MAY BE THE ANSWER TO ALL OUR PROBLEMS."
COME ON! WE'RE HITCHING A RIDE!
WHAT IF THEY TRY TO RAM SOMETHING WHILE WE'RE UNDER HERE?
THEN WE WILL HAVE A MUCH FASTER-- AND SHORTER-- TRIP.

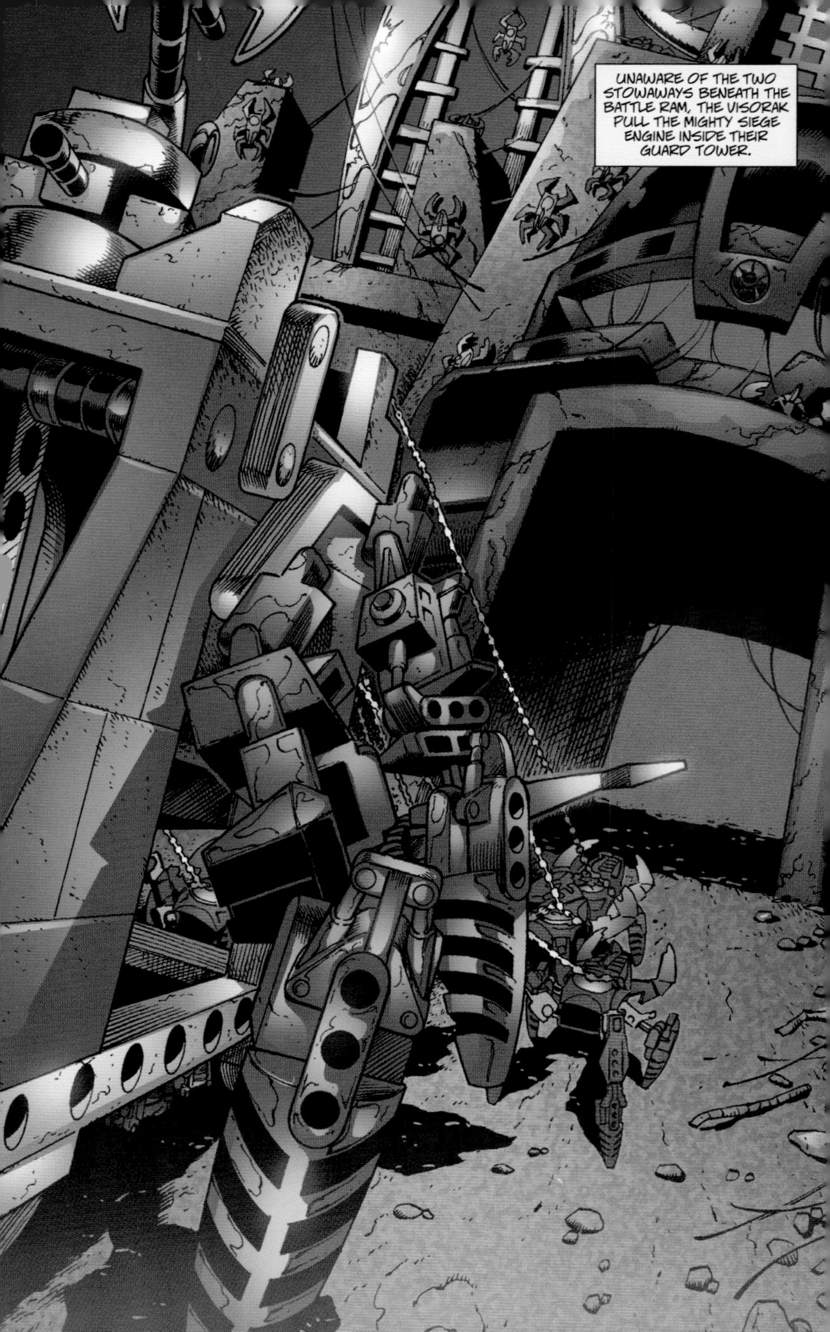
UNAWARE OF THE TWO STOWAWAYS BENEATH THE BATTLE RAM, THE VISORAK PULL THE MIGHTY SIEGE ENGINE INSIDE THEIR GUARD TOWER.

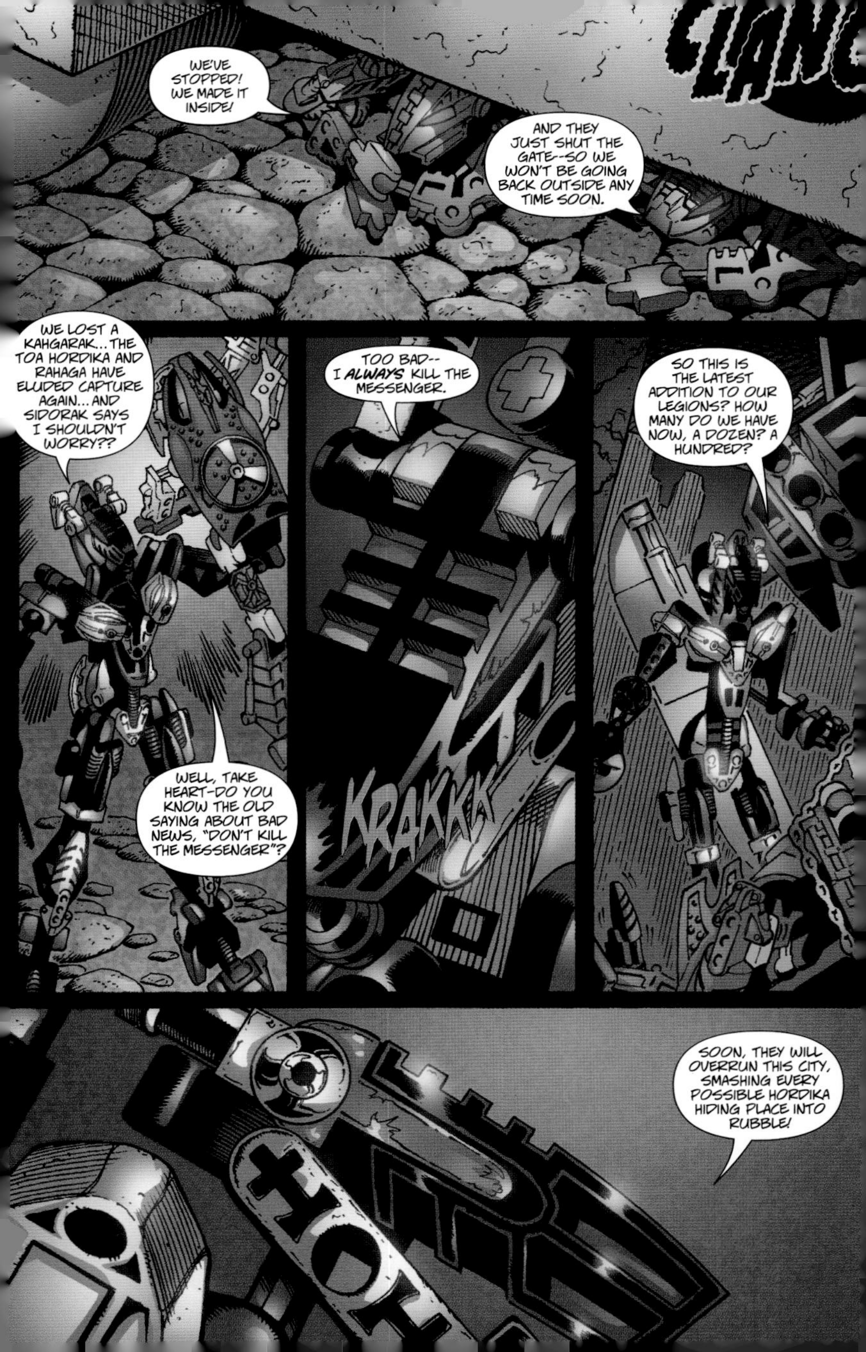
CLANG
WE'VE STOPPED! WE MADE IT INSIDE!
AND THEY JUST SHUT THE GATE--SO WE WON'T BE GOING BACK OUTSIDE ANY TIME SOON.
WE LOST A KAHGARAK... THE TOA HORDIKA AND RAHAGA HAVE ELUDED CAPTURE AGAIN... AND SIDORAK SAYS I SHOULDN'T WORRY??
WELL, TAKE HEART-DO YOU KNOW THE OLD SAYING ABOUT BAD NEWS, "DON'T KILL THE MESSENGER"?
TOO BAD-- I ALWAYS KILL THE MESSENGER.
KRAKKK
SO THIS IS THE LATEST ADDITION TO OUR LEGIONS? HOW MANY DO WE HAVE NOW, A DOZEN? A HUNDRED?
SOON, THEY WILL OVERRUN THIS CITY, SMASHING EVERY POSSIBLE HORDIKA HIDING PLACE INTO RUBBLE!

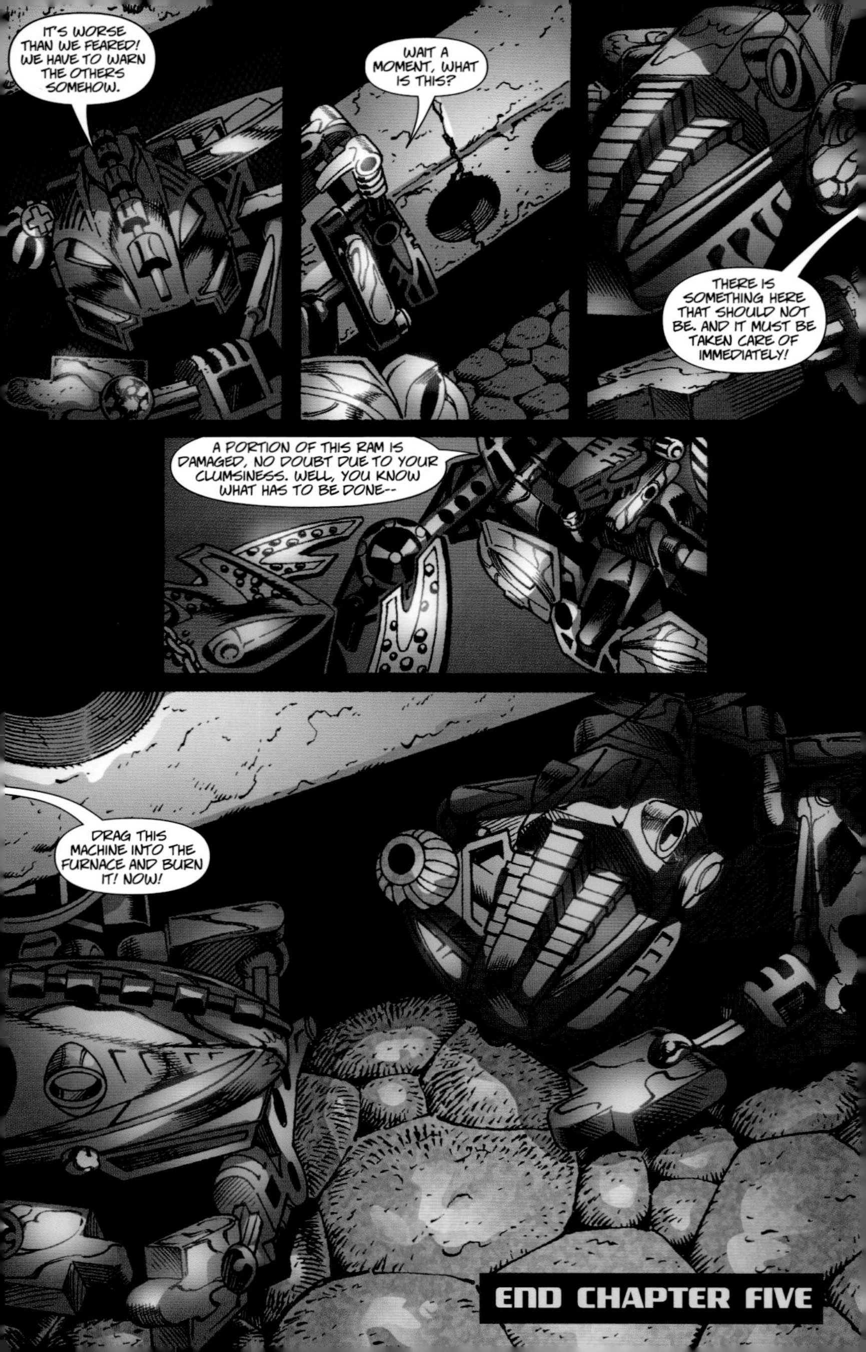
IT'S WORSE THAN WE FEARED! WE HAVE TO WARN THE OTHERS SOMEHOW.
WAIT A MOMENT, WHAT IS THIS?
THERE IS SOMETHING HERE THAT SHOULD NOT BE. AND IT MUST BE TAKEN CARE OF IMMEDIATELY!
A PORTION OF THIS RAM IS DAMAGED, NO DOUBT DUE TO YOUR CLUMSINESS. WELL, YOU KNOW WHAT HAS TO BE DONE--
DRAG THIS MACHINE INTO THE FURNACE AND BURN IT! NOW!
END CHAPTER FIVE

TRIAL BY FIRE
CHAPTER SIX

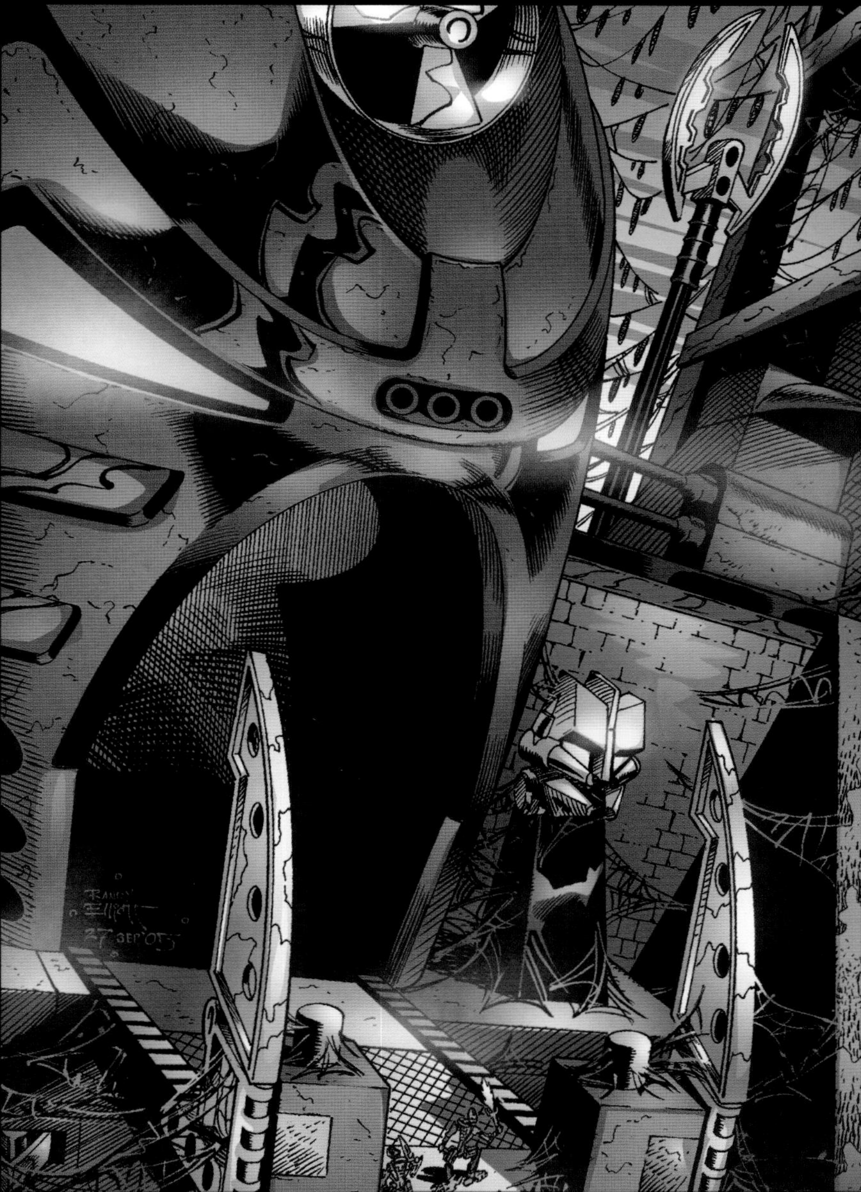

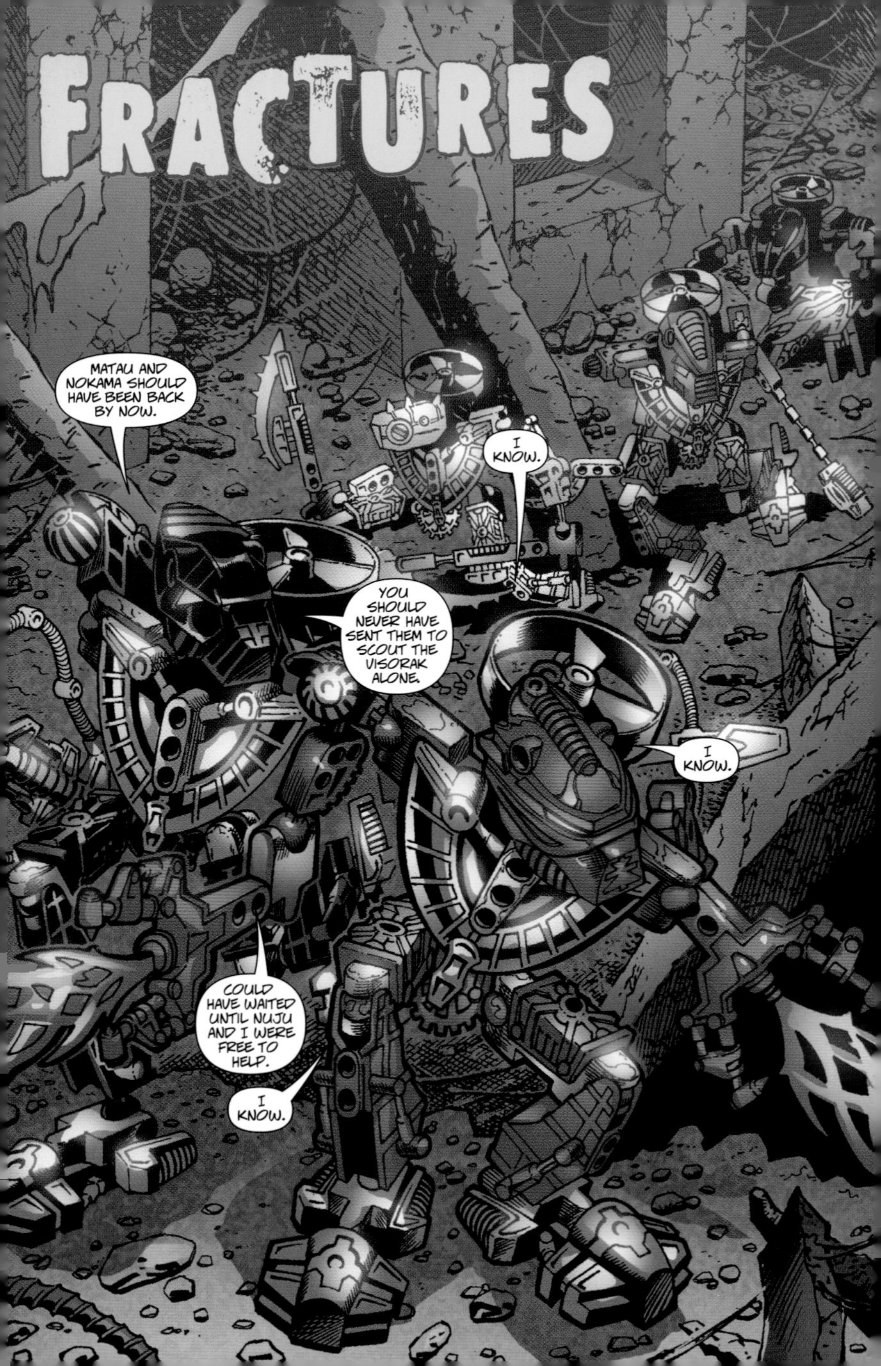
FRACTURES
MATAU AND NOKAMA SHOULD HAVE BEEN BACK BY NOW.
I KNOW.
YOU SHOULD NEVER HAVE SENT THEM TO SCOUT THE VISORAK ALONE.
I KNOW.
COULD HAVE WAITED UNTIL NUJU AND I WERE FREE TO HELP.
I KNOW.

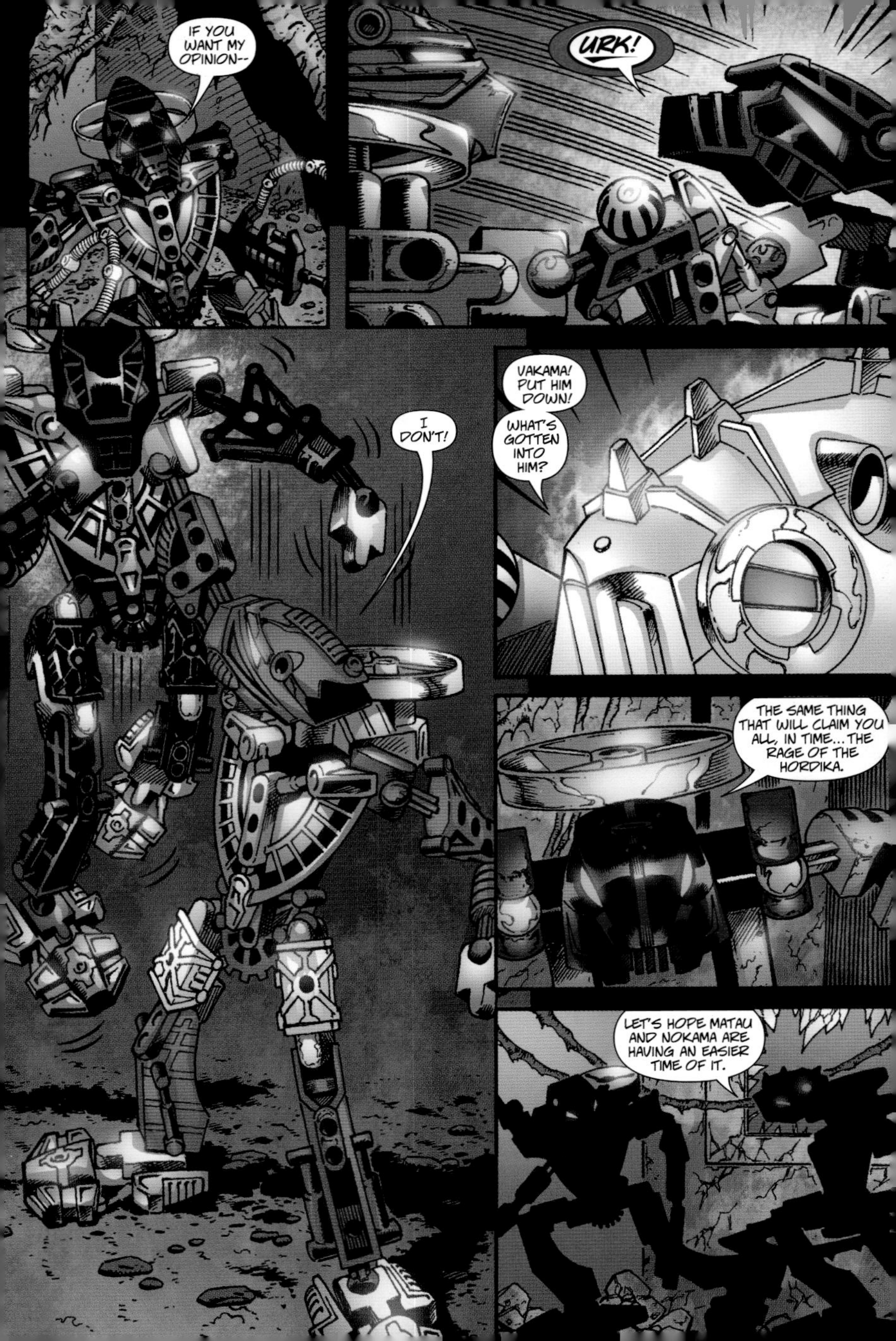
IF YOU WANT MY OPINION--
URK!
I DON'T!
VAKAMA! PUT HIM DOWN!
WHAT'S GOTTEN INTO HIM?
THE SAME THING THAT WILL CLAIM YOU ALL, IN TIME... THE RAGE OF THE HORDIKA.
LET'S HOPE MATAU AND NOKAMA ARE HAVING AN EASIER TIME OF IT.

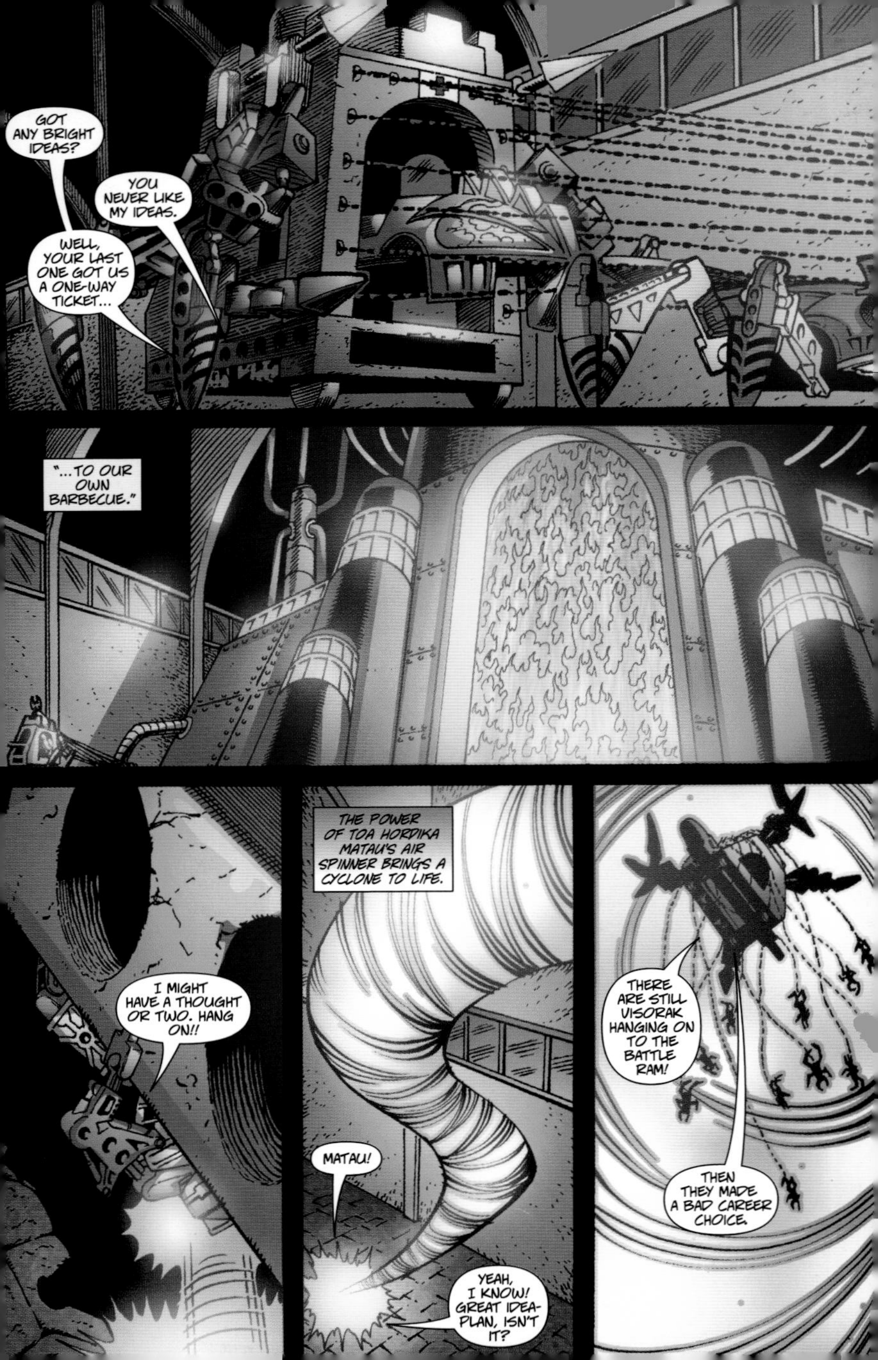
GOT ANY BRIGHT IDEAS?
YOU NEVER LIKE MY IDEAS.
WELL, YOUR LAST ONE GOT US A ONE-WAY TICKET...
"...TO OUR OWN BARBECUE."
I MIGHT HAVE A THOUGHT OR TWO. HANG ON!!
THE POWER OF TOA HORDIKA MATAU'S AIR SPINNER BRINGS A CYCLONE TO LIFE.
MATAU!
YEAH, I KNOW! GREAT IDEA-PLAN, ISN'T IT?
THERE ARE STILL VISORAK HANGING ON TO THE BATTLE RAM!
THEN THEY MADE A BAD CAREER CHOICE.

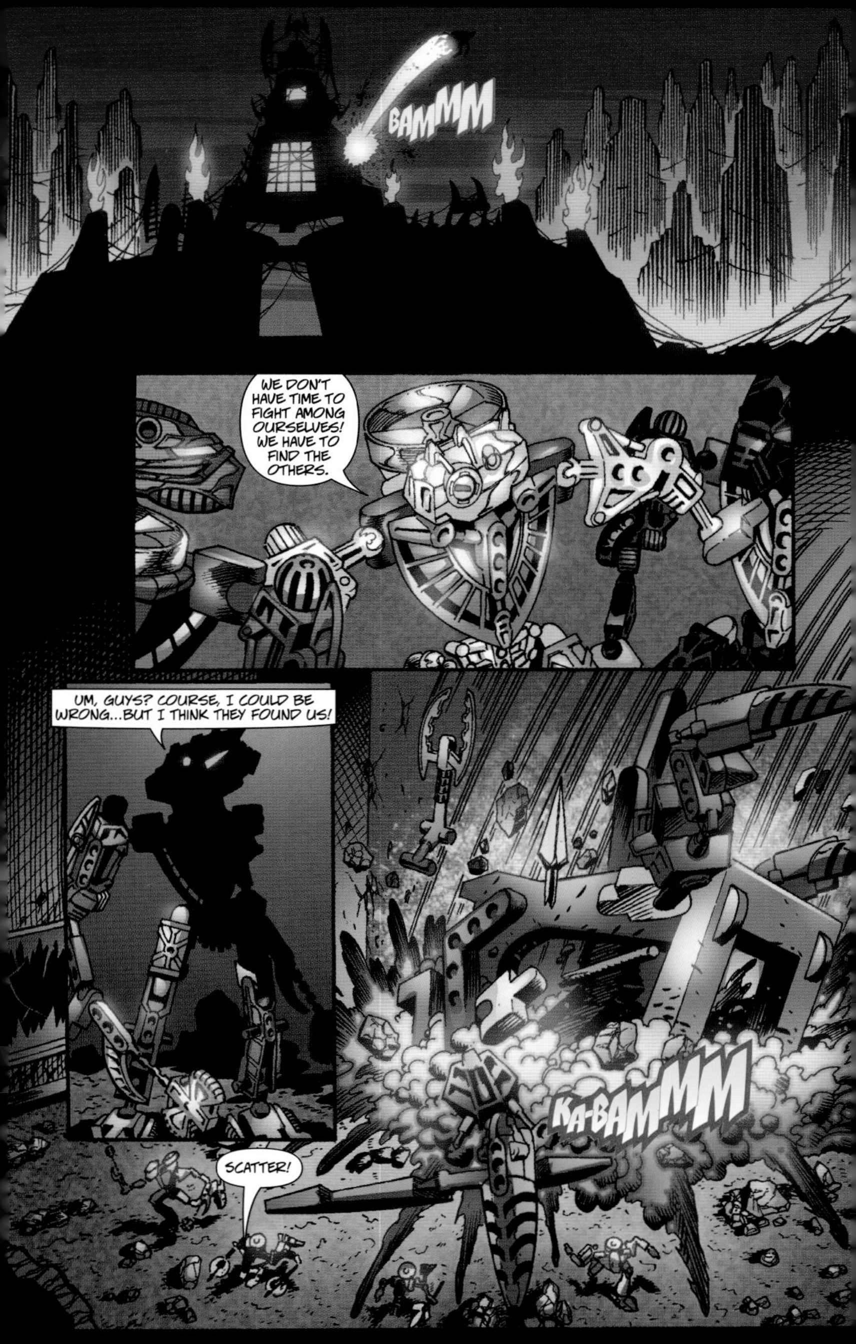
BAMMM
WE DON'T HAVE TIME TO FIGHT AMONG OURSELVES! WE HAVE TO FIND THE OTHERS.
UM, GUYS? COURSE, I COULD BE WRONG...BUT I THINK THEY FOUND US!
KA-BAMMM
SCATTER!

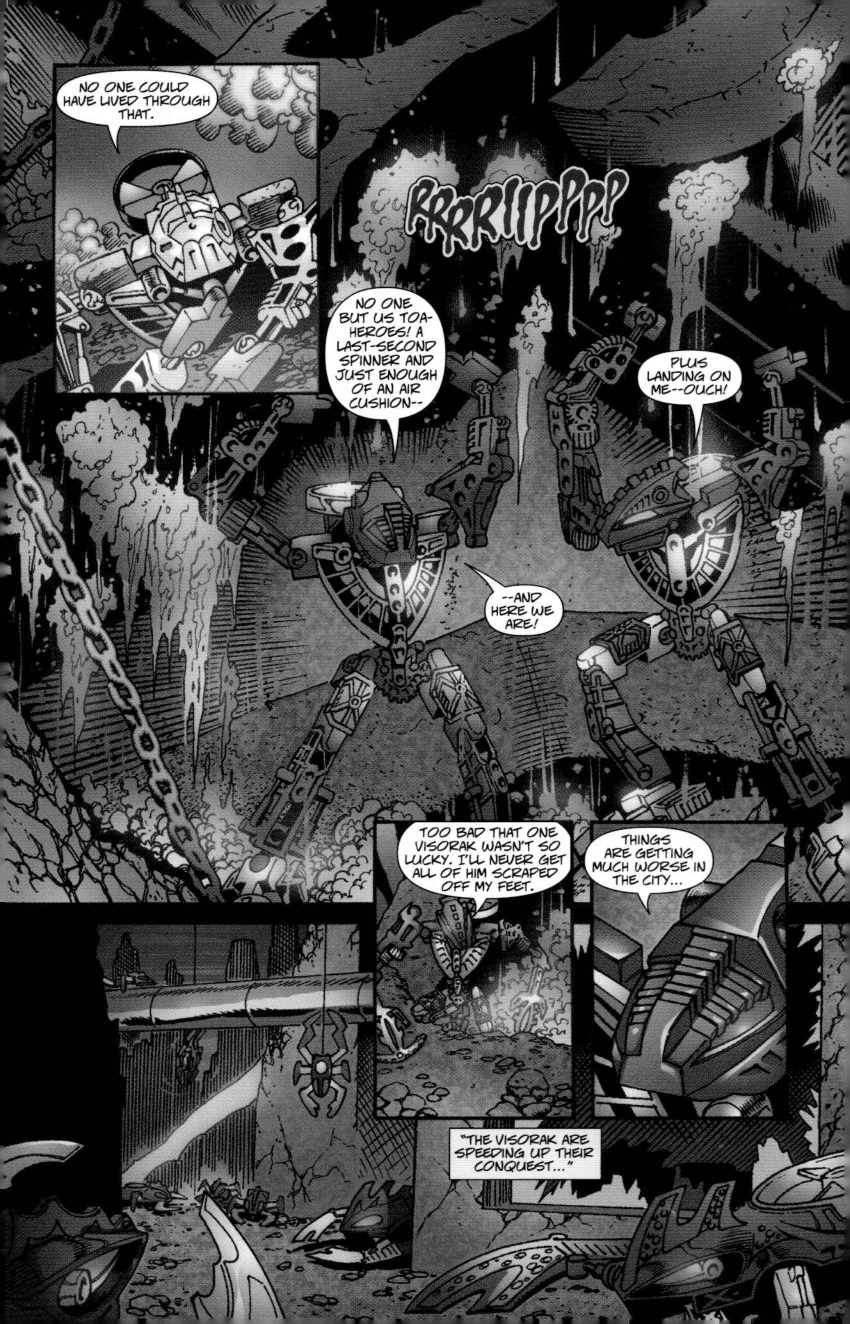
NO ONE COULD HAVE LIVED THROUGH THAT.
RRRRIIPPPP!
NO ONE BUT US TOA-HEROES! A LAST-SECOND SPINNER AND JUST ENOUGH OF AN AIR CUSHION--
PLUS LANDING ON ME--OUCH!
--AND HERE WE ARE!
TOO BAD THAT ONE VISORAK WASN'T SO LUCKY. I'LL NEVER GET ALL OF HIM SCRAPED OFF MY FEET.
THINGS ARE GETTING MUCH WORSE IN THE CITY...
"THE VISORAK ARE SPEEDING UP THEIR CONQUEST..."

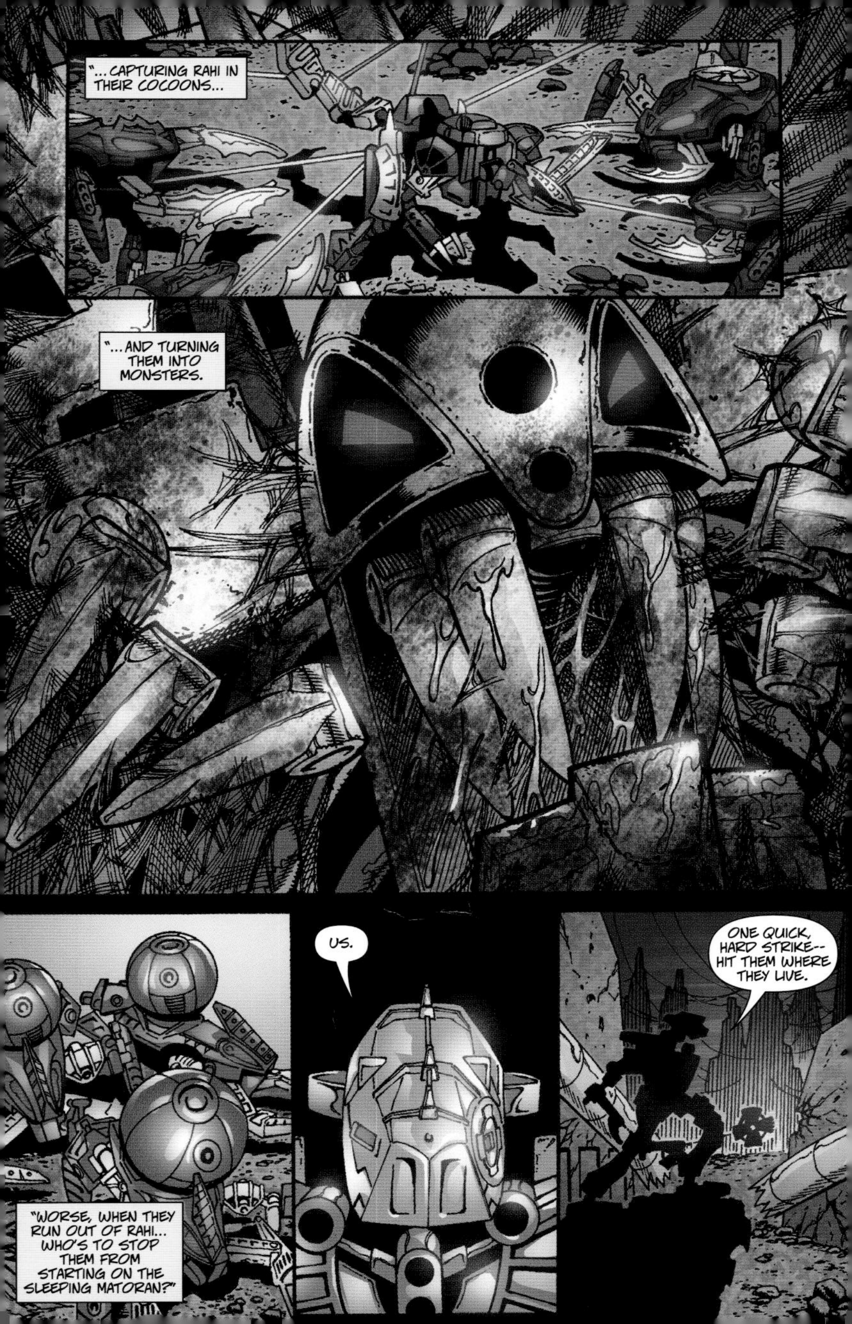
"...CAPTURING RAHI IN THEIR COCOONS...
"...AND TURNING THEM INTO MONSTERS.
"WORSE, WHEN THEY RUN OUT OF RAHI... WHO'S TO STOP THEM FROM STARTING ON THE SLEEPING MATORAN?"
US.
ONE QUICK, HARD STRIKE-- HIT THEM WHERE THEY LIVE.

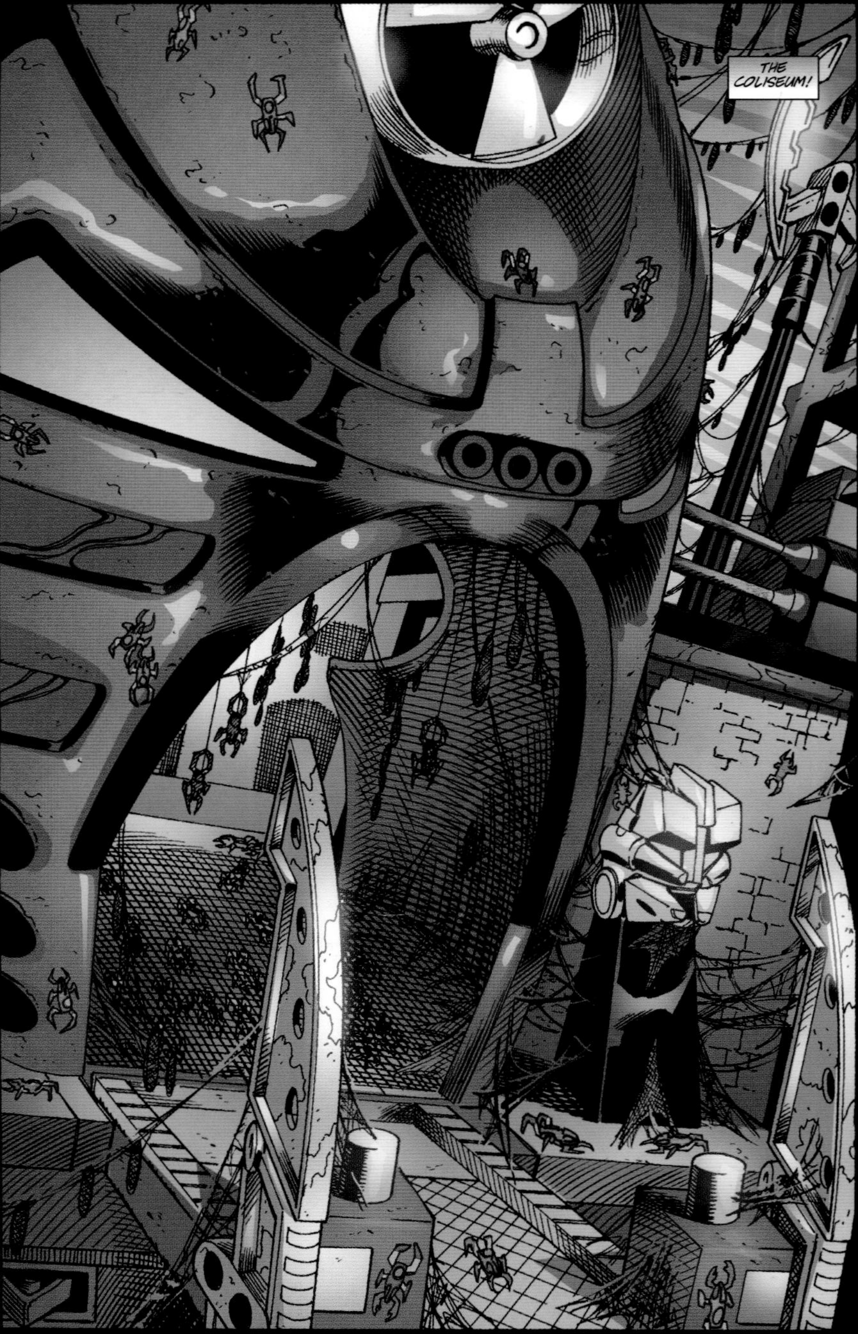
THE COLISEUM!

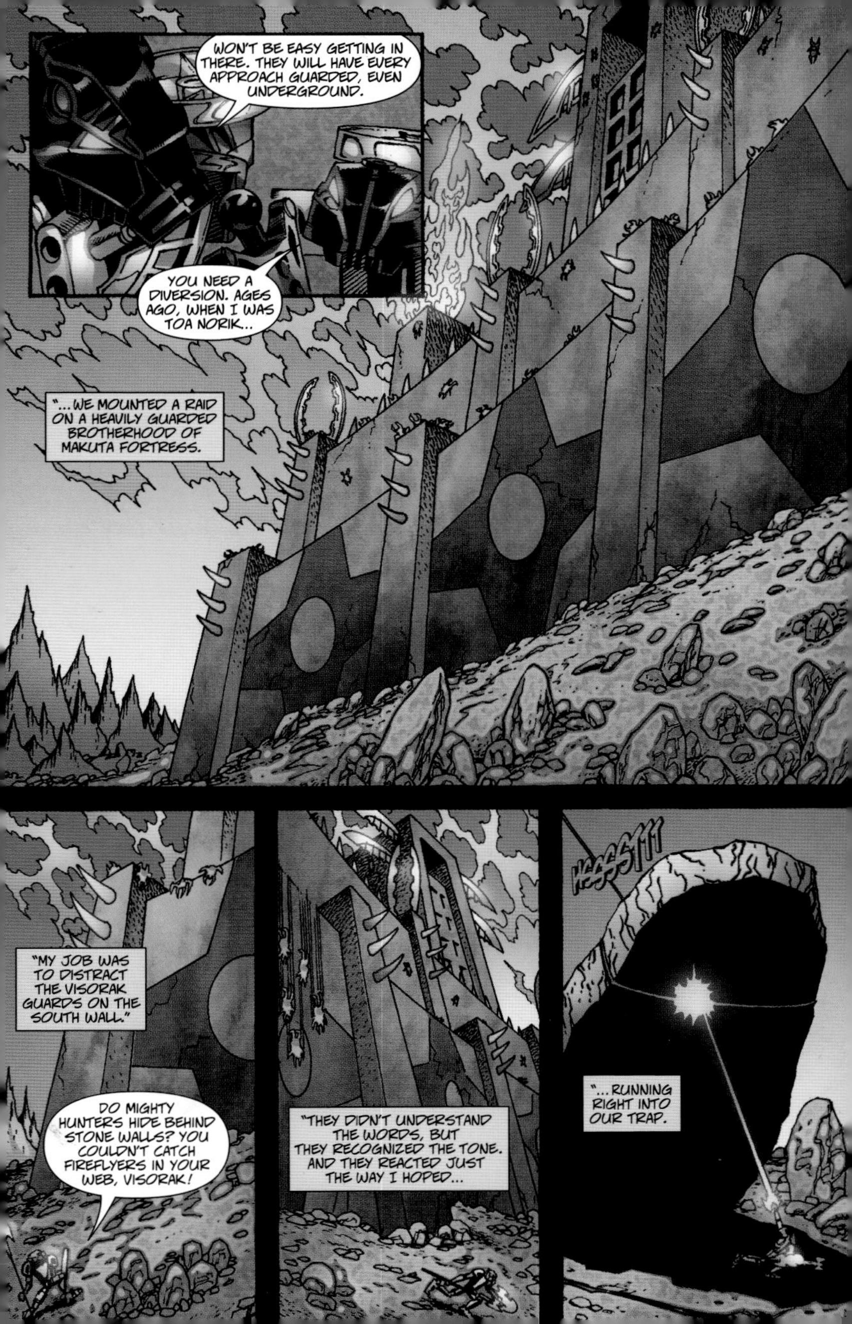

WON'T BE EASY GETTING IN THERE. THEY WILL HAVE EVERY APPROACH GUARDED, EVEN UNDERGROUND.
YOU NEED A DIVERSION. AGES AGO, WHEN I WAS TOA NORIK...
"...WE MOUNTED A RAID ON A HEAVILY GUARDED BROTHERHOOD OF MAKUTA FORTRESS.
"MY JOB WAS TO DISTRACT THE VISORAK GUARDS ON THE SOUTH WALL."
DO MIGHTY HUNTERS HIDE BEHIND STONE WALLS? YOU COULDN'T CATCH FIREFLYERS IN YOUR WEB, VISORAK!
"THEY DIDN'T UNDERSTAND THE WORDS, BUT THEY RECOGNIZED THE TONE. AND THEY REACTED JUST THE WAY I HOPED...
HSSSTTT
"...RUNNING RIGHT INTO OUR TRAP.

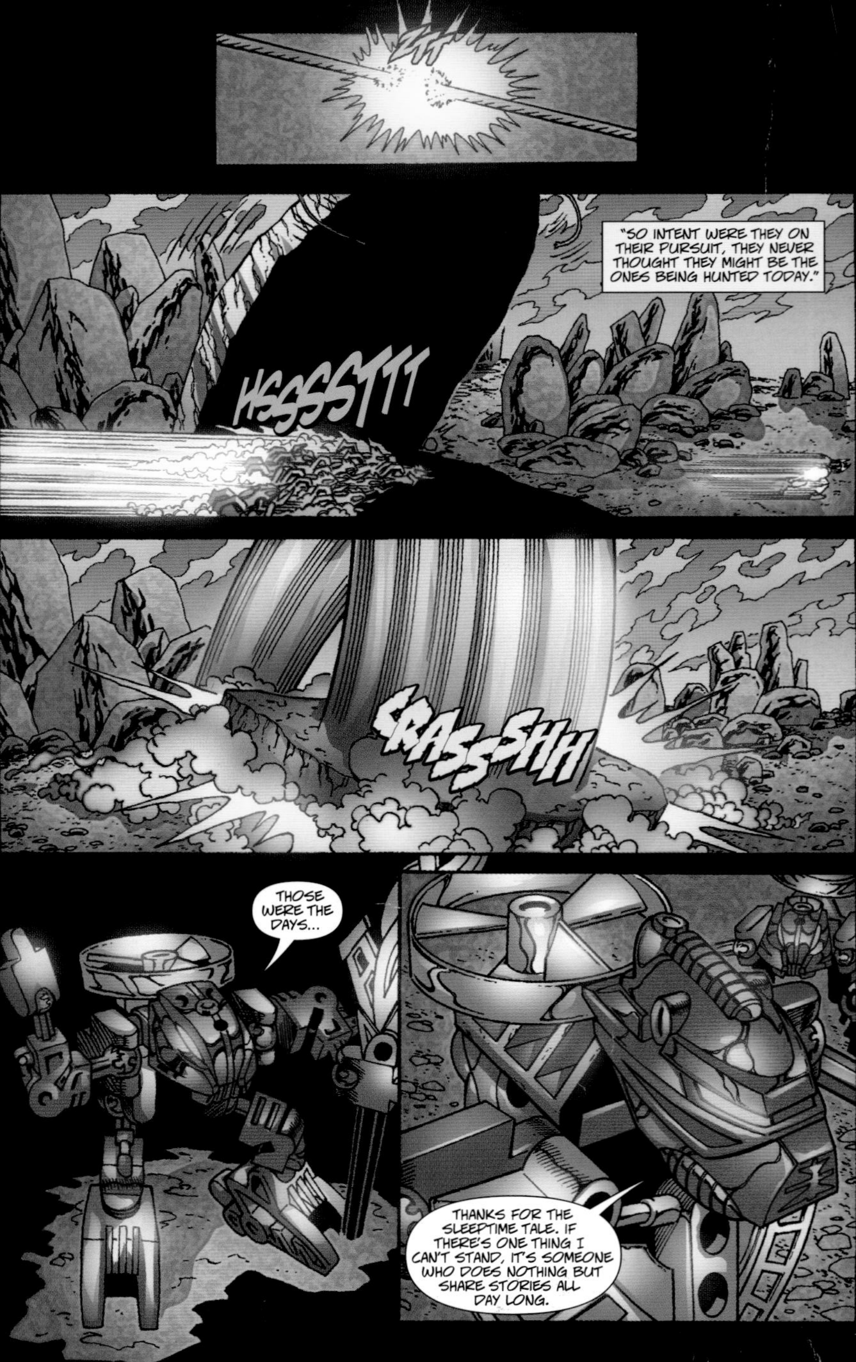
ZZT
"SO INTENT WERE THEY ON THEIR PURSUIT, THEY NEVER THOUGHT THEY MIGHT BE THE ONES BEING HUNTED TODAY."
HSSSSTTT
CRASS-SHH
THOSE WERE THE DAYS...
THANKS FOR THE SLEEPTIME TALE. IF THERE'S ONE THING I CAN'T STAND, IT'S SOMEONE WHO DOES NOTHING BUT SHARE STORIES ALL DAY LONG.

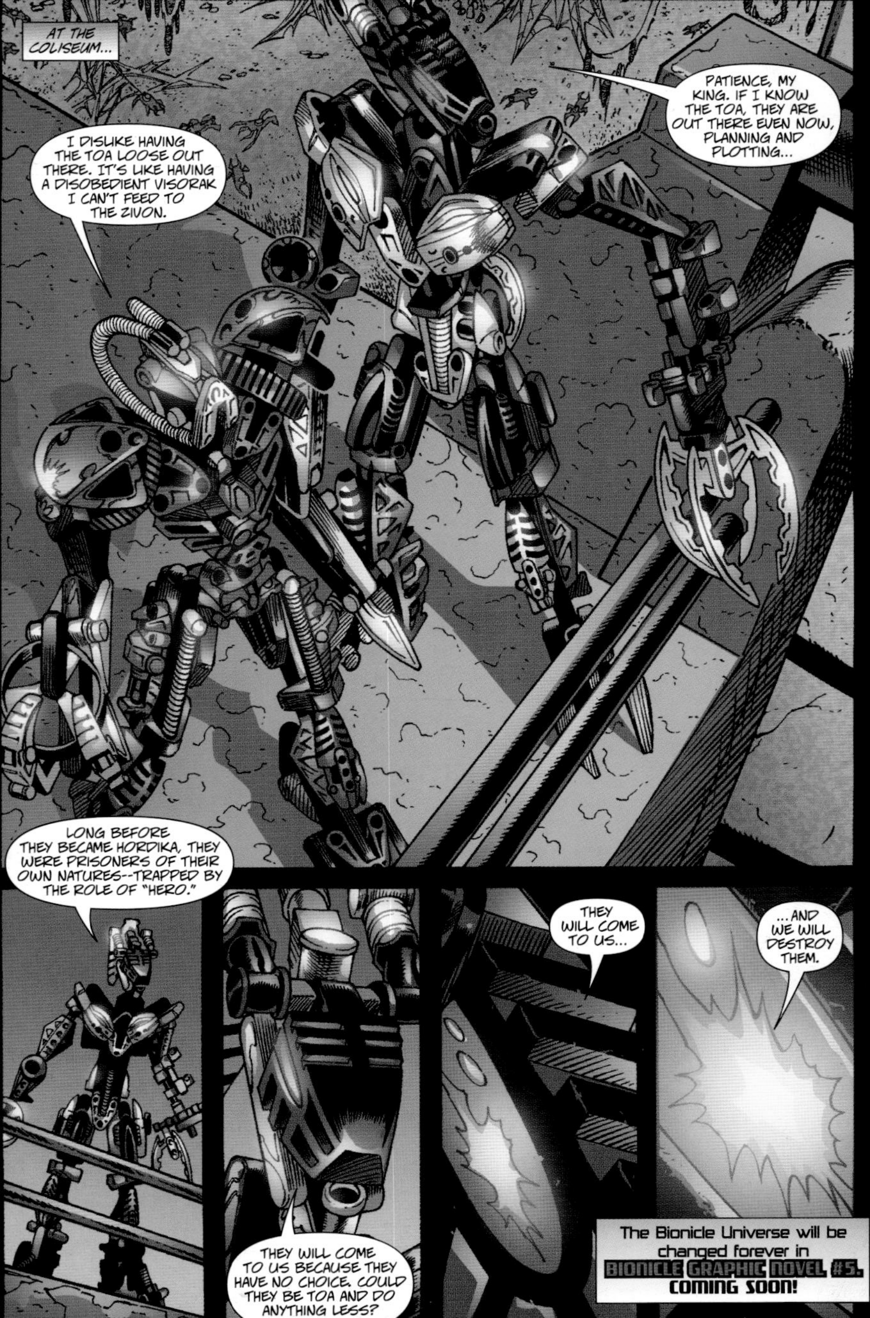
AT THE COLISEUM...
I DISLIKE HAVING THE TOA LOOSE OUT THERE. IT'S LIKE HAVING A DISOBEDIENT VISORAK I CAN'T FEED TO THE ZIVON.
PATIENCE, MY KING. IF I KNOW THE TOA, THEY ARE OUT THERE EVEN NOW, PLANNING AND PLOTTING...
LONG BEFORE THEY BECAME HORDIKA, THEY WERE PRISONERS OF THEIR OWN NATURES--TRAPPED BY THE ROLE OF "HERO."
THEY WILL COME TO US BECAUSE THEY HAVE NO CHOICE. COULD THEY BE TOA AND DO ANYTHING LESS?
THEY WILL COME TO US...
...AND WE WILL DESTROY THEM.
The Bionicle Universe will be changed forever in BIONICLE GRAPHIC NOVEL #5. COMING SOON!

WATCH OUT FOR PAPERCUTZ™

Welcome to a scary edition of the Papercutz Backpages, the place to find out all the latest news about the graphic novel publishers of THE HARDY BOYS, NANCY DREW, TALES FROM THE CRYPT, BIONICLE, and CLASSICS ILLUSTRATED. I'm Jim Salicrup, your Editor-in-Chief, and prime Papercutz promoter! We've got lots to talk about, so let's get right to it...

Things have taken a scary turn here at Papercutz! Don't panic --we're not talking about any of our graphic novels suddenly vanishing from bookstore shelves! We're not talking that kind of scary! Thanks to your continued support, our sales are stronger than ever, and if any of our titles have vanished off the shelves, it's only because they are temporarily sold out! No, we're talking TALES FROM THE CRYPT scary -- and how it's suddenly seeming to take over the pages of CLASSICS ILLUSTRATED and CLASSICS ILLUSTRATED DELUXE!

CLASSICS ILLUSTRATED #4 features world-famous cartoonist Gahan Wilson's creepy cartoons illustrated Edgar Allan Poe's "The Raven and Other Poems." And if that wasn't scary enough, CLASSICS ILLUSTRAT-ED DELUXE #3 features an all-new adaptation by Marion Mousse of Mary Shelly's monster-masterwork "Frankenstein"!

Why have our CLASSICS ILLUSTRATED titles turned into a virtual vault of horror? The answer is obvious! After all, what is a "classic" if not a story so powerfully compelling that it leads to countless retellings? But we suspect that you've never experienced Poe's poems as seen through macabre cartoonist Gahan Wilson's bloodshot eyes, or the tale of Victor Frankenstein and his monster as dramatically brought to life, so to speak, by the dark visions of Marion Mousse.

Despite how many times the Frankenstein story has been told, it's as thought-provoking and as frightening now as the day it was when originally published in 1818. If you've never read the original novel you may be surprised that it's not the over-the-top crazy story so many adaptations may imply, but rather it's a serious tale tackling many major issues. Mousse takes great pains to restore many of Victor Frankenstein's motivations that lead to his "mad quest" to solve the ultimate mystery of life and death (as opposed to simply creating a monster).

In the pages that follow you'll see for yourself, the skill and artistry that Mousse brings to faithfully adapting this terrifying classic. Keep in mind, that the pages of CLASSICS ILLUSTRATED DELUXE are much larger than these pages, so to truly savor these pages, and to avoid eyestrain, be sure to pick up CLASSICS ILLUSTRATED DELUXE #3!

Thanks,

JIM

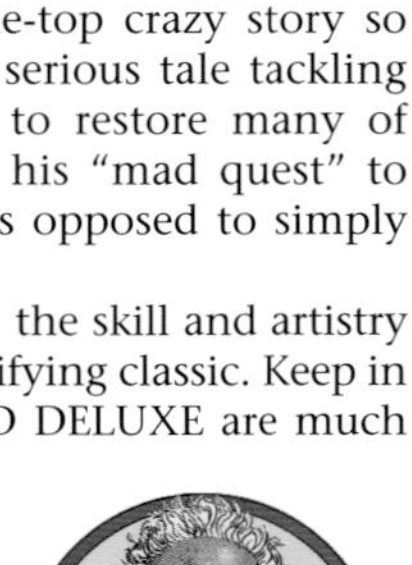

THE OLD EDITOR
Caricature by Rick Parker

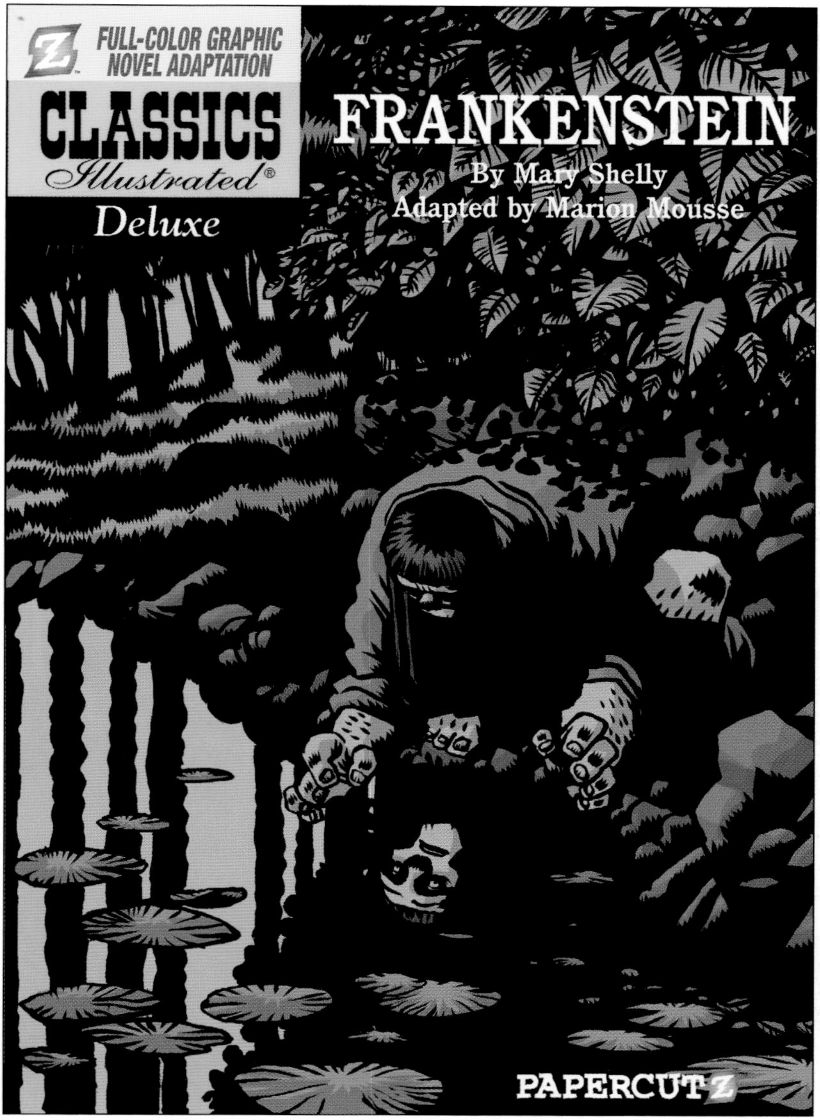
FULL-COLOR GRAPHIC NOVEL ADAPTATION
CLASSICS Illustrated®
Deluxe
FRANKENSTEIN
By Mary Shelly
Adapted by Marion Mousse
PAPERCUTZ

FOR MORE THAN A YEAR, I STUDIED ALL THE FORMS AND CONSE-QUENCES OF DEATH: THE FLESH DECOMPOSING, SLOWLY ROTTING...

...THE MATTER OF WHICH WE'RE ALL MADE, DEGRADING AND WASTING AWAY BEFORE VANISHING AS THOUGH THROUGH MAGIC.

FRANKENSTEIN...

...OUR LOCAL CELEBRITY HARD AT WORK.

...

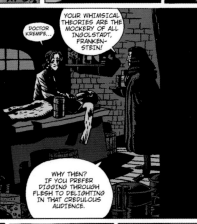

DOCTOR KREMPE.

YOUR WHIMSICAL THEORIES ARE THE MOCKERY OF ALL INGOLSTADT, FRANKEN-STEIN!

WHY THEN? IF YOU PREFER DIGGING THROUGH FLESH TO DELIGHTING IN THAT CREDULOUS AUDIENCE.

STILL CHASING AFTER YOUR MAD HEROES?! CORNELIUS AGRIPPA, PARACELSUS...

DON'T TELL ME THAT YOU'RE STILL A DISCIPLE OF THOSE COOKED-UP ABSURDITIES?!

PHILLIPUS AUREOLUS VON HOHENHEIM, KNOWN AS PARACELSUS, EMINENT ALCHEMIST, WHO CLAIMED TO HAVE EXPERIMENTED ON THE FAMOUS ELIXIR OF ETERNAL YOUTH AND CREATED...

...THE HOMUNCU-LUS, A SMALL LIVING BEING IN THE FORM OF A HUMAN!

I KNOW ALL THAT, FRANKENSTEIN!

SO YOU CONTINUE AND CONTINUE TO PERSIST! YOU PERSIST IN RIDICULING YOUR PROFESSORS, IN DISCREDITING OUR HON-ORABLE INSTITUTION?!!

WELL THEN! SO, I HEREAFTER FORBID YOU TO USE COURSE MATERIAL SUCH AS HUMAN REMAINS OUTSIDE OF YOUR COURSES!

UNTIL NOW, I'D MADE NO ASSUMPTIONS ABOUT YOUR CHARACTER, YOUNG MAN.

YES, I WAS HESITATING...I WAS HESITATING BETWEEN A YAHOO AND AN ENLIGHTENED SCIENTIST...NOW I KNOW.

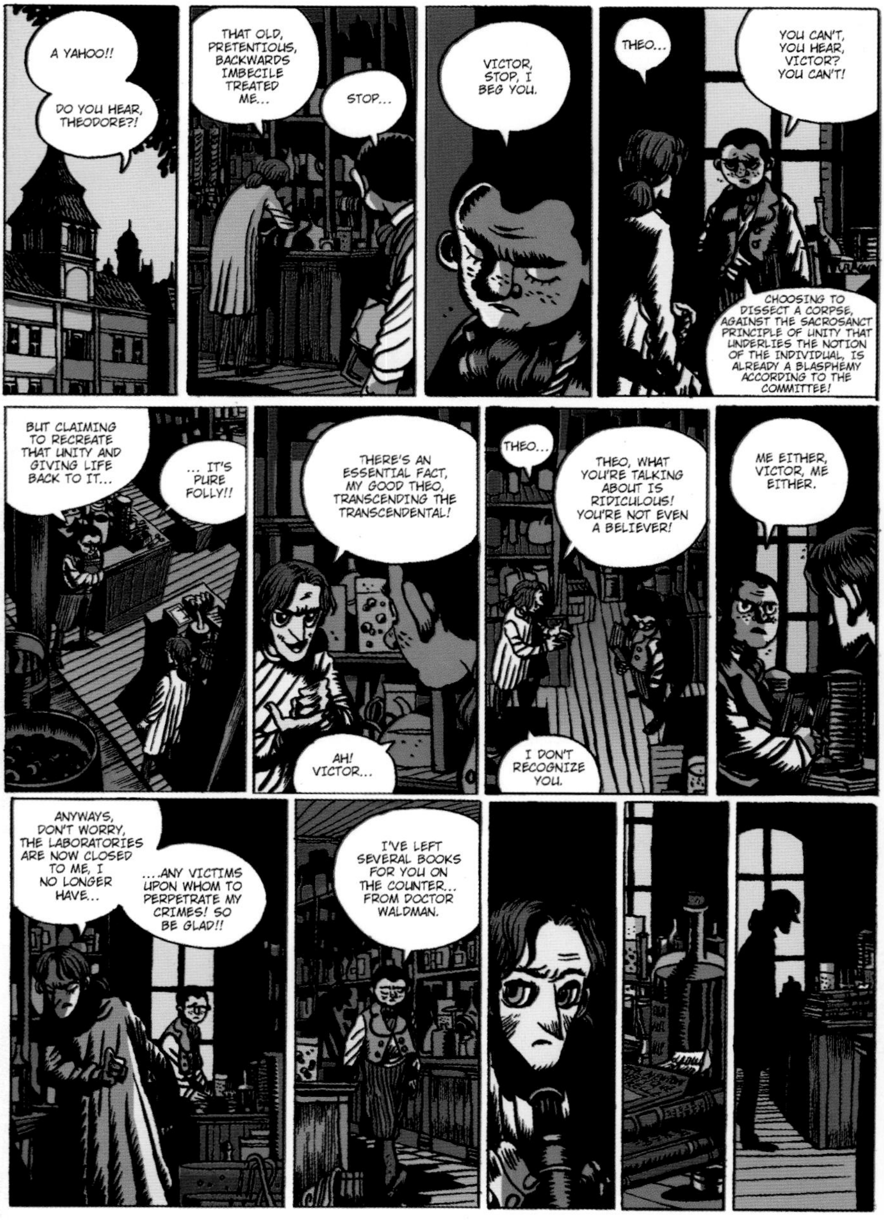
A YAHOO!!
DO YOU HEAR, THEODORE?!
THAT OLD, PRETENTIOUS, BACKWARDS IMBECILE TREATED ME...
STOP...
VICTOR, STOP, I BEG YOU.
THEO...
YOU CAN'T, YOU HEAR, VICTOR? YOU CAN'T!
CHOOSING TO DISSECT A CORPSE, AGAINST THE SACROSANCT PRINCIPLE OF UNITY THAT UNDERLIES THE NOTION OF THE INDIVIDUAL, IS ALREADY A BLASPHEMY ACCORDING TO THE COMMITTEE!
BUT CLAIMING TO RECREATE THAT UNITY AND GIVING LIFE BACK TO IT...
... IT'S PURE FOLLY!!
THERE'S AN ESSENTIAL FACT, MY GOOD THEO, TRANSCENDING THE TRANSCENDENTAL!
AH! VICTOR...
THEO...
THEO, WHAT YOU'RE TALKING ABOUT IS RIDICULOUS! YOU'RE NOT EVEN A BELIEVER!
I DON'T RECOGNIZE YOU.
ME EITHER, VICTOR, ME EITHER.
ANYWAYS, DON'T WORRY, THE LABORATORIES ARE NOW CLOSED TO ME, I NO LONGER HAVE...
...ANY VICTIMS UPON WHOM TO PERPETRATE MY CRIMES! SO BE GLAD!!
I'VE LEFT SEVERAL BOOKS FOR YOU ON THE COUNTER... FROM DOCTOR WALDMAN.

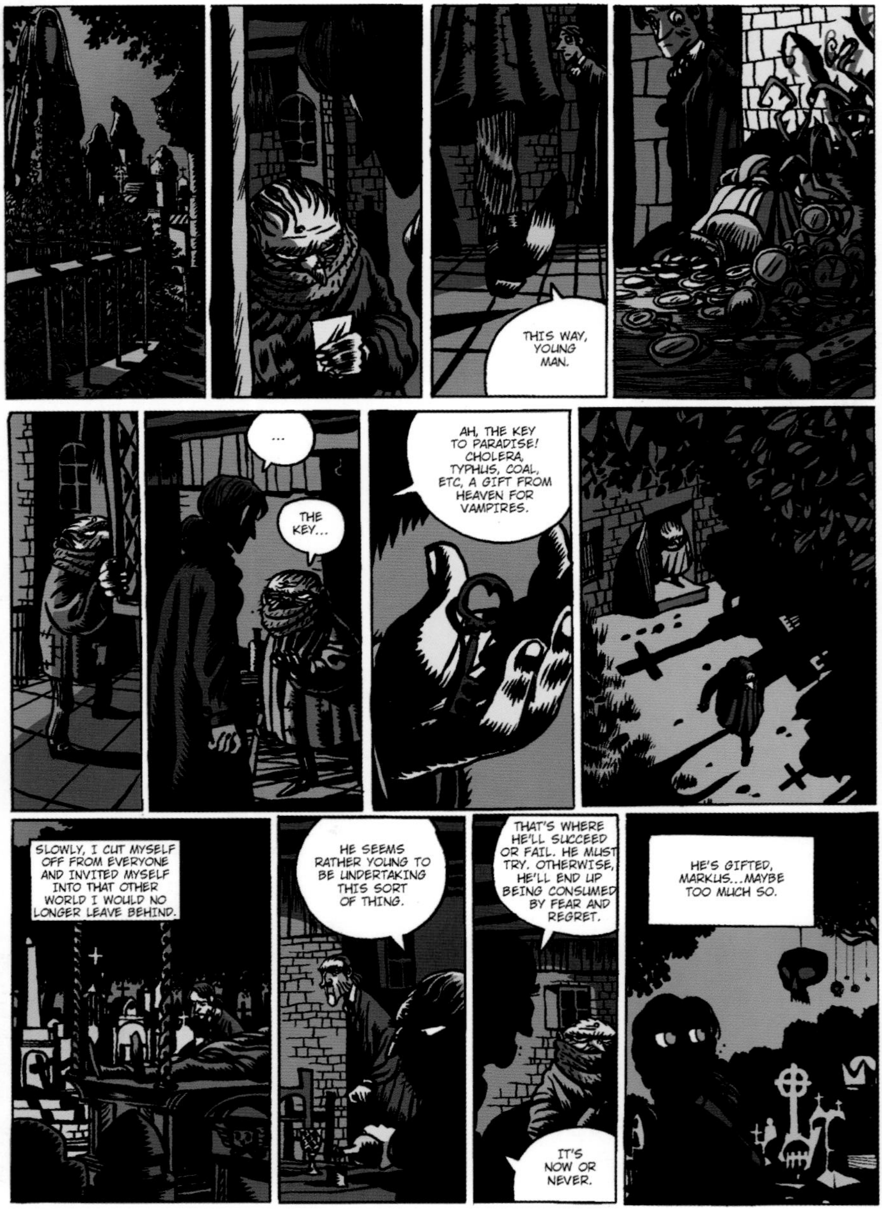
THIS WAY, YOUNG MAN.
...
THE KEY...
AH, THE KEY TO PARADISE! CHOLERA, TYPHUS, COAL, ETC, A GIFT FROM HEAVEN FOR VAMPIRES.
SLOWLY, I CUT MYSELF OFF FROM EVERYONE AND INVITED MYSELF INTO THAT OTHER WORLD I WOULD NO LONGER LEAVE BEHIND.
HE SEEMS RATHER YOUNG TO BE UNDERTAKING THIS SORT OF THING.
THAT'S WHERE HE'LL SUCCEED OR FAIL. HE MUST TRY. OTHERWISE, HE'LL END UP BEING CONSUMED BY FEAR AND REGRET.
IT'S NOW OR NEVER.
HE'S GIFTED, MARKUS...MAYBE TOO MUCH SO.

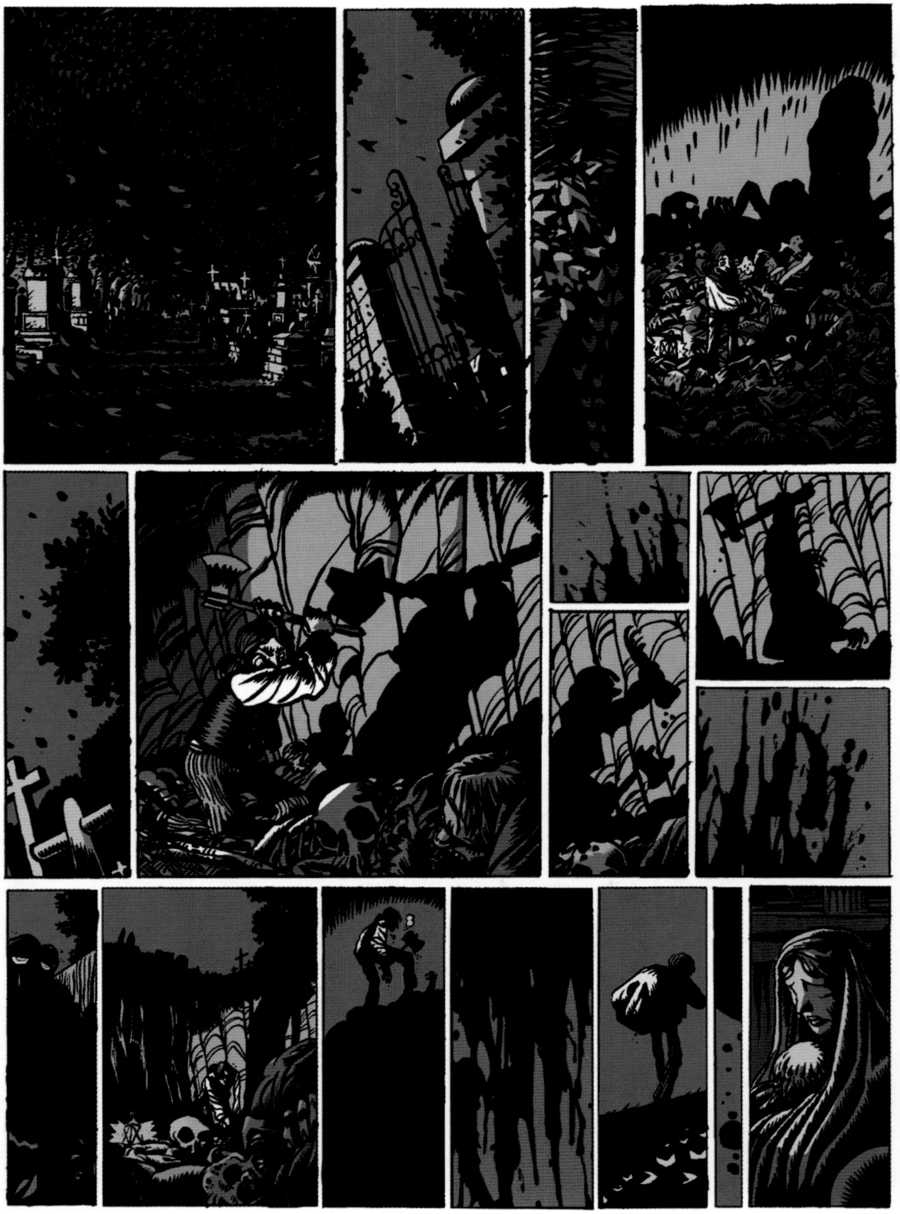

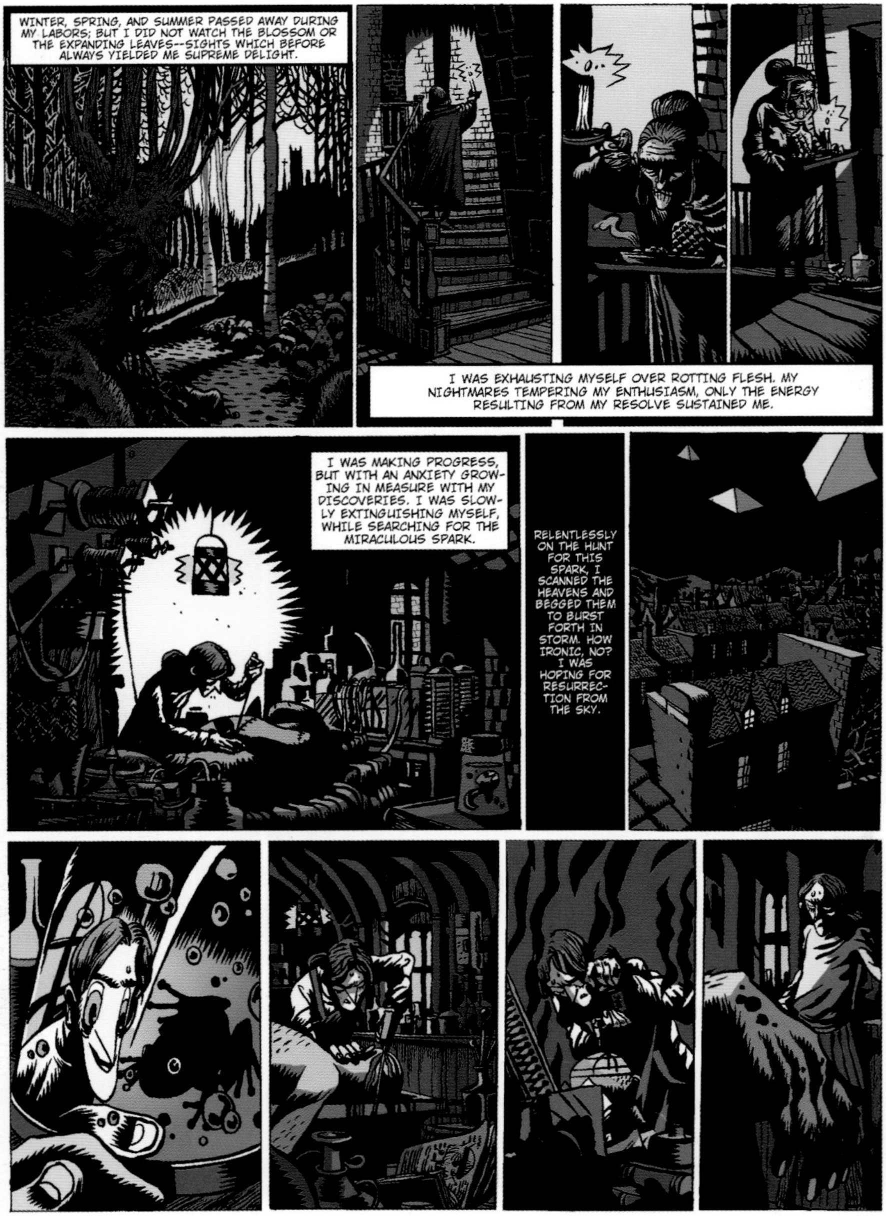
WINTER, SPRING, AND SUMMER PASSED AWAY DURING MY LABORS; BUT I DID NOT WATCH THE BLOSSOM OR THE EXPANDING LEAVES--SIGHTS WHICH BEFORE ALWAYS YIELDED ME SUPREME DELIGHT.
I WAS EXHAUSTING MYSELF OVER ROTTING FLESH. MY NIGHTMARES TEMPERING MY ENTHUSIASM, ONLY THE ENERGY RESULTING FROM MY RESOLVE SUSTAINED ME.
I WAS MAKING PROGRESS, BUT WITH AN ANXIETY GROWING IN MEASURE WITH MY DISCOVERIES. I WAS SLOWLY EXTINGUISHING MYSELF, WHILE SEARCHING FOR THE MIRACULOUS SPARK.
RELENTLESSLY ON THE HUNT FOR THIS SPARK, I SCANNED THE HEAVENS AND BEGGED THEM TO BURST FORTH IN STORM. HOW IRONIC, NO? I WAS HOPING FOR RESURRECTION FROM THE SKY.

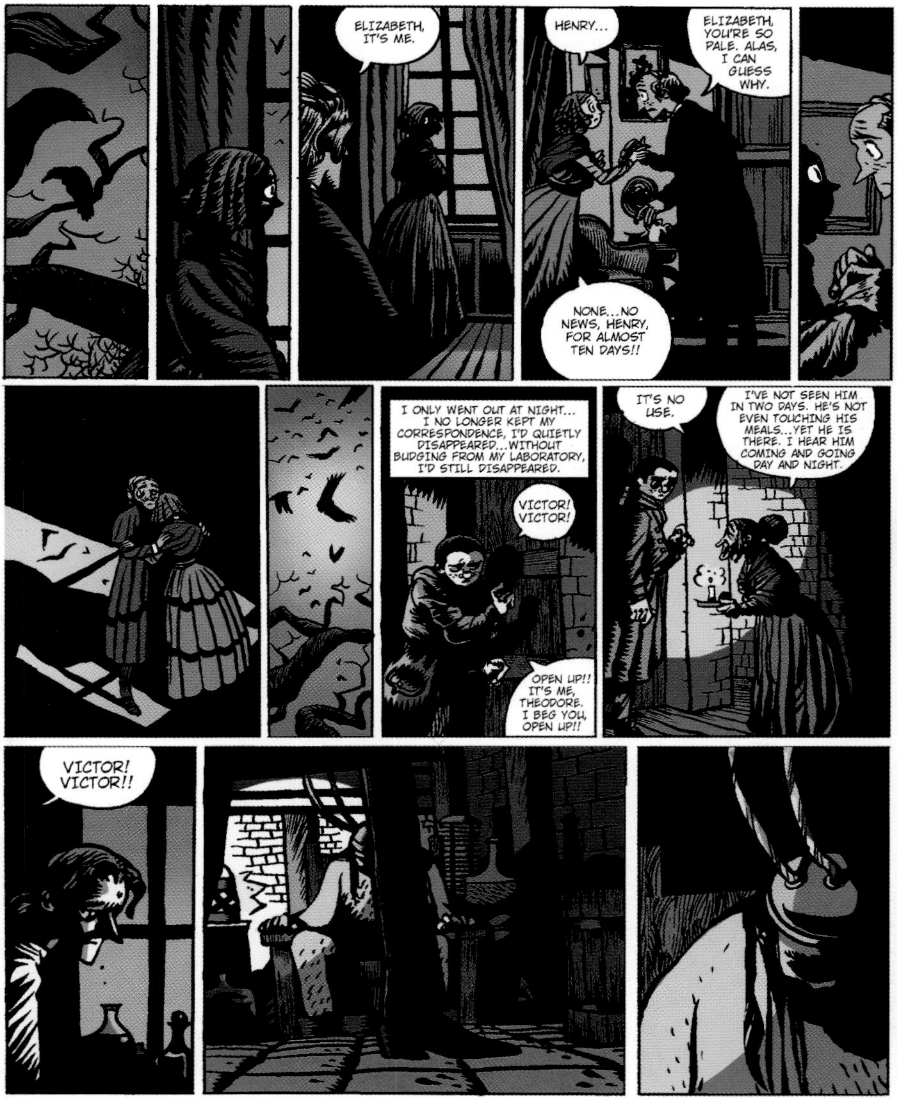
ELIZABETH, IT'S ME.
HENRY...
ELIZABETH, YOU'RE SO PALE. ALAS, I CAN GUESS WHY.
NONE...NO NEWS, HENRY, FOR ALMOST TEN DAYS!!
I ONLY WENT OUT AT NIGHT... I NO LONGER KEPT MY CORRESPONDENCE, I'D QUIETLY DISAPPEARED...WITHOUT BUDGING FROM MY LABORATORY, I'D STILL DISAPPEARED.
VICTOR! VICTOR!
OPEN UP!! IT'S ME, THEODORE. I BEG YOU, OPEN UP!!
IT'S NO USE.
I'VE NOT SEEN HIM IN TWO DAYS. HE'S NOT EVEN TOUCHING HIS MEALS...YET HE IS THERE. I HEAR HIM COMING AND GOING DAY AND NIGHT.
VICTOR! VICTOR!!

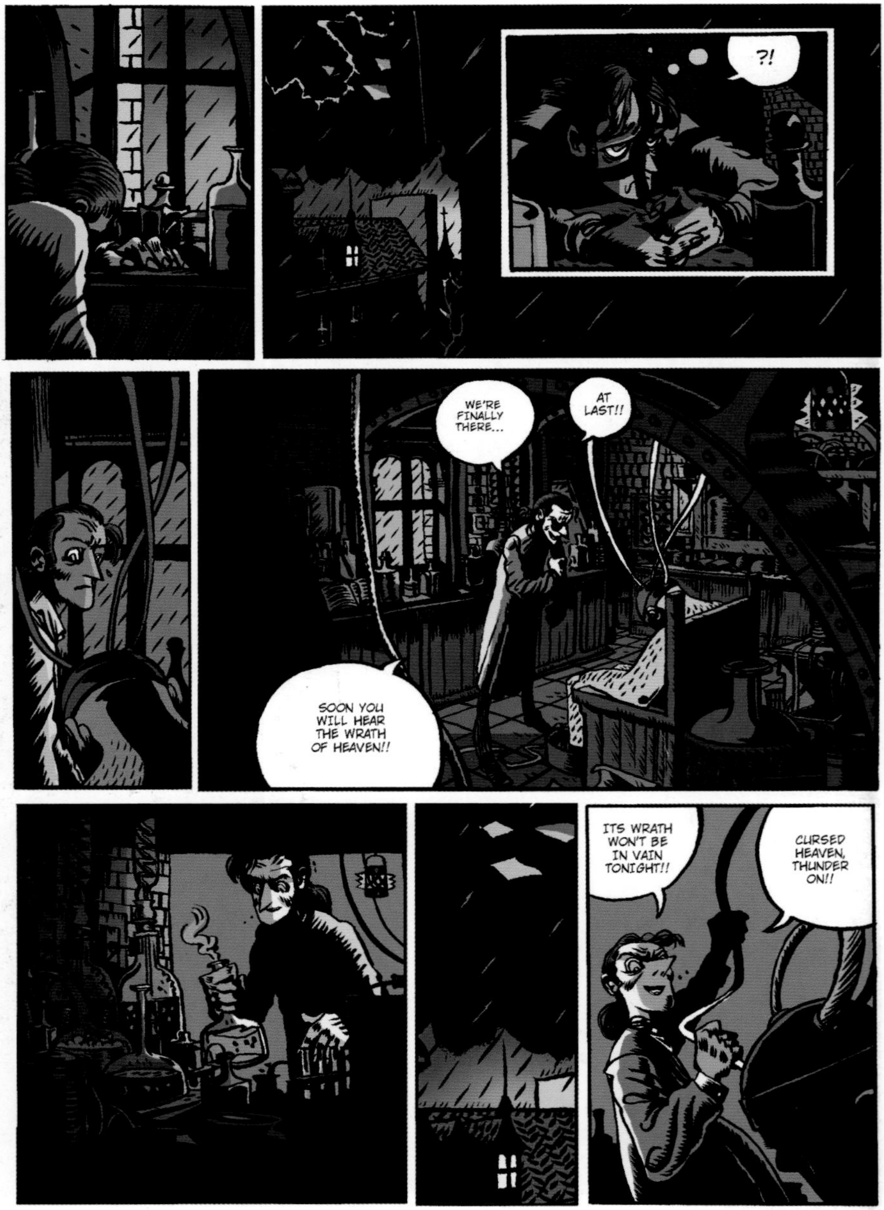
?!
WE'RE FINALLY THERE...
AT LAST!!
SOON YOU WILL HEAR THE WRATH OF HEAVEN!!
ITS WRATH WON'T BE IN VAIN TONIGHT!!
CURSED HEAVEN, THUNDER ON!!

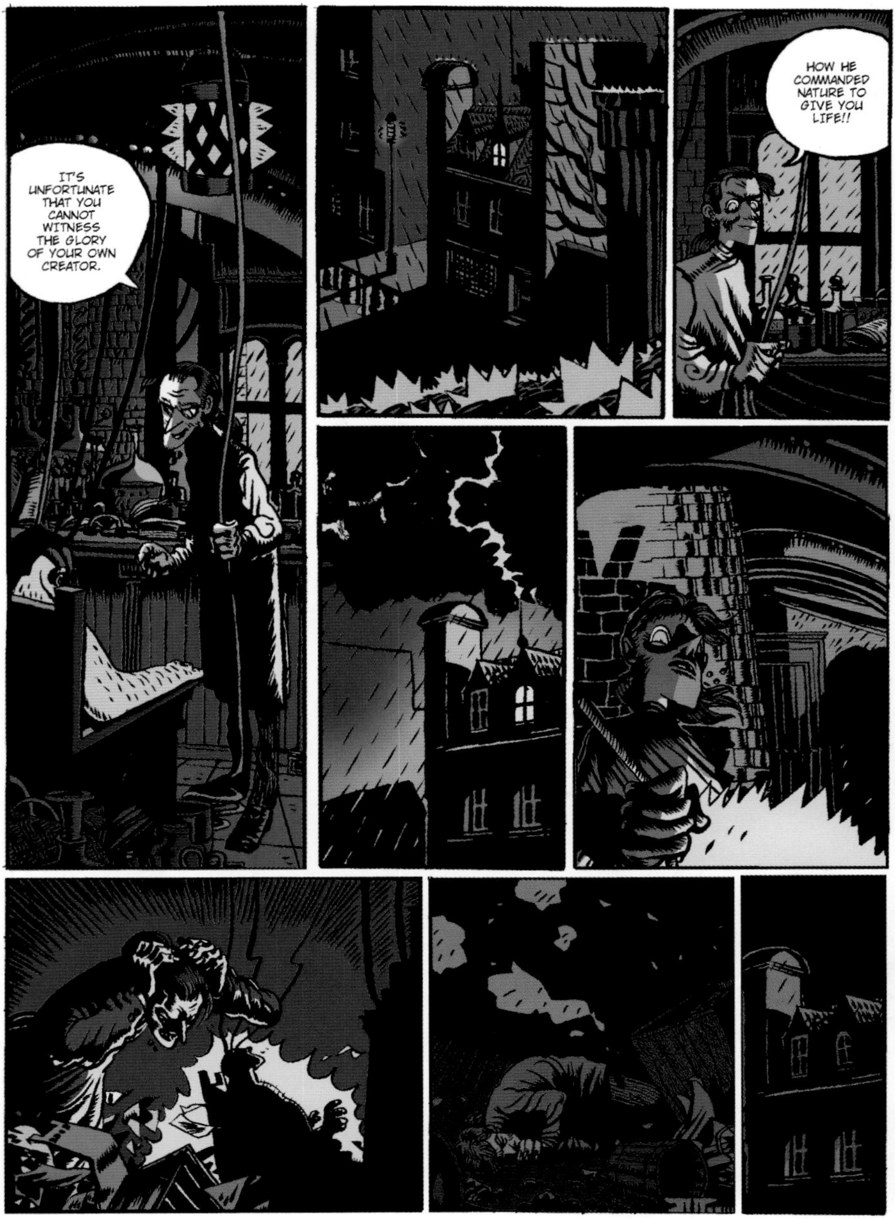
IT'S UNFORTUNATE THAT YOU CANNOT WITNESS THE GLORY OF YOUR OWN CREATOR.
HOW HE COMMANDED NATURE TO GIVE YOU LIFE!!

Don't miss CLASSICS ILLUSTRATED DELUXE #3 – "Frankenstein"

E.C. FANS!

YOU'VE WRITTEN!
YOU'VE E-MAILED!
YOU'VE PHONED!
YOU'VE THREATENED US!
YOU'VE DEMANDED!
(BUT WE'RE COMING OUT WITH
THESE COLLECTIONS ANYWAY!)

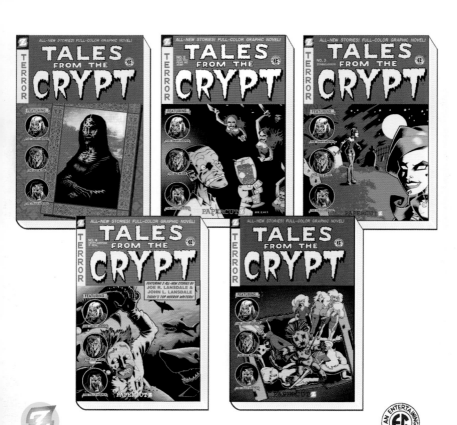

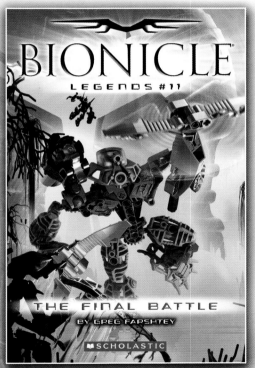

THE **HARDY BOYS**®

A NEW GRAPHIC NOVEL EVERY 3 MONTHS!

ON SALE NOW!

#10 – "A Hardy Day's Night"
ISBN – 978-1-59707-070-6
#11 – "Abracadeath"
ISBN – 978-1-59707-080-5
#12 – "Dude Ranch O' Death!"
ISBN – 978-1-59707-088-1
#13 – "The Deadliest Stunt"
ISBN – 978-1-59707-102-4
NEW! #14 – "Haley Danelle's Top Eight!"
ISBN – 978-1-59707-113-0
Also available – Hardy Boys #1-9
All: Pocket sized, 96-112pp., full-color, $7.95
Also available in hardcover! $12.95 each.

THE HARDY BOYS
#1-4 Box Set
5x7 1/2, 400 pages, full-color, $29.95
ISBN – 978-1-59707-040-9
#5-8 Box Set
5x7 1/2, 432 pages, full-color, $29.95
ISBN – 978-1-59707-075-1
#9-12 Box Set
5x7 1/2, 448 pages, full-color, $29.95
ISBN - 978-1-59707-125-3

CLASSICS *Illustrated*®

Featuring Stories by the World's Greatest Authors

NEW!

#1 "Great Expectations"
ISBN – 978-1-59707-097-3
#2 "The Invisible Man"
ISBN – 978-1-59707-106-2
NEW! #3 "Through the Looking Glass"
ISBN – 978-1-59707-115-4
All: 6 1/2 x 9, 56 pages, full-color

At bookstores or order at Papercutz, 40 Exchange Place, Ste. 1308, New York, NY 10005,
1-800-886-1223 (M-F 9-6 EST) Please add $4.00 postage and handling, $1 each additional item.
Make check payable to NBM publishing. MC, VISA, AMEX accepted, Distributed by Macmillan

PAPERCUTZ.COM

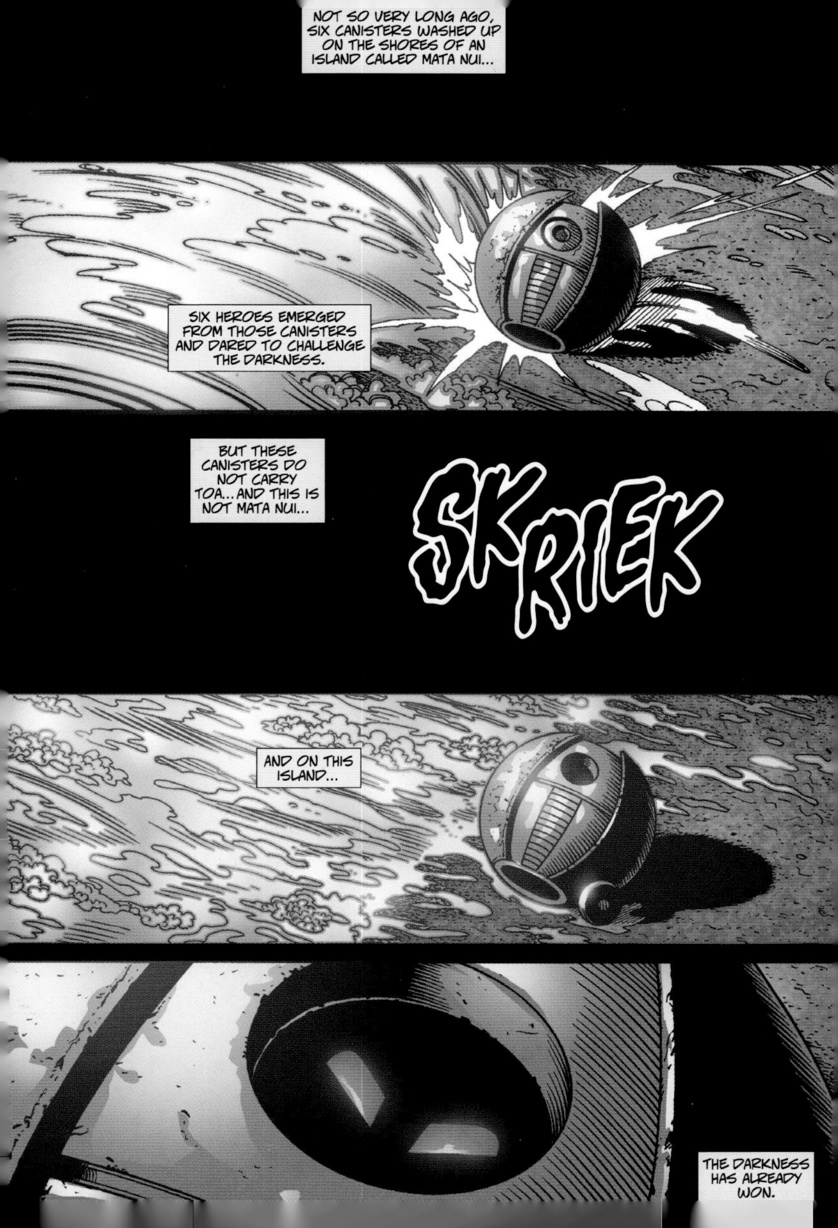
NOT SO VERY LONG AGO, SIX CANISTERS WASHED UP ON THE SHORES OF AN ISLAND CALLED MATA NUI...
SIX HEROES EMERGED FROM THOSE CANISTERS AND DARED TO CHALLENGE THE DARKNESS.
BUT THESE CANISTERS DO NOT CARRY TOA... AND THIS IS NOT MATA NUI...
SKRIEK
AND ON THIS ISLAND...
THE DARKNESS HAS ALREADY WON.

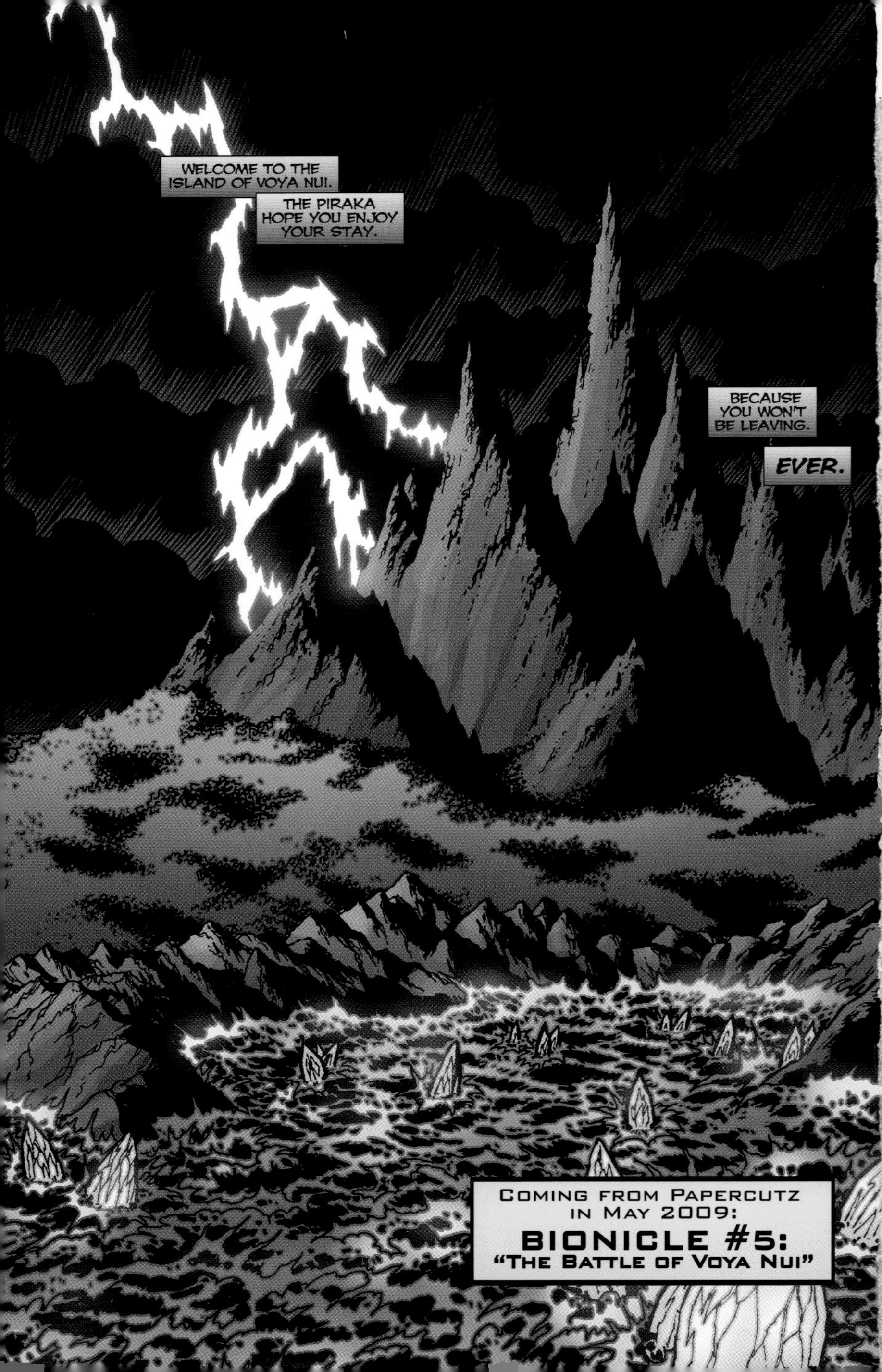
WELCOME TO THE ISLAND OF VOYA NUI.
THE PIRAKA HOPE YOU ENJOY YOUR STAY.
BECAUSE YOU WON'T BE LEAVING.
EVER.
COMING FROM PAPERCUTZ IN MAY 2009:
BIONICLE #5:
"THE BATTLE OF VOYA NUI"